MORIBUND EARTH

SURVIVORS OF ZEETA 21

Cover art 'Breath' by Max Bedulenko

Water in Black Productions
Moribund Earth's and Zeeta 21's title designs by Douglas P. Lobo
Interior illustrations and concept art by Armand Luro, art direction by Douglas P. Lobo

This novel is entirely a work of fiction.
The names, characters and incidents portrayed in it are the work of the author's imagination. Any resemblance to actual persons, living or dead, events or localities is entirely coincidental.

Paperback edition 2024

Editor: Bonnie Wong
ISBN-publisher: AnyBook Press, Amsterdam

ISBN/EAN: 978-90-833751-5-1

Printed using Amazon's print-on-demand service. Units are produced as they are ordered, which reduces excess production and contributes to environmental sustainability.

Independently published.
Please leave a review on Amazon or Goodreads, thank you!

For more content from the author please visit MonkWax Studios on Youtube, Twitter and Instagram

This book was previously published under the title 'Tofu Brains: Life On Zeeta 21'.

Praise for Moribund Earth: Survivors of Zeeta 21

"Author Lars Koch has crafted a detailed novel with a chilling premise that provides a glimpse into a future where societal norms and environmental stability have crumbled… The dialogue is compelling but never overdone or overspilling with emotion, yet the pain of the central figures is obvious and heartfelt, making readers ponder the future of our planet and the potential allure of escape to the stars. Overall, I would highly recommend…for cyberpunk dystopian fans everywhere, and I eagerly await what comes next in the series".

K.C. Finn for Readers' Favorite

"…A captivating and imaginative sci-fi book that took me on a thrilling journey through a distant future. Lars skilfully blended elements of technology, adventure, and mystery to create a great narrative.
The characters… are well-developed and relatable. I became emotionally invested in their struggles and triumphs".

★★★★★

Amazon

"Koch's vision of the future is both terrifying and hopeful, reminding us that even in the face of adversity, humanity has the capacity for resilience and adaptation…I highly recommend this book to anyone looking for a fresh take on the science-fiction genre or just sci-fi in general or Fallout series".

★★★★★

Goodreads

ZEETA 21

Trajectory Override Console

EMERGENCY? SAFELY STEER ZEETA BACK TO EARTH!

BLOC 13

TRASH-DAY? NEVER AGAIN...

FILE UNDER: VDSG VTB-001-15

PROPERTY OF THE ARAND CORPORATION

Kalopsia:
Sounds of a Moribund Earth

Original soundtrack
by Nobody's Nail Machine

Available on:
Spotify, Apple Music, YouTube Music, Amazon & Deezer

In loving memory of
Jytte & Karl Koch

Zeeta 21 Mission Archives

Prologue

It happened in the year 3239: the Year of Death. Humanity had finally pushed itself to the brink, effectively depleting Earth's resources, and people grew reckless in desperation for food, clean water, and safe living space. Simultaneously, their ability to reason diminished; nations became paranoid and hostile. It was only a matter of time before the Final World War would break out. No one knew who had started the war, and no one cared. The sky rained fire and fury for months. Bombs of incredible potency carried destruction over continents and filled the oceans with poison, rendering life nearly impossible. Sophisticated cyber-attacks spread panic and confusion at the speed of wildfire. People turned hostile; neighbours were fighting neighbours, husbands killing their wives, and women abandoning their children.

The End of Things was nigh.

Before the war broke out, the remaining superpowers, the United States of the Western World, Greater Russia, and the Chinese Empire, had joined forces in a final attempt to save Mankind. They built a domed mechanical city set to be launched into space to allow humans to prosper in a new and safer environment. It was called Zeeta 21, conceived to carry 20,000 people on a fixed fifty-year flight trajectory before landing back on Earth. Earth's time was running out; it was time to find another solution for humanity.

The year is 3246, and we are starting the final preparations for Zeeta's launch. Pockets of survivors are scrambling to survive on the Earth's burnt crust, living in isolation from one another. Some have heard about Zeeta, but most are oblivious to its existence.

Our story begins at the Monastery of Our Good Lord. It comprises a group of zealous monks led by the Abbess. The monks dedicate their lives to technology and serve as Earth's last hub for development and research. They form the last civilised bastion where nations can meet to discuss.

Chapter I: Launch of Zeeta (Year 3246)

Leaders of the Surviving World

The Abbess looked at the Old Clock. It was ten forty-three in the morning on the eighteenth of May, 3246. She was about to chair an important meeting with the Leaders of the Surviving World Committee, or the LSWC. This group was composed of representatives from nation-states that still had the capacity to communicate with the outside world. After the Seventy-seventh World War ended in 3239, many countries were desolate from radiation and pollution. The populations which had inhabited the land were decimated.

The meeting today was crucial. It was the two hundred and seventy-second discussion about Mission Zeeta 21.

The Abbess started getting impatient. There was usually a lot of commotion before meetings, but today was special. The meeting was taking place in the Monastery's main hall, a large dome-shaped room filled with technological gadgets. It could seat up to three hundred and fifty people, and she expected it would almost reach capacity.

But a lot of things were not going according to plan. The monks misplaced the representatives' nametags from New Uruguay and Greater Russia, a misstep capable of causing a diplomatic crisis and tainting the impeccable image of the Monastery. Luckily, she spotted it in time.

Overwhelmed by the number of guests, the monks also struggled to purify enough water to fill the drinking cups in the welcome salon. Fortunately, they compensated by serving more Buckwheat Beer. This year, the Brothers achieved an unprecedented alcohol percentage, which improved everybody's mood.

The Abbess was particularly upset when a young and zealous monk named Brother Francis, ecstatic to have outsiders visit the Monastery, tried to hug one of the guests. Any form of physical contact was, of course, strictly forbidden.

More worrying, the Abbess had received late notices from several Committee members informing her they would not show up. Several of them bluntly said they would no longer support Zeeta 21 financially, withdrawing all their funds from the project. She feared the entire project might be at stake.
The Old Clock was visible out of the corner of her eye. It was ten fifty-eight, and the meeting was about to start. As she approached the speakers' podium, a million thoughts raced through her mind. Despite her internal struggles, she had to keep up appearances. They needed to get Zeeta off the ground — it could be humanity's last hope.

"Honourable World Leaders,
Distinguished Members of the Committee,
Dear friends and Master Teachers,
We are gathered here today at this crucial juncture of our shared journey.
The bombs fell a little over six years ago. The Seventy-seventh World War was unprecedented in scope and scale, reducing most of the Earth's crust to a barren wasteland. Life has since then been hazardous and even impossible for millions of innocent people.
However, we here at the Monastery of our Good Lord have remained vigilant and hopeful. And indeed, you have given us hope. You, great leaders, …" the Abbess choked as she despised lauding war-hungry tyrants, "... have offered us a hope for a better future, for all humanity." Faint applause was heard in the crowd.
"In your great wisdom," she continued, perceiving the taste of vomit in her mouth, "you decided that conflict and strife was not the way forward. No, cooperation and common understanding were needed. Indeed, under the humble guidance of our Monastery, you agreed to seek a peaceful solution. You decided to come together to construct Zeeta 21. A city built for space travel, Zeeta 21 would offer humanity a new chance to live, breed, and prosper outside the hemisphere of Earth's boundaries."
The Abbess took a deep breath. "It seems we took life's frailty for granted here on Earth. Maybe there's a better chance for our survival in space?" She added the question impromptu and with more emotion than planned. She saw her trusted Brothers look at

her nervously, but apart from some scattered and uneasy coughing, no one in the audience seemed to notice much.
She regained her focus and resumed.
"Therefore, dear World Leaders, dear LSW Committee members, it is imperative that we finalise the great work that has begun. We cannot afford to cease the enormous efforts which have led us to this great day. Doing so could prove fatal – for all of us.
The construction of Zeeta 21 is almost complete. With less than six months to go, we will, at last, be able to rejoice in the fruits of our labour. The end is nigh. The end of humankind's despair hails the dawn of new hope. Zeeta 21 is that hope; it is the light we need to shine into this world.
Zeeta will fill our skies with peace. Our Brothers here at the Monastery continue to pray that the men and women chosen to go live in space breed a new generation of children full of zest. We pray those children will eventually return to Earth enlightened with new ideas and fresh perspectives. May they achieve what we have failed to do: to live in peace and harmony with one another in full respect of Mother Nature.
I wholeheartedly thank you, dear World Leaders, for your continued efforts and the trust you place in the Brotherhood. We strive to warrant your kindness and goodwill." The Abbess paused and gave a long bow.
"Now, having concluded the formal introductory part of this session, I would like to give the floor to Ms Dorateen 'Scorpia' Fernandez. Ms Fernandez is heading up the United Southern American Conglomerate, whom we particularly thank for their exemplary pecuniary kindness over the years." She turned to face Scorpia and bowed again.
"Ms Fernandez will brief you on the latest status of Zeeta and announce the next steps to be taken."
Dorateen Fernandez, born in the Mexican Republic, was a long-standing member of the LSW Committee. She had been promoted to the highest diplomatic ranks in her home country, then became de facto Chairwoman of LSWC due to her formidable ability to reach consensus, often by intimidating those who disagreed with her. She was an impressive woman due to her large size and strong character. She did not insist on formalities, though, and always insisted that people simply called her 'Scorpia'. Her late mother

gave her that nickname. It meant to celebrate her ability to survive in harsh conditions at any cost, even if it required poisoning those in her way.

"Thank you, cherished Abbess," Scorpia said as she walked to the podium. She wore a turquoise green jacket and skirt, and her extended eyelashes were a bright purple.

"It's most certainly a pleasure for me to speak here today. As rightly said, we stand at an important crossroads. The Monastery has served as an impeccable arms provider for so many years. Our greatest conflicts wouldn't have been possible had it not been for their expert research and development. Remarkable work on new laser and plasma technologies has been carried out for centuries in this very facility. Let's hear a round of applause for the Abbess and her diligent monks!" Applause filled the room. The Abbess took it in silence.

"Now, let's cut the crap. We all spend a lot of money. I mean, I've seen the Monastery's latest budget forecast, and phew! Trust me, some serious cash is flowing through this place. That's why I, and others, suggested ten years ago: why not spend at least part of the money on a common project?

"Of course, military expenditure is and will continue to be needed. In this day and age, each National Conglomerate needs to protect itself, no doubt about that. We have rogue survivors, pagan cavemen, in almost every part of the world. Uncivilised, threatening our way of life! Plus, we've got these new … creatures. Radiation brought those about, and no ordinary weaponry can kill them. Only a plasma rifle to the head will do. Trust me. I've seen it!" Scorpia took a sip of purified water from her personal canister. She started sweating. She loved going off a tangent like this; sometimes her speeches would last for hours.

"Yes, military funding is still needed, and I've personally told the Abbess to place special emphasis on hydrogen-driven long-range missiles. We at the Southern American Conglomerate are driven to make the next large-scale conflict as environmentally friendly as possible, reducing greenhouse emissions by up to twenty-seven percent!" Scattered applause and cheering were heard.

"And this is why I'm up here; we need to talk about the future. Like I said, it was decided after the last World War that the Leaders of the Surviving World needed to come together. Since

then, twelve percent of the Monastery's annual budget has been allocated to a common peace project. Sadly, we've gone slightly over that. Six years ago, we estimated we needed forty-seven billion dollars, but, so far, we've spent nearly sixty billion." The last statement prompted a stream of expletives from the crowd.
Scorpia spoke sharply into the microphone to rein in the crowd, "Now, now. Hold your horses! Your investment is worthwhile. We've cut some corners to make it work. Some of the underground parts of the city will remain unfinished for now to shave off unnecessary expenses. But it's important we all stay on track. After all, what good are we as nations if we have no enemies to fight? People need to survive for us to exist!" Scorpia drank the last of the water in her canister, then angrily signalled to the monks that she needed more.
"That's why we decided to build Zeeta 21. Zeeta is the first city ever built and designed for life in space. In a nutshell, we ran out of safe living space here on Earth, so we figured going outside Earth was the only option. Pretty smart, right?" Scorpia glanced at the Abbess who was still wearing her traditional helmet, which obscured her entire face and made her expressions impossible to read.
Scorpia continued, "Zeeta 21 will house twenty thousand of the best and brightest minds of what's left on Earth. We've been drafting people intensively for twenty-seven months, and, so far, there are 18,761 on the list." She paused, raised her finger, and forced an enthusiastic smile. "Some had to be coerced, but most came voluntarily." At this point, she was getting weary of being on stage.
"But enough from me. For more detailed explanations, let me hand the floor over to Dr Alois Lechowsky, Director of New Business Ventures at the Arand Corporation. He'll give you further info on where we are." Scorpia stepped aside but remained on stage.
Lechowsky was a tall man with long hair and a well-kept beard. He had a friendly demeanour and addressed the crowd in a clear, bright voice, "Why, yes. Thank you, Scorpia. It's certainly a great honour to be up here again. It's been a while. The last time I had the pleasure of speaking to this fine assembly was three years ago when we ran into some troubles designing the main reactor core

of Zeeta. Regrettably, this caused some delays and further expenditure, but rest assured that everything is back on track, and we're hungrier than ever for results! The ship is nearly ready."
Lechowsky brought up a holographic image. "As you can see on this detailed replica of Zeeta, all major parts of the ship are now ready. We have a fully habitable surface, which resembles a real city, complete with houses, skyscrapers, Jonny-bot taxis, and soon, human life." Lechowsky smiled at Scorpia, who was busy putting a young monk in his place for taking too long with the water.
"The only thing missing is the lower western section of the ship, which currently is empty except for the main infrastructure. As this is underground, we focused first on the main compartments, such as the main city, the engine rooms, and the navigational system."
He continued as he slowly strolled across the stage. "I'm happy to say, ladies and gentlemen ...", Lechowsky, an experienced speaker, paused to draw in a deep breath to evoke suspense, "... Zeeta 21 will be ready to launch five months from now, as planned, on October twentieth, 3246!" He opened his arms for dramatic effect; the crowd remained still.
"Of course, Zeeta 21 is much more than its technological prowess, which by the way, ladies and gentlemen, I assure you is top-notch! Zeeta features an artificial ecosystem capable of simulating oxygen production and even mimicking plant life. Imagine that. Sitting in a perfectly manicured park with synthetic trees that never wither and foliage that doesn't grow dull. Just gazing at the stars." His smile grew bigger. "But coming back, Zeeta is about more than a beacon of human advancement. It's a platform for humanity to prosper. It's about its people! Oh, yes. We're doing our utmost to ensure safe living quarters and living conditions for our lucky future inhabitants. Each of our 18,761 residents will be treated with the care and respect due. They'll be given the highest possible level of comfort."
Scorpia returned to the front of the stage and stood next to Lechowsky.
He continued, "Just to give you some details, the entire mission, I'm happy to say, will be led and supervised by the Arand Corporation. As Arand's Director of New Business Ventures, I'll

of course join the mission and it's my responsibility to ensure that everything goes smoothly. We'll have a form of soft central 'governance', although I don't like that term, from Arand and a police unit known as the Enforcers. Trust me. This is just so that people feel safe. The Enforcers will have limited powers and will certainly not interfere in anyone's life. Now, let me tell you all about how gummy bears will be produced in space from recycled chewing gum. In fact —"

"Your plan is a fucking travesty. It's amateurish bullshit, and it's never going to work," a voice echoed throughout the entire assembly.

Lechowsky, cut off in mid-sentence, briefly hoped he could ignore the outburst and get on with his presentation.

The full-throated voice continued, "I've never seen such a load of drivel from supposedly distinguished officials like yourselves!"

The automated LED beams scattered across the room, trying to identify the surprise speaker. The monks had to manoeuvre them by hand.

"There's a plethora of things I want to know here. What surveillance system have you set up? How will the Enforcers maintain law and order? Where are the penitentiary facilities? Who will control the food supplies, and how will you keep people from running amok in case of general shortages?"

The bluish beam had now tracked the speaker down. He was sitting in the back rows, looking relaxed and leaning into his chair in a comfortable manner. Lechowsky felt cold and miserable, taken aback by the hostile questions. Squinting his eyes, he saw the man sitting in the Northern European Conglomerate pod but could not make out which country he represented.

After a brief pause, it was Scorpia who spoke. "And who might you be, exactly? State your name, affiliation, and ranking, please."

"I think it matters less who I am and more what I can bring to this project," the man retorted.

"Look, sir. Quit clowning around and let the assembly know who they have the pleasure of listening to, I implore you. We have an agenda to get through, and I really can't tolerate this much longer." Scorpia was sweating profusely; that damn LED beam did not help.

The man got up and slowly walked towards the stage. He was now standing some ten metres away. Two others were following behind him. Scorpia noticed that he was dressed in blue pants, a decent suede jacket, and a tie. Not a diplomat, for sure, but he looked civilised enough.
"My name is Sunny Bridges. My team and I ...", he paused to gesture towards the woman and man just behind him, "have intricately studied your latest designs for the past sixteen months. Now that the mission is entering the final stages, we want to present our recommendations to make it a success."
Lechowsky eventually mustered the courage to step in. "Well, while your suggestions might serve the general interest, I must remind you that Formula 27B-6 would have to be duly completed and filed with the Arand Development Office. Provided, of course, your Formula 79U document has already been approved. Otherwise, we couldn't possibly be required to look at any such —"
"The expedition you are about to embark on will be an utter disaster," Sunny interrupted. "People will die, and your reputation will forever be tainted with sin and shame." Sunny looked at Scorpia as he spoke. He ignored Lechowsky and continued, "My crew and I have composed a list of 1217 changes to be implemented and operational before launch. The changes can be grouped into three categories: 'a', mainframe optimisation; 'b', security, and 'c', governance. Without our input, you're doomed to fail." Sunny's stern eyes rested on Scorpia.
She had been in thousands of top-secret meetings and dealt with people from all walks of life. But, something in Sunny's ferocious manner surprised her. He seemed intelligent and even elegant in some strange way. She was willing to hear him out.
Misreading the situation, Lechowsky oafishly said, "Come on. Can we get this man away from the stage? Can someone call Brotherhood Security? This has gone on long enough. We'll miss the noon mass if we don't —"
Scorpia flashed him a glare. "Shut your fucking mouth!" she hissed. Someone turned the mic off just in time to spare the audience.
"I want to hear what he has to say." Then, she faced and addressed the audience. "Honoured delegation! Please allow a small

deviation from our schedule. I'll be dedicating some time to a private discussion with this individual and his … cohorts. Do excuse us. This afternoon's programme will proceed as planned." Scorpia left the stage with Sunny's entourage. Lechowsky meekly followed behind them.

Sunny Steps In

Scorpia and Lechowsky stood with Sunny and his two followers in a dimly lit room with monitors of every size lining the walls. Lechowsky started feeling claustrophobic; plus, he was still uneasy not knowing the motives of these strangers. They sat down at the table in the middle. Scorpia was eyeing the three. They all sat and looked at her with focused stares.

She took control of the floor."So, are you going to tell me what this is about?" she asked. "Why don't you start by introducing yourselves." It was an order, not a request. Sunny quickly replied as if he had been waiting for the cue to do so. "As mentioned earlier, my name is Sunny Bridges. I'm a Chief Engineer specialising in AI system design." He then gestured towards his male companion. "To my right here is Robert Bacon. He's an advanced mechanical engineer and one of the main architects of Zeeta's engines. He's been working on the project since the very beginning."

Looking left, he continued, "And this is Kira Berezin. Her field is Advanced Agro-Engineering technologies. Kira deals with food engineering, a multidisciplinary field combining microbiology, physical sciences, and chemistry. In short, she'll be producing the food on Zeeta.

"Together, we'll eliminate uncertainty from the equation to ensure everything runs according to plan once we launch Zeeta."

Lechowsky struggled to find the right moment to interrupt, and this seemed as good as any. "But, wait, wait, wait! Hold up! You three, you're some magical troika that pops up out of nowhere with a slew of answers to questions no one has even asked yet, solving problems no one has even addressed —" He looked at

Scorpia. "I mean, what, er, who are you? Why should we trust you?" Scorpia nodded in silent agreement.

"We're specialists from the Northern European Conglomerate assigned by our respective Nation States to this project," Sunny explained calmly. "We're hired by the Arand Corp as contractors, albeit working quite independently from the central organisation. As such, we've been actively contributing to the construction of Zeeta. Now we wish to come to you with our proposals. That's all there is to know. As things are, we naturally don't feel any particular, hm, affiliation to our home countries."

Scorpia gauged him. "In other words, by coming directly to me, you hope to circumvent your hierarchy back home. About the people paying you to work on Zeeta, I take it you've had some falling out with them or carry some sort of grudge? Or perhaps you feel you're more likely to succeed in your endeavours by coming directly to me instead of going through usual channels. If you are indeed contracted by Arand, you know our administration can be quite … difficult. It's not always easy for new ideas to get through."

Sunny glanced at Scorpia. She was quick to make correct assumptions. She was a woman with a great deal of intelligence and strong will: a dangerous cocktail.

"I take it then," Scorpia paused, got up, and strolled through the room with her hands behind her back before continuing, "you're vigilantes? Rebels, acting on your behalf for a cause you deem righteous, just, or perhaps simply self-fulfilling. Can I assume that much?"

A serious expression appeared across Sunny's face. It showed a sensitive side of him, fragile even. Scorpia thought this was a man who spends many hours alone, pondering.

"You could in some sense label us, uh, outcasts, I suppose. But humans are complex beings. And I'm not one to assign any rudimentary nomenclature for what essentially constitutes an intricate web of emotional and practical drivers," Sunny said. He had regained his impenetrable demeanour.

Scorpia sat back down. "Listen, chump. You managed to grab my attention and fuck up my meeting schedule. But you better make it worth my while. So, tell me exactly what the hell it is you three came here to do."

A light immediately sparked in Sunny's eyes. He had been waiting for this moment.

"In essence, we want to solve your biggest problem: control. Pulling twenty thousand people from their natural habitat into space is both unprecedented and risky. There's no way of knowing how people will react. And although you have some law enforcement measures in place, the risk is high."

Scorpia and Lechowsky gave each other incredulous looks.

Sunny continued, "We're going to install an all-knowing artificial intelligence system called NADOSH on the ship. The system will tie into every possible nook and cranny of the ship's controls. This entails everything from monitoring people in their homes and controlling when and how individuals take their meals and prescribed drugs. Also, NADOSH is intrinsically linked to the ship's engine controls." Sunny turns towards Bacon. "This will allow the Commander in Chief to instantaneously get detailed reports about the ship's trajectory, energy use, et cetera."

Emphasising an important sidenote, Sunny said, "of course, Mr Bacon here will manage the operation of the engine systems. No interference is allowed, and any communication is for data-exchange purposes only.

"Kira has devised an ingenious system to optimise food supplies. With her techniques, we can produce synthetic meals rich in nutrients and extremely cheap to make. Most of the base ingredients comprise recycled waste from organic and non-organic sources. Crucially, various drugs can be added to the food to either experiment with mind-controlling techniques or at least render subjects more docile, if need be."

Lechowsky was about to talk, but Scorpia shushed him. "Indeed, that might prove useful," she said while pondering the possibilities.

Sunny explained, "What's more, we've invented the XZ-9000 Cybertronic device. This gun will essentially lobotomise any subject that refuses to obey orders by inserting a thin needle through the eyeball, piercing the front lobe of the brain, and

extracting serotonin-filled brain juices. This procedure effectively turns people into zombies and renders them unable to work or perform any but the most menial tasks. Thus, it's naturally to be used exclusively for the most extreme cases of non-conformity."
Gesturing again towards Kira, Sunny continued. "Our expert has even made a special brand of edible food paste to feed these wretched souls. It's called: Tofu Brains — a mix of ninety-nine percent synthetic human brain compounds and one percent liquorice. I can assure you no actual human specimens are used to produce it. And it'll keep the zombies calm, keep them from acting upon their cannibalistic tendencies. In other words, we suppress their hunger for human flesh. Ideally, this will ensure they'll still be able to carry out some menial tasks."
Scorpia was about to speak, but Sunny did not let her. He finished what he wanted to say. "Oh, and we plan to start mass-producing XZ-9000s early next month. One in five Enforcers should carry one and receive advanced training to use it. Trust me. It'll be needed after we launch."
Scorpia left the table briefly to take a call from her superiors. She returned, her expression changed but secretive, and sat in silence. So, Lechowsky jumped in. "But hold on for a second here, people! I mean, is this all just done and dusted? You speak about installing some omnipresent AI to control Zeeta. I mean —" he meekly looked at Scorpia, "we can't accept this. It wasn't in the protocol. It would have to be studied in detail, looked over by the Launch Planning Committee, who would first need the greenlight from the steering board before we could even think about mentioning it under AOB with the LSWC members." Lechowsky was out of breath.
For the first time, something Lechowsky said caught Sunny's interest. "Ah, yes. That's a good point. I should underline the fact that NADOSH is already up and running. We have her connected to all the different subsections of the ship, whose functioning isn't possible without her. So far, people believe these are merely autonomous sub-sections of the main data access network while, in reality, NADOSH is running everything. The only thing left to

do is activate her central avatar, the 'person' the Chief in Command will speak to."

"Whaat!" Lechowsky spat, incensed. "This is outrageous! Where are the guards? I want these people removed! We can't —"

Sunny continued to speak, unperturbed by the outburst. "NADOSH is programmed to react with hostility towards anyone compromising her or the mission. Thus, de facto, any opposition towards her will lead, eventually, to the death of that individual. Locking us up won't make much difference. I'm merely trying to convey that I hope to have you as active partners in this project as it makes things … less messy."

"You fucking rat. I'll throw you to the monks! Their torture chambers were designed for people like you. Hope you like acid!" Lechowsky thundered.

Looking at him, Scorpia said, "You will do no such thing." She folded her hands.

"We'll consider what these men are saying and assess their proposals. NADOSH sounds like an adequate main interlocutor for this mission. Indeed, she could help us make wise decisions for Zeeta and keep its people and processes under control. It seems like a possible way forward."

Lechowsky was flabbergasted, his rage mixed with profound insecurity. "But this is insane! How can you accept this so quickly? I mean, these people just walked into the room. We can't just take what they're saying at face value. The entire thing could be an elaborate hoax for all we know. What the hell does N-A-D-O-S-H stand for, anyway? Probably some smart-ass technical acronym. I promised people utopia, not a machine that would run their lives." His eyes were bloodshot.

Scorpia started pacing the room while thinking about it out loud. "What I've heard for the last twenty minutes makes loads more sense than anything your empty-skulled brainstorming committee ever came up with." Scorpia sighed. "It's our responsibility to ensure that Zeeta and its people are safe and adapt well to their new lives. Clear boundaries are crucial for any child as it helps them develop healthily, and so it is with nascent civilisations.

We'll give people clear limits and harsh repercussions for anyone stepping outside those limits."

To Lechowsky, she said, "I've just received a call from the Judge. The Superiors have decided it shall be this way." He gulped.

Scorpia had changed her expression completely. Management made it clear she had to follow orders and let Sunny carry out his ideas. Her mind was racing with all the possibilities presented by the radical proposals of these three uninvited guests. Don't know why, but they seem trustworthy enough, she thought to herself. At least until the operation gets going. I can get rid of them if needed.

To the others, she smiled and said,"I believe it's indeed better to keep this under wraps. Everything that we've discussed here will be our little understanding, OK? I don't want this, shall we say, detail to reach the Leader of the Surviving World Committee. Anyhow, they've entrusted us with organising operations as we see fit. And we don't want to bother them with such technicalities at this critical juncture when their resources are better spent elsewhere. Do we agree?" Her eyes pinned down Lechowsky. The smile was gone.

He averted his gaze and sunk into his chair. That was exactly the kind of concession Scorpia was expecting.

"Good. Unless I change my mind, we shall do as Sunny and his two, um, partners propose." There was a gleam of malice in Scorpia's eyes. "On one condition ..." She looked at Sunny. "I want to join the expedition as a Member State representative. I want to be on Zeeta 21 as a privileged diplomatic member with complete immunity. I want luxury and freedom. I won't answer to anyone." Lechowsky gestured wildly.

Scorpia gazed into the air. Her look reminded Sunny of an excited child, carefree and ready to run across a busy road to get what she wanted. While admirable in an infant, that was a dangerous quality in an adult.

She took two steps forwards and spun around. "I want this to serve as a common understanding between us. It won't be written or recorded and will simply be a tacit agreement amongst us here in the room.

"I will function as Executive President of Zeeta 21, and you will all answer to me. Lechowsky will keep his position as Director at the Arand Corporation, serving as a puppet for all accountability and responsibility of the mission. He'll also be the face of project Zeeta 21. De facto, it will be me, Sunny, Bacon and, uh, what's her name …" Scorpia glanced at Kira, "who makes the decisions. That's how Zeeta will be run. Give me a night to sleep on it, but that's what I'm thinking. It's the will of the Judge and the Arand Corporation."

Scorpia's word seemed so final that no one bothered to interject. Lechowsky tried adamantly to save what little self-respect he had left. He puffed up his chest and said, "I know just the man to lead the Enforcers. Lieutenant Horrigan will be the iron fist we need."

Sunny looked at Kira and Bacon and nodded. Their plan was approved, and the real work was about to begin.

Brother Francis Brings the Holy Receptacle

It was an exciting day, almost too much so. Brother Francis was called upon by the Abbess herself to carry out a range of distinguished tasks, usually given to higher-ranked monks. She put him in charge of overseeing that all delegations had ample water supply during the conference, which was no small feat; Ms Scorpia drank all the extra supplies they had. The Abbess also gave Brother Francis the responsibility of placing name tags and country flag labels for each delegation. Unfortunately, he misplaced the flags of Greater Russia and New Uruguay. Luckily, giving them extra homebrewed Buckwheat Beer rations settled the mishap.

He was in a rush. The Abbess had told him that the mysterious guest, Mr Sunny Bridges, was going to attend a private work session with a few trusted companions. It was of utmost importance that their flasks be filled with clean water to ensure maximum efficiency during the meeting.

Francis was running around in such a frenzy that he spilled most of the water from the flasks. He became flustered with embarrassment when he realised they were not closed properly.

But the flask for Mr Bridges he kept safe and secure under his robe.
He approached the meeting room where the Abbess said the private work session was being held. It was, of course, in the secret underground passages of the Monastery, away from prying eyes and used only for exceptional occasions. Francis took a deep breath and gently opened the door.
“You fucking imbecile! Is that all you’ve got?” the loud voice of Mr Bridges thundered through the room; Francis felt the weight of Bridges’ words suspended in the air.
“We haven’t gotten this far … No, we’re not going to be stopped or even delayed by a simple-minded fucking simpleton like you. Because, you know, that’s what you are. A simpleton. A fucking idiot not capable of understanding things greater than yourself!” Sunny’s words hammered down like an acid hailstorm.
Francis noticed Sunny’s two friends from the meeting and a fourth gentleman in the room. It was an Arand technician.
Sunny was the only one standing up, pacing the room while spewing obscenities at the Arand representative seated with his back towards him. Francis made a mental note to pray that the Good Lord cleanse his ear canals after this ordeal was over.
Silent as a mouse, Francis walked up to Sunny. “Your fresh water supply is here, sir. I’ve filled up the fl-fl-flasks personally,” he stammered.
Sunny turned towards him abruptly, his face red with rage. Without a word, he forcefully knocked away Francis’ tray. Francis, completely in awe and perplexed by the enormous presence of this great man, fell to the ground. He was still clutching Sunny’s flask and did not know what else to do but hand it to him.
Sunny’s lips broke into a sad smile, ripe with deceit and self-loathing. He took the flask and threw it at the technician’s head. “Maybe this jester is eager for a fucking sip of water. That might make him more cooperative.” The flask bounced off the back of the unlucky man’s head with a loud thwack!
Francis was beside himself. The weight of all the stress and anxiety preparing for the LSWC crashed upon him. He was also

struck with fascination for this Sunny Bridges character, about whom he had not heard until only a few hours earlier. He felt tears of pride come to his eyes; this was a sign of destiny at work. That he was to behold such a divine sight as watching one of the creators of Zeeta making final preparations was simply too much. He wept.

Francis quickly snatched up the empty flask from the ground. "This is it. The Holy Receptacle. Sunny's flask. I shall hold on to it and protect it with my life," he solemnly vowed.

He thought better of staying in the room much longer. Instead, he clutched the flask and sped for the door. Better to be off before a new torrent of abuse came, this time directed at him for his poor performance as drink-bringer.

As Francis was about to close the door, he heard a gun go off. "None of my business … Better not bother the Abbess with such affairs," he thought as he ran off, brimming with equal measures of fear and joyful bliss.

Back in the room, Bacon looked at the corpse flopped over the table, the – now-former – Chief Technical Adviser for the Arand Corporation. Sunny had been vociferously questioning the man for an hour non-stop; the atmosphere was tense.

"Sunny! What the hell? You shouldn't have done that! You risk getting us all killed, jeopardising the whole thing!" Bacon exclaimed.

The gore in front of them was appalling. Half of the balding man's scalp was missing, and blood was still oozing onto the table. Kira turned her head in disgust.

Sunny dismissed Bacon's concern. "We'll write it off as suicide. He was dead weight anyway. We can't have such incompetent crewmembers." He was still worked up and was rapidly pacing back and forth. "Yeezus! Is no one around here capable of explaining to me, in simple terms, for how many nanoseconds the Orbiter Vehicle will remain attached to the 2xTurbo Rocketdyne RS-255 main engines at launch?"

"Don't worry about the details. Just let the machine do all the calculations," Kira spoke softly. Her voice was so sexy, Sunny realised. “After all, it’s what you’ve built her for. Let NADOSH take control of everything. No human interference is needed. We’ve already tested this setting in the beta version." She smiled at Sunny in a very endearing way.

Bacon stood up; a verbal explosion ensued. “Thanks for bringing that up, Kira. Would now be a good time to remind us all that we can’t do half the fucking things that Sunny promised? Would now be a good moment to highlight that the artificial intelligence you call NADOSH is nowhere near as functional as Sunny just promised everyone at Arand Corp!? We’ve been trying unsuccessfully for months to get NADOSH to react to even simple air quality control and lighting commands. FAILED. As things currently stand, that hunk of metal is not getting off the ground, let alone capable of housing human life for more than ten minutes before they all suffocate from lack of oxygen.” Bacon let out a huge sigh. “Maybe now’s a good time to call it quits? Admit to Scorpia that we oversold this whole thing and just accept that Arand will do whatever they want and probably fail miserably? Hell, I’d rather be on a ship with people running around like headless chickens than die from radiation poison or whatever the hell comes next on Earth.” He sighed bitterly.

“I need the original code. It’s the only way," Sunny muttered. He had not been listening to Bacon’s rant. “With the chip from the original AI, I can build it into Zeeta’s mainframe and run it directly.” Sunny was still gripping the laser pistol tightly. To his disgust, he noticed some goo from the body in front of him stuck on his hands. “I have … I have studied the Pendleton file to death. I know all the ins and outs. The cyborg used for that mission, NADOSH, was incredible. She was a machine, but she showed such adaptability and managed to survive impossible odds. She was just a machine disguised as a woman, but she completed her mission and even developed compassion. Despite being a machine, she developed compassion for Pendleton until the very end.”

Bacon was trying to ignore the fresh corpse. Holding up a handkerchief, he sputtered, “Oh, here we go again with the fucking Pendleton fairytale. What does it matter that a convict sentenced to live on a planetary rock in exile fell in love with a cyborg? That's all she was, Sunny, a fucking cyborg sent to cure a doomed man of his loneliness. That's it. If you feel certain that old tech can run an entire spaceship, you're lying to yourself. The reality is we have no goddamn way of knowing if your little programming routine can run Zeeta 21. You made a good speech at the council meeting, sure. Got Arand's ear, who, by the way, we don't work for anymore since they fired us, remember? And, you just conveniently omitted all the unknowns. What happens when we let an untested and possibly independent AI loose in a city of twenty thousand hapless people? She might turn us all into slaves as far as I'm concerned."

Sunny looked to the ground. He was immersed in his thoughts. It was impossible to tell if he was still aware of the people around him. "All my problems will be solved when I get the original code," he said. "It's the only way. NADOSH is our only option. We'll set her to self-aware mode the second we leave Earth's atmosphere. I'll program her consciousness to ensure my well-being. If she was capable of loving Pendleton, she'll be capable of loving me too. And all the people of Zeeta. She'll be kind and merciful to anyone who lives there. I and only a few others will have the password to overwrite the trajectory coordinates. That means only a select few can steer Zeeta back to Earth before the mission ends if needed."

Kira shifted in her chair. "That sounds awfully dangerous. I mean, what if something happens to you or you're somehow left unable to act? In a case of a major emergency, that could compromise the entire ship," she said.

"I'll inject a neurotransmitter into my body. That way, NADOSH will constantly be aware of my vital signs. Her first mission will be to keep me alive. I'll also code an emergency response in case we need to crash-land on Earth. NADOSH and I will live - and die - together," Sunny said while gazing off into the distance.

Kira and Bacon felt the oppressive atmosphere in the room. They realised they were taking a huge gamble literally travelling into the unknown with Sunny. However, they felt reassured by Sunny's presence; he exuded an inexplicable calm. It felt right being around him, and he was comforted by the idea that they could rely on each other.

Bacon took a sip of water. "After we take off, I want to be left completely alone. My team and I will continue working in the engine rooms without interference from the outside. This will give me time to continue my research," he said.

Kira looked at him. "You mean you're still adamant about doing gene manipulation on humans to see if they can evolve? Sure, humans aren't perfect, but I think it's beyond the scope of this mission to create different forms of life."

"Humans are the reason we're in this fucking mess to begin with!" Sunny roared. "Our species somehow has an unquenchable thirst for self-destruction. Indeed, if Bacon is right, there might be something after us, such as the transmutation of our species, the next step on the evolutionary ladder. Maybe going beyond our human frailties is the way to save our planet and future generations." His words were tinged with both hope and spite.

Bacon felt satisfied with the support of his comrades. "Very well. It seems we're all in agreement here. Let's carry this through. Sunny, whatever you do, I advise you to move quickly. Last I heard, they plan to launch a few months from now, so we don't have much time to get NADOSH working properly. Whether we can do that in time seems to be the biggest unknown here." Bacon got up.

He sensed romantic tension between Kira and Sunny. "I'll leave you two in case you have, um, other things to discuss." He left the room.

Alone now, Kira and Sunny sat down next to each other. Sunny let out a huge sigh and let his head drop into his hands. "No one fucking understands me… The load and pressure I'm carrying on my shoulders. I just want to make it right," he said. "I know there's hope for humankind; it can't end this way."

Kira was touched by his vulnerability; it was the first time she saw him open up like this. "I understand it's a lot. But you shouldn't feel alone. We're here to help you," she said as she rubbed his shoulder.

Sunny noticed she had taken off her shoes. She had painted her toenails with three colours of polish; the sight of her feet aroused him.
He took her hand gently, and he started caressing her cheeks. She smiled at him, and they kissed. Sunny felt a bolt of lightning traverse his entire body. She was soft, and her lips felt like balm on an open wound. He slowly ran his fingers through her hair, short, silky curls. He looked into her deep brown eyes.
Sunny felt hard already. He got up and pulled her body against his. He lifted her skirt, then her one leg. He pushed himself into her with a determined thrust. He moved. Timid at first, then harder and faster. They both moaned in enjoyment as they extracted mutual pleasure from each other's bodies.
Just before he came, Sunny thought there might be some things worthwhile in life after all. He let the orgasm run through his body, his every nerve ending tingling with emotion.
Then he opened his eyes and realised the dead man was lying there next to them. There was still work to do.

Sunny Sees the Abbess

Sunny must have been waiting only five minutes, but it felt like an eternity. His palms were sweaty, and he could barely remember what time of day it was. So many things were racing through his mind: calculations, potential outcomes, all that could go wrong.
But he needed to convince her; he needed to see the Abbess.
Her presence caused an invisible veil of tranquillity to come over the tiny room they were in. Sunny had managed to get an impromptu meeting with her in one of the most Eastern towers of the Monastery. They were, as far as he could tell, completely alone.
As soon as she walked in, he closed his eyes and took a deep breath. Somehow, he felt like everything was going to be alright. The Abbess looked menacing. Her towering figure was dressed in a multi-layered gown best described as flexible war armour decorated with golden patterns reminiscent of ancient Rome. On her hands were white gloves from which an unknown gooey

substance appeared to drip. Her face, as usual, was completely covered, this time by a bulky-looking helmet with no visible passages to let air circulate.

"I… I'm Sunny Bridges. We must speak."

The Abbess put her hands together. "I know who you are. The Judge and the Arand superiors told me about you. Now, make haste. Tell me why you have beckoned me."

Sunny nodded and explained. There was no time to waste.

"The Pendleton file, I've studied it in minute detail. The cyborg used for that mission, she survived. I want to transfer over the AI to control Zeeta. I need access to her mortal remains and extract the chip myself. It's the only way." Sunny, realising he was in the presence of a great being, was humbled.

She remained silent, so Sunny continued. "I've laboured for weeks attempting to copy the code. But I need the source material. I need the actual cyborg and her memories. Before Pendleton passed she … she showed remorse. She showed him love and kindness. This AI clearly has immense learning and problem-solving abilities, and it can do what's best for Zeeta. Keep the people safe. It's our only hope." Sunny felt a lump in his stomach. Everything depended on the Abbess and her reaction.

"I have foreseen your request; your contribution to the meeting earlier caused quite a furore. My meditations have guided me. And I shall grant your wish. You will be given access to Nadia, the cyborg host with the AI you seek. Since the Pendleton mission, we have kept her functional here at the Monastery. You know that from the documents, I presume."

Sunny felt a burden lift from his shoulders. There was hope yet.

The Abbess continued, "I ask but one thing: be truthful to your heart. Do everything in your power to succeed. I fear what might happen once Zeeta takes off. Dark visions have clouded my mind. Nadia was one of our finest prototypes. She was conceived as a manual labour cyborg, built to serve here at the Monastery. But she turned into so much more. Be conscious of your actions. Do what you can; keep your spirit pure." The last statement carried a firm, if not menacing, undertone.

"My monks will guide you to a secret location in the dungeons underneath this very Monastery. You will have twenty minutes with the specimen, no more." As soon as she finished, the Abbess turned and left the room.

Two monks immediately entered, gently blindfolded Sunny, and took him away. Many chambers of the Monastery were kept secret from the outside world; this was one of them.

He regained his senses in a small sterilised room, partially lit by pre-war monitor screens and a few fluorescent overhead lights. A few monks were preparing for the operation, but Sunny ignored them.

He was looking at her — Nadia.

She lay there on the table, her mortal remains looking innocent and peaceful. Her entire face had been blasted off by a gunshot, exposing the circuits and wires inside her head. Dried blood stained her clothes. Why the monks had not cleaned her in all this time, he did not know nor bothered to ask. It was clear she was a machine. Tubes and electrical cables were keeping her online. It felt unreal to see the woman he had read so much about.

The monks nodded at him, and he stepped back. He watched as they cleaved her skull open and worked their way towards the core. Much damage had already been done to her metal cranium, so there was no point in being delicate. They extracted the main controller chip and gently placed it in a foam-lined box. The machines were turned off, and Nadia was no more; the only thing left was the chip containing NADOSH. Sunny took the box from the monks and left the room.

It took him another four months of non-stop labour to install Nadia's chip into the NADOSH mainframe. When he finally succeeded, Zeeta 21, docked at the take-off pad close to the Monastery, lit up the entire desert like a beacon of light, all systems functional.

Brother Francis ran to his window when the blinding rays penetrated his tiny tower room. A tear trickled down his cheeks.

Ready for Take-off

It had been a few months since Lechowsky last saw Sunny and the two others. He still carried a grudge and spent much time pondering the rude way in which they interrupted his presentation at the last assembly, making him look like a fool in front of the entire delegation. And Scorpia. His blood boiled as he imagined the many ways he would like to exert his revenge.

Apparently, Scorpia had given Sunny free access to Zeeta during off-hours, meaning he was pretty much free to tinker with whatever he saw fit. This was completely out of protocol, of course. God knows what the hell he was doing there, but Scorpia remained convinced that installing the super AI was the right thing to do. I really hope Scorpia's telling the truth. That the Judge supports this like she says, Lechowsky thought.

At least she had promised Lechowsky that they would get Sunny out the way as soon as possible. She, too, agreed that he was too much of a liability. They just needed to get Zeeta into orbit, get everything stabilised, and then he was no longer of use.

To keep occupied, Lechowsky was finalising his work on the Jonny-bots. The robots would serve the people of Zeeta, doing menial tasks like cleaning, cooking and taxi services.

He had approved the final list of friendly phrases the bots would use to communicate. Fifty years was a long time to be away from Earth, and he saw it as a personal responsibility to make talking to the bots as varied and agreeable as possible. His favourite line so far was, "Have no fear, your friendly Jonny-bot's here!"

At that moment, one of the monks clumsily opened the door to his office. "Ex-excuse me, sir, but this, er, person wanted entry. He wouldn't wait any longer," he said while tripping over the hem of his robe. A smile broke on Lechowsky's face.

A man wearing a massive set of power armour walked in. A mask made of high-grade aluminium, almost like those ancient gladiators wore, covered his face. Behind him was another soldier dressed in civilian clothes. Although maintaining a calm demeanour, their propensity for violence was evident.

"I've just gotten some jolly news. It seems my men and I are going after all," the armoured man spoke. His mask made his voice

distorted and frightening. Lechowsky's smile grew bigger. Just as he thought: it was Horrigan, all right.
"Indeed!" Lechowsky sprung from his chair. "I managed to get approval from the Board. You and your men are welcome to join Zeeta when it launches just a few weeks from now! I'm thrilled we've managed to make it work. But let me just say that it was no easy feat!"
Horrigan, all emotion masked by his gear, nodded. "Affirmative. What made them change their minds? I thought the previous decision to ban ex-military staff had been final."
"Aha, well, belonging to a former secret military service is one thing, Horrigan, but the real problem was the numerous atrocities committed by yourself and your fine assemblage of…'', he glanced at the man behind Horrigan, "killers."
Lewchowsky continued, "I did the best I could to cover it up, but it was just too much for the Arand Board. Even in this day and age, there are limits to what the remnants of our once civilised society can do. The stuff your crew did still gives me nightmares."
Horrigan remained neutral and emotionless.
"So, yes, the good people at the Arand Corporation were nervous about allowing you and your rogue band of mercenaries on board. Understandably so, I might add. I mean, I wouldn't want to be confined in a space-city with women and children murderers." Lechowsky struggled to speak casually; the trickle of sweat on his forehead revealed his anxiousness. "But, I made them decide otherwise in the end."
"What changed?" Horrigan demanded, discretely communicating that the build-up wasn't necessary. He just wanted facts.
Lechowsky put his hands behind his back. "Well, we need protection on this mission, Arand Headquarters must be kept safe at all times. A new guy, fucker named Sunny, made all this clear to us. Let's just say he changed the, er, dynamics of how we plan to run Zeeta. I was taken aback at first, but then I decided to make the most of it. Hence, I'm appointing you Commander of the Enforcers, Horrigan! You will de facto oversee our entire police force, reporting directly to me."
Horrigan nodded.

"I hope this is somewhat, er, pleasing, to you. Zeeta 21 should be a pleasant experience. For sure, it'll be better than getting scorched by the radiation on this hell-hole Earth has become. I foresee a great career opportunity for yourself, and your closest cohorts." He smiled at Horrigan's partner. The name tag read 'J. Blakemore'.

"I don't fucking work for anybody," Blakemore spewed. A young boy of ten or eleven timidly clung to his knee. Lechowsky figured it was Blakemore's son.

Lechowsky maintained a mock smile, then looked at Blakemore and said, "Now let me just make one thing clear to you two motherfuckers. I'm giving you the chance of a lifetime to leave Earth and repent for the sins you've committed. Lord knows there have been plenty. Here, you're treated like scum. On Zeeta, you'll be first in command. But don't you ever forget that you fucking work for me. Whatever you do, my safety is your priority. You got that?" He continued, "You want to know how I got you a place on board? By stripping you of your humanity, that's how. The fact that you agreed to undergo a complete cyborg-transformation means that anything left of that, shall we say, delightful personality of yours will be gone. Eradicated. The only thing left will be a hunk of metal with a huge gun that serves me."

He calmed down and continued, mostly speaking to himself, "Lord knows this is stupendous. What the hell am I getting myself into? That Sunny boy gave me a good scare. If indeed people turn into barbarians, I need to be safe. I'll be the Leader of the Arand Corp on Zeeta and force those ants to obey." He chuckled quietly with boyish glee.

Blakemore crossed his arms over his chest. This was not the first farcical power display he had seen. He felt his son hold on to his leg. Blakemore had been trying to provide for him as best he could since the boy's mother passed. But life on Earth was increasingly tough even for a well-paid mercenary. He hoped Zeeta would be a safer place for them both.

"Affirmative, sir. I'll start training and prepping the men. We'll be ready for Zeeta's scheduled launch," Horrigan said and left the room.

"You'd better be," Lechowsky murmured bitterly to himself. "You'd fucking better be." And to Horrigan he said, "Oh, and don't forget. You have your transformative surgery tomorrow at nine a.m. I told the monks to keep that pretty face of yours in a jar somewhere when they cut it off."

October 20th, 3246: Launch of Zeeta 21

Scorpia was frantically pacing back and forth. Two weeks had passed, and the last-minute preparations for Zeeta's launch had gone mostly according to plan. Large parts of the ship's underground remained unfinished, but there was no more money to complete the work. They had to make do with what was there.

Lechowsky had insisted an army of goons, one of whom looked like an armour-clad tank, be brought along. Not exactly whom she would have chosen, but she did not object. She was, frankly, exhausted. From the beginning, she felt the whole weight of the mission had been on her shoulders. Between negotiating financial support from the countries and presenting numerous progress reports to the LSW Committee, her batteries were drained. Oh, how she dreaded sharing the stage with Lechowsky, listening to his utopian fairy tales. It had all taken a toll on her, physically and mentally. Her feet were feeling tired; she sat down.

But everything was going to be okay. Today was the launch of Zeeta, and she would finally reap the fruits of her hard labour. She imagined a long journey through space where she would be treated like a queen. She would make decisions and work when necessary, but mostly she would enjoy life and make sure Lechowsky stayed in line.

She had not heard from Sunny in a while, but her sources reported that he had been quietly prepping Zeeta as agreed. She hoped he would not betray her, but that remained to be seen.

Her thoughts were interrupted when the door-gong sounded. The monks had those stupid bells installed in each room in the visitors' quarters. It made this skull-cracking low-pitched tone the people of religion seemed to find soothing. It went off four times; that meant the Abbess was visiting.

The Abbess came into the room as quietly as a feather. Scorpia looked at her. The Abbess was wearing a large gown made of dark brown textured leather and elegant fabric in a similar shade. On her head was a disturbing two-horned goat-head. Scorpia wondered what the Abbess' face looked like; apparently, no one had ever seen it.

"Forgive me, Abbess, but your dress today, it's really … astounding. What does it signify? I know you told me something about suffering …", Scorpia trailed off.

The Abbess sat down on a wooden bench and spoke gently, not the least taken aback by the question. "Indeed, here at the Monastery of Our Lord we proudly display our suffering on the outside rather than keeping it hidden within our souls. That way, we give it room and space to grow, so we can share it with others and ultimately transcend our pain." She paused briefly. "Thank you for enquiring about our ways. We're grateful and humbled when outsiders are interested in our way of life."

I was just wondering why you dress like a freak, Scorpia thought. She said aloud, "Yes, er, well, I take it you didn't come here to exchange fashion advice. As you know, Zeeta will be leaving in a few hours, so I need to get ready. My boarding escort will arrive shortly." Scorpia had the impression that Abbess was wearing a smile heavy with sorrow under her mask.

"Soon, you and thousands of others will fire up Zeeta's engines for the first time and take to the skies in a blaze of glory. Your journey around the Earth will bring clarity to mind and soul. Whereafter, you'll surely land back on Earth to bring new enlightenment and hope to the world. We're all so proud and hopeful of what you can achieve," the Abbess said kindly.

"Alas, fear and a heavy heart weigh on me and disturb both my sleeping and waking moments. I worry. I worry gravely for what's about to become of you. And of us." The Abbess' words drove an ice pick through Scorpia's heart. She elegantly expressed the mix of excitement and fear they all felt. Although they tried to conceal it, Scorpia's entire staff were somewhat fearful of leaving.

The Abbess nodded as if she had read Scorpia's mind. She solemnly put her hands together. "So far, I've contained my pain and suffering through meditation. But the Brothers have started to feel it as well. I sense the same anguish running through our beloved Monastery. Although Lord knows the monks are working as diligently as ever. They'd never let fear get in the way of their duties." The Abbess sounded so warm and proud when she spoke. Scorpia thought she was probably a beautiful woman beneath the witch-like exterior. Her feet were feeling better, so she got up to take a glass of fermented water, what the monks called beer. "Why, yes, umm, the monks surely have done great deeds. Without them, this whole operation wouldn't fly. We would be … grounded, for lack of a better term," she said absent-mindedly.

The Abbess sighed. "I've prayed day and night for you and the ship's crew members, all 18,765 of you. I pray you'll stay safe. And wise. That's what worries me the most: that a stroke of fear or panic will cause bad decisions to be made and things spiral out of control."

Scorpia, her mind still elsewhere, took another sip and put down her glass. She opened her mouth to speak but quickly lost her train of thought.

"I know about the changes to the interior design. And I know about NADOSH," the Abbess said. Her tone was firm but not accusatory. "Mr Sunny Bridges made quite an impact with his speech at the last Committee meeting. I can understand why you took on his proposals. I'm not sure I would've made the same decisions, but I can understand your reasoning. After all, one doesn't argue with the Judge and the Arand superiors." She didn't seem to hold any grudges and was merely stating facts.

Scorpia froze. How the hell did this lady know about the changes she had greenlit Sunny to make. Did she know about the Enforcers as well?

The Abbess continued, "I'm not here to cause strife or influence you in any way. Once Zeeta leaves the Earth's atmosphere, you're on your own. Only your love for God and your common sense can guide you. Our Brothers and I will remain in contact by radio with the ship, but our powers to intervene are limited. Therefore, I beg of you, be wise. Trust the inner good within yourself and in others. Don't make decisions out of anger, fear, or spite. Look for the unlimited ocean of consciousness within yourself and pray that you can find it in your fellow men as well. Don't let this become a tragedy. We, and all the people on Earth, are counting on you for hope and strength. We'll await your return with eagerness and faith."

The Abbess got up and started to leave. This was not a discussion but rather the Abbess asserting her views. Scorpia sat back down, the sour taste of low-grade beer still burning the back of her throat. She received another call from the Judge and took his instructions in silence. Her thoughts were swirling inside her head like a tornado, triggering a migraine.

"I need to get high. This fucking pain is too much," she mumbled while rubbing her temples. Her stomach felt as if it were ready to crawl out of her mouth, spilling its contents in the process.

Then, the dreadful gong sounded again. This time it was her escort group. It was time to board Zeeta for the final take-off. Her escort was professional and comforting. Four rather handsome men in Arand uniforms arrived in a small electric vehicle to drive her to the Zeeta take-off site.

The car drove up to an elevated platform where the Arand directors were sitting. Scorpia joined them and started watching all the equipment and groups of people be loaded into the Zeeta spaceship. There was a long line of people slowly walking up the boarding platform. All happened peacefully and quietly. The monks stood around giving out desiccated flowers and praise to anyone passing by. Scorpia thought they looked like idiots.

"When this thing takes off, we initiate our contingency plan. Immediately," she said to Lechowsky, who was standing with a few others. He was discernibly taken aback by her blunt statement.

"I have the greenlight from the Arand superiors. The Judge himself approved it."

"Holy fuck," he murmured to himself. He stumbled over some metallic crates as he moved closer to where Scorpia sat. He was now within whispering range.

Scorpia frowned, and her voice turned dark and hostile. "I don't trust any of these people, not a single one! Just after we take off, I want to turn on the heat. Unleash the Enforcers. Everyone is

confined within their cubicles. Complete order and control will be upheld from our side. Arand will run the entire show. And anyone who opposes us will be quelled."
"But-but I thought we would wait a little bit, at least a few months, to see how people behave, how things progress, before —"
Scorpia ignored Lechowsky's concern and interrupted him. "And I want constant surveillance of Sunny and his band of merry men. Just to make sure they don't step out of line. If they do, we clamp down on them. Immediately."
This pleased Lechowsky, who now seemed more at ease with the order. He called Horrigan over and whispered something to him.
Scorpia watched a pregnant woman in the crowd. Her belly was huge; she held onto it while smiling at someone helping her up the steps. Scorpia frowns. What a pathetic fool, she thought. I'll wipe that grin off her face soon enough. I'll make every one of you respect me.

The pregnant woman gave birth to a beautiful girl called Lily about a month after take-off. Like all mothers, her mind was filled with hopes and dreams that her little girl would grow up happy, strong, and eager to make a positive impact on the world. Little did she know that Lily, and the rest of Zeeta 21's populace, would spend their lives in captivity.
Soon, all the remaining passengers and Arand staff members boarded, and the launch protocol was initiated.
A pleasant voice filled the ship's passenger sections as the engines fired up and the doors were sealed triple-shut. "Greetings, fellow space travellers, space explorers, and space cadets! Welcome to Zeeta, your home away from Earth! I'm sure you're all fired up to get moving, so listen carefully, and we'll be on our way. Now's the time to take your designated seats and hold on close to your mummy, daddy, or designated legally viable warden. We're just about to take off! Drinks and other refreshments will be provided to you shortly. In case of ANY questions or requests, grab the plastic tube in front of you and inhale as deeply as you can. It'll send you straight to dreamland, so you can forget about your troubles. Please be aware that the Arand Corporation can

absolutely not be held liable in any form or manner in case of unwanted illness, discomfort, or deaths that may or may not occur anytime before, during, or after our initial flight schedule has concluded.

"That does it for the formalities. All that's left to do now is sit back and relax. And remember, folks: smile happy, smiiiiile Zeeta!" The voice was replaced by a busy rustling of people settling into their seats.

And without further ado, Zeeta 21 carved its way through what remained of the Earth's atmosphere, slowly making its way towards the stars.

Chapter II: Hope Flies High (Year 3263)

Brother Francis Looks to the Sky

Francis sat down and looked at his mechanised pocket watch. It was ancient, handed down from his Elder Brother and mentor at the Monastery. He was immensely proud of it.

The year is 3263, seventeen years since Zeeta left Earth; much had changed there in the meantime.

The Great War broke out in 3248, only a few years after Zeeta was launched. The tenuous peace pact between nations of the Surviving World gradually rusted away. Building Zeeta 21 was extremely costly, and what little resources each country had left was squandered on meaningless defense programmes. In fact, each country built up armies and invested in technology to wage war as their leaders grew increasingly paranoid. Adding fuel to the fire was the increased radioactivity and rampant environmental degradation. In short, Earth was becoming a hostile place to live. Consequently, the members of the LSWC were desperate to appease their population to limit riots and unrest, a task that became even more thankless after Zeeta launched. People asked themselves, Why was I not chosen to go? Why did my kids not deserve the chance at a better life?

Unable to provide good answers, nations did what nations have always done: create an image of the enemy, of the Other. In desperate times, people need to point the finger at someone to blame for life's shortcomings. It is intrinsically human and destructive.

Francis sat by himself, as he often did, while pondering all of this. The Brothers had shown him images from the Monastery's reconnaissance satellite. The war had caused unspeakable destruction, devastating the western part of the world.

And for the first time in history, the Monastery itself had been under direct attack. The Abbess said this had never happened before; the Monastery was supposed to be a haven for dialogue

and understanding between parties. It was also where nations bought their guns and technology.
The Brothers dealt with the attack swiftly; the enemies were burned to cinders. Alas, two ballistic warheads hit the western dome of the Monastery's cathedral. Four Brothers died, and seven more were burned severely. One of Francis' close friends nearly had his entire face burned off by the plasma; it was not a pretty sight. The attack also smashed the satellite the Monastery had been using to maintain radio contact with Zeeta. Francis and the Brothers spent months trying to fix the desecration.
The Abbess said that identifying the assailants was impossible as anyone could have hired the attacking mercenary ships. She also believed they should not bother trying as nothing good would come of it.
Francis let out a huge sigh and gulped down some dirty water. He had not even bothered to purify it. Dum spiro spero, he whispered to himself. While I breathe, I hope. The Abbess always said to maintain hope and have faith that Zeeta 21 would be successful, eventually bringing more peaceful times to Earth.
But is there still hope? Francis wanted to believe the Abbess, but he remained anxious about everything that could go wrong. Also, on one side of his stomach was a hard, painful and pulsating lump. I should tell someone about it.
The Abbess kept the Brotherhood together the best she could. But he knew she worried too. She would often wear the ceremonial goat-head mask, which she only wore in times of disquiet. He focused on the task ahead of him. Francis and a few others were to scout around the Monastery for traces of edible plants or animals, the latter preferably not too radiated. He zipped up his fabric black leather coat and strapped on his full-visage helmet. Leaving home had become a dangerous endeavour. After the last war, radiation storms and weather hazards became frequent. He had also heard tales of beasts the size of fifteen men roaming the land. As he stepped outside, Francis switched his helmet to night mode as it was the only way to see through the sandstorms. He glanced at the sky. I hope and pray the people of Zeeta are safe

and will return to us with new ideas and a fresh outlook on humankind's survival. A small tear trickled down his left cheek.

Digging Through the Past

Lieutenant Horrigan stomped on moribund individuals and cadavers, crushing them under his heavy armour as he made his way towards the spot indicated by the Jonny-bots.

He had been ordered to retrieve three specific individuals from the Disposal Site. It was essentially a huge hole, one hundred metres deep and fifty metres wide, where all dead or dying citizens of Zeeta were dumped. The stench bore witness to that.

"We estimate with a seventy-eight percent certainty that we have correctly identified the third and final specimen, sir," the Jonny-bot said. His colleagues responded with affirmative beeps. Failing to receive any visible reaction from his superior, the bot tentatively added, "Our proposed course of action is to return the specimens to headquarters for further testing and final identification, sir."

Horrigan hazily regained focus. "Load them into the transporter, and let's get the fuck out of here," he said while waving his hand and turning his back to the bots.

The operation had changed him. Since becoming a cyborg, he had struggled to concentrate on anything outside the orders given by his superiors. Still, he was annoyed the entire morning about this mission, which he had received at six a.m. while tending to other more urgent tasks.

His superior at the Arand Corp, Lechowsky, had personally insisted that Horrigan oversee and carry out the mission, then report back immediately upon its completion. Horrigan was given a ridiculous number of Enforcer squads, troops that could have been put to better use elsewhere, to go to the Disposal Site of all places. It was by far the most miserable task he had had to do during his seventeen years of service on Zeeta.

The Jonny-bots were busy hauling up the final raggedy bastard, who supposedly was still breathing. One of the bots slipped and landed face down onto a cluster of fresh corpses, smearing its immaculate blue plastic uniform with blood and gore.

At least one thing to amuse me this morning, Horrigan thought grimly behind his metal mask. While making his way back towards the hover van, his right boot got stuck in a dead man's jawbone. As he was about to raise his left foot to crush the skull and free himself while relieving some aggression at the same time, he saw a peculiar electronic device sticking out of the corpse's upper-right chest pocket. About the size of a hairbrush, it had a handle and a small screen with a metallic matte grey finish. The man, a worker before meeting his final fate, was wearing a blue and yellow jumpsuit, characteristic of the laboratory staff of the Arand Corp. Horrigan picked up the metallic display device and turned it on. The device flickered, then a piece of text started scrolling down the screen. A pleasant voice narrated a video depicting sketches and designs of the Zeeta spaceship. It was a promotional video distributed to people on Earth leading up to Zeeta's launch, enticing them to sign up.

Welcome to Zeeta 21: Your home away from Earth!

An introduction to our glorious* and congenial city*[1]
Are you tired of living under the constraints that life on Earth imposes on us: pollution, gravity, taxes? Do you ever dream of something else? Something bigger? Well, so do we!
Welcome to Zeeta 21: the first city outside Earth. Zeeta is a $57.490 billion space project set to launch on October twentieth, 3246. We've brought together the world's leading nations to offer something unique. Zeeta is a city designed for space travel built on a massive steel platform measuring eleven-squared kilometres and covered by an impressive plexiglass dome to shield its inhabitants from space hazards. It has some spectacular and ultra-modern features, including a simulated day-and-night cycle, lush parks with synthetic trees made of the finest plastic fibres modern science has to offer, and a breathtaking view of nearby stars and solar systems. What's more, you can expect a host of mind-numbing and regularly scheduled events and activities — everything you and your family could ever want!
Zeeta will primarily be inhabited by the best and brightest minds from a multitude of nations, comprising leading scientists, doctors, and engineers. But don't fret. There's room for you too!
We guarantee employment if you choose to move here, and you and your family will be given free accommodation and food. Everything is paid for by the Arand Corporation!
Our Jonny-bots will make sure you enjoy a life of ease and comfort. These jolly fellas accompany you throughout your day. Forget about annoying tasks related to transport, grocery shopping, and healthcare. All you have to do is (work and) enjoy.
And did we mention the estimated negative zero point one percent crime rate[2]? Clearly, this is the best place for you and your family to prosper in a safe, carefree environment.

---

[1] The terms 'glorious' and 'congenial' might not necessarily apply to the city in question. Facts/statements in this informational brochure may have been altered/fabricated, and the facts/figures herein could have possibly been slightly/significantly changed to the point where they might/might not represent a correct depiction of the city in question.

[2] Official figures. Actual statistics may differ.

Now can you think of one good reason why you shouldn't come here? We can't either! Don't hesitate. Sign up now!
Do as so many have done before you: come help make our great city even greater. We already have nearly eighteen thousand confirmed inhabitants and are always looking for more people to join our army of people that helps make life on Zeeta simple, satisfying, and safe.
Join us now!! And be part of the future.

Remember, folks: smile happy, smiiiiile Zeeta!

Copyright: Arand Corporation, Marketing Bureau of Zeeta 21, 3246.

The video ended with a picture of an early Jonny-bot model when they looked even more mechanical and disturbing. The device flickered again before powering down indefinitely; the storage conditions in the worker's pocket had not been optimal.
Horrigan discarded the device amid the human bodies and ran a diagnosis report of the area on his built-in mainframe.
The following facts and figures started scrolling in front of his pupils:

Zeeta 21 status report by NADOSH … proprietary Arand Corporation software v. 1.6.9.420 …
… classified…

Current location> Sector 4B, Disposal Site (above ground). Friendly territory, controlled by Arand Corp.
<<>>>Risk of accidental death> less than 4,2%.

Adjacent location> Sector 5B, engines and machinery (underground). Neutral territory, controlled by Specials.
Characteristics:
Technicians and engineers, dispatched by Arand Corp. Runs engines and machinery of Zeeta.
Isolated group of individuals > mutations possible, unknown if allegiance to Arand Crop still exists.
<<>>>Risk of accidental death> estimated at 10-12%.

Unknown location>system error< sector unclassified (underground). <<>>>Hostile territory, controlled by Fallen.
Characteristics:
Group of outcasts hiding from Arand Corp.
Status: Warning! Warning!
Do not approach without greenlight from superiors. Highly dangerous.
<<>>>Caution! High risk of accidental death> estimated at above 96%.
Arand casualties sustained since launch … *calculating* … 1,276
<<<report concluded>>>

Horrigan's blood boiled thinking about the Fallen, a wretched clan of lowlifes who hid like cowards underneath the city's surface. Swear I'll personally execute every last one of them! He thought. Hate was the only human emotion he was still allowed to feel.
He then received a call from an Enforcer officer on his wrist-AI, a personal computer implanted into the lower-left wrist of each Zeeta citizen to facilitate communication with (and tracking of) individuals. "Sir, reports of attacks in Sector 14Z, likely instigated by members of the Fallen. Do you want to assist in the clean-up action?" Horrigan declined the distress call after a brief hesitation. "Take two hover vans there and get the situation under control. I need to report back to HQ."

The Arand Corp HQ

The trip back to the Arand HQ seemed to last an eternity. Horrigan was seated in the first hover van, surrounded by elite Enforcers. Behind them was the carrier with the three newly acquired bodies. Horrigan looked out on the streets. People in the sector around the Arand Corp's main tower were calmly going about their daily business. There was a heavy presence of Enforcers and Jonny-bots, ensuring safety and comfort for the citizens. It was perfect, exactly what Zeeta was conceived to be.
Unconsciously thinking about the Fallen, Horrigan was filled with rage, infuriated with the imbeciles trying to destroy the harmony Arand had brought. Without paying attention, his knuckles tightened under his metal gloves.

“Lieutenant, we’ve arrived at Arand’s main tower and will proceed with the task at hand. You’re free to report to Commander Lechowsky and inform him of the success of your mission.” The Enforcer struck a perfect balance between being professional and respectful, the mark of a good officer. Horrigan got out of the hover van while giving the officer a quick nod.
“Time to see the boss”, Horrigan thought while looking up at the impressive Arand building. He somehow knew the next part of his day would be less pleasant.

The elevator ride to Lechowsky’s office on the 21st floor felt like an eternity, and Horrigan’s head swirled with personal and illegal thoughts. He disagreed with the orders he was given and was annoyed at having wasted good officers’ time digging through graveyards. He would have to put such free-thinking away: they were not part of his mandate as a lieutenant.
His mind cleared as he entered the office, which was the Arand Corp’s main control room. The large room was filled with screens and counterintelligence equipment which covered the ten-metre walls. It was usually neatly kept, but today the place was a mess. There were synthetic paper transcripts scattered everywhere, and multiple surveillance monitors displayed scenes of chaos, riots and disruption in several of Zeeta’s key sectors.
The executive summary report Horrigan drew up earlier was already outdated; more Arand casualties had been added in the meantime. On top of that, Lechowsky was having a heated discussion with NADOSH, the AI controlling Zeeta’s key functions. He was talking to her avatar displayed on a large OLED monitor in front of him.
“Listen. I don’t fucking care about your estimations and mumbo-jumbo. I want to find that fucker ASAP. I don’t have time to wait forty-eight hours until the final identification is made. And I care even less about recovery schedules to get him back to good health. Pick out the info I need from his brain with a rusty metal shard if you have to, and discard the rest. Is that clear, you dumb bitch?” He was exasperated. “Or do I fucking need to write it in C++ coding language for you?”
NADOSH seemed unfazed by the emotional outburst and replied in her usual neutral tone. “Commander. I can //confirm//

successful identification of specimen#1. Result: DNA //not matching// the sought-after individual. //Positive ID// made for middle-grade technical engineer John Frye, inhabitant #11389. Not possessing crucial knowledge. Specimen#1 will be //disposed of//. Immediately." Lechowsky, visibly still terribly upset with the situation, let out a great sigh of irritation. Who programmed NADOSH's dialogue module? It's choppy as hell, he thought.

NADOSH continued, "Consequently. Required identification time for two remaining //subjects// reduced to…*calculating*... thirty-six hours, eighteen minutes, and fifty-five seconds. Both //specimens// badly injured. Consequence: limited teeth samples available. Regrettably, parallel //rehabilitation process// hampered by lack of medical bots; sixty-eight point seven percent of fleet stationed in the //outer sectors//. Commander, next report will be //provided// ASAP." NADOSH's avatar then gave a subtle and decisive nod towards Horrigan, who was still standing at the back of the room.

Lechowsky, still slumped over the main control board, looked behind his shoulder, and made a jerky movement to wipe the sweat off his brow. "Ah, yes, Horrigan. Please do come in," he said as he tried to make his shoulder-length grey and white hair look presentable. "Leave us now, if you will," he said to NADOSH. She gave a polite smile before the monitor turned off. Lechowsky crawled down on the floor and disconnected the cables attached to the central monitor. He wanted to be certain no one could listen in on the ensuing conversation.

Walking towards Horrigan, he said, "Sorry you had to witness that, grown-up business." While under pressure, Lechowsky would often make witty remarks before announcing bad news. Horrigan hated it when he did that. Scenes of riots continued playing on one of the screens. Noticing that Horrigan was bothered by it, Lechowsky quickly switched it off via voice control.

"Horrigan, I wanted to thank you personally. Your intervention was a complete and utter success: no casualties and three living specimens were recovered. Quick in and out, just like in the old days." With that last remark, Lechowsky tried to force a convivial smile to placate Horrigan; it did not work.

Horrigan, in his usual robotic and cold manner, said, “Sir, I respect your authority as my commander in chief, but sending officers to a dump site to pick out corpses is a suboptimal use of their time. You are well aware that my men and I have more pressing matters to attend to.” He gestured towards the recently switched-off monitor.

Lechowsky took a deep breath. He thought to himself, I hope this tin can isn’t going to go all smart-ass on me. What the fuck is it with these robots, thinking they’re entitled to their own opinion like that?

But he smiled, looked meekly at the monitor, then back to Horrigan, and replied, “Trust me, Lieutenant. I know. You’re the best man I have. Slayer of evil, upholding justice. All that good stuff." Once again, Lechowsky failed to charm Horrigan, so he switched to a more official tone. He was wearing his usual white uniform with golden shoulder pads and gloves. At first glance, he looked like a leader who could maintain order.

“Look, the mission you carried out was highly important, even crucial for Zeeta’s survival. Sorry for the last-minute briefing, but we couldn’t risk any leaks.” Lechowsky looked toward the OLED monitor and paused briefly before continuing.

“You see, the individual we’re looking for has important knowledge that we need to, uh, help us get Zeeta back on track. He knows all about steering the ship and, most importantly, has the manual override codes which allow Zeeta to deviate from the set path. In fact, this person was the chief engineer before we had to, uh, silence him."

Lechowsky took another breath, pondering what information to divulge. “The guy’s name is Sunny. Sunny Bridges. Can you believe that? Stupid fucking name, I know. You might remember him as the annoying fuck who barged in on my presentation speech back on Earth all those years back. No? Anyway, he was unfortunately included in the last round of eliminations a week ago. Hence, he was at the Disposal Site. You know, suspicion of high treason and all that. Smart guy for sure. Unfortunately, he became a liability.”

Horrigan indeed knew all too well. His men were ordered to track down any threat to the Arand Corp. He was hard-wired to keep things peaceful on Zeeta by neutralising the resistance.

“Please advise on the next steps, sir,” Horrigan said. He was clad in full-body metal armour but without his mask. Lechowsky got a look at his appalling ‘face’. Only the bald, pale forehead and some skin on the cheeks remained. His eyes had been replaced with brown sockets, and his jaw and the rest of the skull were metal. Lechowsky shivered, averting his eyes.

“Listen, Lieutenant, it’s a complex matter, I know. That’s exactly why I didn’t want to bother you with the details. We’re doing everything needed to make this a success and get us back on track. I promise.” Lechowsky spoke decisively but with a hint of self-doubt.

“What I need you to do now is lead your Enforcers. We need the troops to focus. Convince them that we’re on top of things. Hold down the resistance, like we used to."

Horrigan kept his reaction short. “Affirmative, sir.”

For the first time during the conversation, the concerned look on Lechowsky’s brow dissipated, if only slightly. “Excellent, jolly good, as they say! Once again, I know I can count on you. But, listen, while your men are doing all the busy work, I have another special mission in mind for you." Horrigan stood motionless. “You see, this Bridges guy is a heavily sought-after individual. We believe both the Fallen and the Specials are looking for him too. You see, his knowledge is extremely valuable. So we’re facing high risks of direct attacks or infiltration attempts. You know those sneaky Fallen bastards, not to mention the traitors everywhere."

Lechowsky paused, expecting confirmation from Horrigan. There was no response, so he continued.“In a nutshell, I need someone to infiltrate the Fallen headquarters. We need to find out how much they know. If they’re mobilising any major attacks, we need to anticipate them. We no longer have the resources to cover all sectors, so we need to flank up strategically. Your task is to find a way to get inside. Crush the foetus before it is born, so to speak. Sorry for the grim analogy."

Horrigan struggled to compute a reply. He was programmed to follow orders, not improvise. Not to mention that it was a near-suicidal undertaking. In the last ten years of open conflict with the Fallen, Arand had never been anywhere near entering the Fallen’s underground base, let alone determining with any certainty their

exact location. Due to the hasty departure, the Zeeta surveillance system had not been sct up in most parts under the city surface. Keeping a straight face, he said, "Affirmative. I'll get on this right away and keep you updated."
Lechowsky stepped towards Horrigan and looked him in the eyes. "I knew I could count on you, son. The entire Corporation is most pleased. Now, if you'll excuse me, I've got some other pressing business to attend to. Dismissed, Lieutenant."
Having returned his superior's honorary greeting, Horrigan left the office and went to the canteen quarters. He still struggled to analyse the situation and calculate a correct course of action. For the first time he could remember, Horrigan registered feelings of doubt and fear. These were illicit emotions, especially to someone of his rank. He needed a strong dose of painkillers and nerve stimulants to make them disappear and called for his personal Jonny-bot.

Horrigan was determined to figure out a plan and execute it. He needed to find someone willing and able to infiltrate the Fallen base, and he already had someone in mind.

Echoes of Hate

As soon as Horrigan left, Lechowsky banged his fist into the nearest computer console. Fool! I'm such a fool! He muttered to himself. He was mad at NADOSH, whom he suspected was hiding something. But most of all, he was angry with himself for not figuring out what it was. He started strolling around the command centre to regain his composure. He was a good-looking man, especially for a man close to sixty. His grey and white hair gave him an air of authority. This is my territory, my palace. Nobody's going to steal it away from me. Not now. I've worked too hard. I crawled to the top, one step at a time. I am the master of Zeeta. His thoughts calmed him down.
At that exact moment, he received a message. His wrist-AI, implanted under the skin of his left underarm, started giving out a soft red light at two-second intervals. Lechowsky let out a sigh. It was a pre-recorded message, and he already knew from whom. It was Her.

Sitting down, he initiated the message with mind control. Then the hissing voice began to speak.
… Sweetheart … My little squirrel … It is meee… Come see me, daaarrrling … Lechowsky always shuddered at the horrible way she pronounced 'darling'.
… Come see me … It is time… I know you have news for me. I know you've been good, my love … I've made contact as we discussed … Come to my cave …
The tone of the last sentence implied she was not happy, which usually was the case. Lechowsky decided to go immediately not to make matters worse.
"Jonny, I will be out of my office for a few hours. Don't tell anyone. If someone comes to the door, you do not let them in. In case of calls, you have authority to simulate my voice but make sure you expedite them in an efficient manner."
The Jonny-bot was nodding while Lechowsky gave his instructions. "Yes, sir. Affirmative, sir," it said, first in its own voice then replicating meticulously Lechowsky's. Lechowsky was always disturbed by that, but it was an effective decoy.

Scorpia's cave was five kilometres west of the Arand Corp's main tower. It used to be an old uranium treatment facility, but it shut down since more efficient operations had been set up underground. Lechowsky travelled incognito, escorted only by two of his most loyal bodyguards. Not even Horrigan could know about his whereabouts.
He reluctantly entered the abandoned compound. As soon as he entered, he lost all WiFi connections; he was effectively untraceable. It was like stepping back into the past. Lechowsky eased through the first set of security doors, which were all open and unguarded since the place had been decommissioned years ago. The deeper he went, the more the steel walls became covered in green and black pus. He entered a great hall, where a moss-like, almost organic substance had infiltrated every nook and cranny. The lights were dimmed in this area. Lechowsky could never figure out if Scorpia needed the dim lights for her comfort or just to seem more imposing.
The pungent smell of Scorpia's presence filled Lechowsky's nostrils, as he struggled to get past some slippery steel beams. She

was a seven-metre-tall beast effectively nailed to the ground due to her massive weight. Sevcnteen years in space had not been kind to Scorpia; any resemblance to humanity was long gone. Her huge oblong head and yellow eyes were those of a reptile. Her skin looked dark green and was covered in scales, although it was hard to ascertain due to the poor lighting. The only visible sign she had once been a woman was her gaping vagina, wide open and spilling with pus. Lechowsky shivered as their eyes met.

"Yooou ..." Coughing and gagging followed Scorpia's first attempt at dialogue. She was not used to visitors.

"Youuu piece of shit." Lechowsky recognised her dark, sour voice immediately. The pre-recorded messages he received were usually produced using the vocal cords of one of her victims after the person had passed.

"Worthless ... worm...," Scorpia drooling as she spoke. Her arms and legs were bobbing up and down in angry excitement.

She struggled to contain her anger. "An agreement was made between usss ... Did you uphold your part of the bargain, ssssslaaave?" She sibilated before breaking into uncomfortable laughter.

Lechowsky mustered up all the energy he possibly could to reply to her.

"Yes, Scorpia, uh, my dear. Our intelligence team went to the Disposal Site and recovered three recently discarded former Arand members, one of whom is probably Sunny Bridges. We already ruled out one, so just waiting for final ID-checks on the other two to see which one is Bridges ...". Despite speaking incrementally louder, Lechowsky was drowned out by Scorpia's loud guttural laugh.

"Intelligence! ... Let me assume the intelligent part came from your computer-lover rather than you," Scorpia said mockingly.

"Well, I —"

"Silence! I demand that you bring me the Engineer. It is my right! Bring me Sunny. He can fix the steering console and bring us home to Earth!" Scorpia was practically screaming at this point. "And I want more juice! Why are you not bringing me more fresh samples, do you want me to perish! You want my beautiful skin to fade? I will tear down the whole city before that happens! Dig

right through you and your puny plastic robots. I have amassed powers you cannot believe."
The juice Scorpia was referring to was a blue liquid primarily consisting of serotonin extractions sucked from the brains of Zeeta's inhabitants. This liquid was believed to make you happy if ingested, but it left the kind donor paralysed.
"Listen, Scorpia, supplies are running low. We, uh, we can't actually afford to lose more people. Whenever we lobotomise someone, it's impossible to get them back to any sort of functional state. They become like zombies. And we've lost a great deal of the XZ-9000 devices. They're in dire need of repair, and we just don't have that kind of expertise anymore," Lechowsky whined.
Scorpia let out a loud noise resembling a snore from a clinically ill person.
He tried to turn the conversation. "But I've brought you a sample. It's the last of the —" He was cut short as a long tentacle-like limb jetted through the air and viciously grabbed the glass receptacle holding the blue liquid. His skin was torn off and he suffered from burns where the slimy limb had touched him. Loud gulping noises came from the back of the room, followed by the crackling of splintering glass.
Lechowsky rubbed his arm to calm the excruciating pain. He half-heartedly expected a kind remark from Scorpia, but knew it was in vain.
"Get out of here … worm." Silence.
"Don't come back until you have more juice. And the Engineer. I want both."

Lechowsky stumbled out the hall to the relative safety of the compound entry. He wept before joining his guards.

Rusted Dreams' Bar

Horrigan had gone incognito and entered Sector 4C, which was close to the Disposal Site. Using his Magnetron-Field-Generator, MGF for short, he made his armour and helmet invisible and now appeared as a common layman. Before entering the bar, two security bots which were fixed to the wall scanned him for any illegal items or substances. Finding nothing, they opened the automatic door. Inside, Horrigan saw about sixty people sitting at different tables.

There were only a few bars on Zeeta, so each one was designed to maximise the seating space. Cramming people into tight spaces was imperative when living in a floating space city. The Rusted Dreams' Bar, albeit Zeeta's largest, was no exception to this rule. It had tables and chairs attached to large vertical columns, like winding staircases, to utilise each square metre of space. The bar patrons did not mind, they were all linked into NADOSH's virtual entertainment program. No one spoke to each other; they all sat facing thin computer screens displaying avatars customised to their liking.

Horrigan quickly scanned the room but registered no illegal thoughts or excessive amounts of happiness. It seemed there was law and order, allowing him to focus on his task.

A floating egg-shaped pod appeared behind him, prodding him to sit down. "What's your pleasure, sir?" was heard from its speakers. "Take me to the bar," he replied, and the pod started gently moving. It stopped at the bar, made of solid aluminium, and a screen appeared in front of Horrigan. He noticed the ten or so other patrons, beverages in hand, also sitting there and looking at their respective screens. His screen flickered, and the barman's avatar appeared. "Yeah, welcome to the Rusted Dreams, finest rusted joint in the universe. What can I getcha? We're outta Moonray Rum and Dome Dew Brew, but don't cry about it, will ya?"

Horrigan leaned slightly towards the screen. "I want to talk to you. Come over here." The barman gave him a strange look but obeyed nonetheless. The screen turned off and lowered back into its slot in the desk. The barman, a middle-aged man with a noticeable under-bite, stumbled over to where Horrigan was seated. He wore a beige gown and had red cables fixed to eight points of his lower jawbone. Where the cables led or what their purpose was remained unknown.

"Listen, partner, I don't know who you are, but I suggest—" Horrigan cut him short. "I'm looking for this man." He quickly displayed a picture in front of him using his wrist-AI. The bartender gave him a sour look and nodded towards an individual

seated five persons to the left of them. Horrigan nodded. “We need to be alone," he said.
“Look, Mr Hot Cakes, I dunno who you think you are, but this is a regulated establishment right here. Enforcer territory, ya dig? If you want to do any of that unpermitted stuff, like having unrecorded conversations with strangers, I suggest you go down below. My cousin once mentioned this place close to the Specials' territory where —” The bartender made a loud ‘oomph’ noise as Horrigan grabbed a handful of the cables tied to his jaw and pulled him closer.
“I need to talk to that man. We want privacy." Horrigan deactivated the magnetic field covering his face for a brief moment. The bartender saw the horrible metal mask covering Horrigan's face and glanced into his dark, copper-coloured eye sockets.
Regaining his senses, the barman muttered, “Uh, of course. Right away.” He turned to his customers. “Boys, time to pack it up. We have a special visitor today." The other pods at the bar were immediately dispersed around the room, and all the screens folded back into the table. The two remaining pods hovered in next to one another. A sonic isolation sphere was lowered to cover both the pods, meaning the two men could hear and see everything going on in the room, but no sound would leave the sphere. They were alone.
Looking towards the other pod, Horrigan could only see a muscular arm reach out to pose his glass. The arm was clothed in a remarkable turquoise armlet. Horrigan knew it was the right guy.
“Listen, buddy boy,” the stranger said while gently pushing his automatic 44. Magnum Pulse pistol against Horrigan's lower abdominal region. “I appreciate the invitation, but I don't like socialising much, so let's get to the point. Who are you, and what do you want?”
Horrigan thought about removing his camouflage but decided to wait.
“I would've thought the unemployed would be more welcoming when a job was being offered to them. Especially those who drink all day instead of looking for one." Horrigan's sarcasm dialogue-module was still functional.

The stranger, an incredulous look painted on his bearded face, turned his pod around. "Horrigan? Is that you? What's up with the camouflage? You look like a bum."
"Jon Blakemore. Some things change, but not your dry humour. Good to see you." Horrigan's outstretched arm was greeted by Blakemore's and accompanied by a quick grin.
"Jon, my emotional intelligence scanner informs me that I should engage in small talk for a few minutes. The goal is to establish a friendly, even open, conversation, which, in turn, makes it more likely that you'll accept the proposition I'm about to make. Unfortunately, my EQ-module is not functioning well after the operation, so I'm unable to do so," Horrigan explained.
"Don't sweat it, Horrigan. You weren't much of a conversationalist even before they made you into a borg. One of the most cold-blooded bastards I ever met back on Earth. Still can't believe they let a war criminal like you on board this ship. Guess it shows what a shit-show this was from the start," Blakemore said sternly while sipping his drink.
"Jon, my analytics tool indicates you are the best Enforcer I have. Statistics prove you killed more Specials and Fallen than any other officer and brought substantial evidence against traitors. I had this data verified before coming," Horrigan said dryly.
"Verified the data? How touching." Blakemore laughed, "And you know I'd do it all again. Problem is, the more you kill, the more they keep on coming." His voice was bitter.
Blakemore used to be one of the top-ranking officers within the Enforcers and had been likely to take over Horrigan's role. However, he had grown tired. He had learned some troubling news regarding his personal life, which made him step back from his duties. Blakemore became gravely depressed, with no will or energy to do his daily work anymore. He stopped going to the Arand Corp, even stopped reporting to his superiors. Worse yet, he had ceased taking the daily mind-stimulants administered by NADOSH. One would usually be interrogated and shot for that, but Horrigan had managed to protect Blakemore from repercussions. So far.
"I'm ... I just have no fucking steam anymore!" Blakemore exclaimed. "Every day, I think about how to stop those bastards. How to drill a fist-sized hole in their fucking beehive once and for

all. If only I knew how. I'd take a squad of our best troopers, get the job done. Once and for all."

Horrigan remained vigilant. He tried scanning Blakemore during their conversation to decipher whether he was being satirical or earnest. But that was impossible since Blakemore was off the mind-control drugs for weeks.

Horrigan said, "I have been given a challenging task by my superiors, a task that I am not fully able to fulfil. However, I estimate with reasonable certainty that the best course of action would be for you to infiltrate the Fallen headquarters. Discover their secrets. Kill their leader, Brian Warner. Doing so would indirectly complete the objectives given by my superiors. This is, of course, top-classified information." Horrigan knew he was overstepping his mandate with all this information, but his estimates show it would increase the chance of success. Blakemore sat back for a while, sipping his beverage. Moonstar Dust with Tomato-Fragrance, from the looks of it. A lot of it too. Horrigan figured he would be well drunk by now.

"What's the story?" Blakemore said, partially as a question, partially as an accusation.

Horrigan lost his composure for a moment, "Well, you're our best man, I thought of you for this mis —"

"Yeah, you said that already Blakemore interrupted. "For you to crawl into this hole and propose something as suicidal and ludicrous as this, there must be a big issue. Or something you're not telling me. So, let's start from the beginning. What's the story?" He asked the question in such a firm tone that Horrigan knew he would have to calculate his reply carefully.

"Jon … this mission, the whole situation, is top secret. I do not have access to the data." He tried honesty; according to his human psychology app, this approach sometimes worked. "Arand is looking for Sunny Bridges and has most likely found him. It seems plausible that the Fallen are looking for him too. And Zeeta and our common mission appear to be in peril." He could not fathom the consequences of what this peril meant exactly.

Blakemore, more perplexed than satisfied with the answer, gave a short nod and took a huge gulp of his beverage. Although he was a machine, Horrigan seemed frank. The Moonstar taste had faded, and only the bitter sting of the synthetic tomato powder remained.

As he turned to Horrigan to pose another question, a huge bang was heard on the door of the bar. Seconds after, the lights were dimmed, and red lasers filled the entire space. The door opened, and four Enforcer troopers came bustling in. Behind them, a flying ED-EE bot followed repeating the message, "Warning. Warning. Non-permitted behaviour detected. This is not a drill. Remain in your positions. Arand Enforcer officials will handle this. I repeat, warning …". The ED-EE bot's tiny speakers were at a deafening volume, jostling the small bot with every syllable. It had two antennae attached to it, and a small plexiglass visor for movement detection mounted on the front.

The Enforcers hastily made their way to one of the front centre tables, acutely aware of their targets' position. It turned out to be a man sitting on the middle row, approximately two metres in the air. The man was glued to his monitor and could not stop laughing. The computer avatar on the screen seemed to have bugged; it repeated the same joke over and over. Each time, the face flickered, and it would start again, making the bar patron laugh harder and harder. In fact, he seemed oblivious to the commotion around him.

All this changed when one of the enforcers took out his Pacifier, a device resembling a large metal spear with a sharp pair of grappling hooks on one end. The Enforcer used the device to latch onto the man's right ankle, tearing off flesh and clothing. Simultaneously, the Pacifier gave the man an electric shock so powerful that he jetted into the air and landed with a blunt thud on the ground. While he was obviously in excruciating pain at this point, things had happened so fast that his grin remained transfixed on his face. Another Enforcer then crouched over the man, fixing the XZ-9000 gun, popularly known as the Lobotomizer, to his forehead.

A third Enforcer shouted, "By Regulation 3246/125/BUZ, encoded in Zeeta's Book of Laws, it is not permitted to experience individual, selfish happiness and/or pleasure induced by natural, i.e. non-administered, means for any prolonged period equalling more than two point seven seconds. Any such feelings beyond this will render the offender culpable with the consequence of having to donate one's happiness to the collective good of Zeeta's population. Consequently, it falls upon us to extract any such feelings from your body, and liquify and donate them to the common good. Non-compliance with this Regulation will result in death."

As he finished reading out the text, the second Enforcer loaded up the XZ-9000 that was now firmly attached to the man's head. The Enforcer shot a long needle next to the man's right eye and into his brain. A thin liquid was extracted from it into a compartment of the device, mixed with a blue compound, and then poured into a glass oblong tube. The Enforcer pulled the needle out and detached the device from the man's head. The whole process took barely two minutes and left the man paralysed on the ground. Blood was pouring from his head and mouth.

Blakemore gave a quick nod to Horrigan, who had been so transfixed on the happenings that he did not notice that all the monitors in the room now displayed NADOSH's avatar. All of them were facing the Enforcers as if to monitor the operation at hand. When the glass canister was safely stowed away, NADOSH remarked, "Good job, //officers//. Running internal error diagnostics … successful. Error found in my //social simulation module//. Data optimisation tool initiated. Have - a - pleasant - day." Her attempt at pleasantries sounded forced and unnatural as always.

The Enforcer who first entered the room, apparently the most senior, made an honorary gesture towards NADOSH, followed by an affirmative nod. It was difficult to tell what his emotions were as all Enforcers wore dark blue dome-shaped helmets, which had an even glass-like finish and obscured the entire face except for the mouth and nose. He did not seem taken aback by NADOSH's intervention.

As soon as the squad left the room, the lights came back on, and everything quickly went back to normal. The bar patrons turned their attention to their individual screens which, after a short flicker, resumed their chosen program. The wounded man still lay shaking on the ground, doomed with paralysis and numbness for the rest of his days. No one seemed in a hurry to help him.

Back at the bar, Blakemore and Horrigan turned their pods around to resume their conversation. They spent some minutes reminiscing on successes of previous missions.

They were interrupted when Blakemore mistakenly knocked over the canister holding his beverage, spilling it on the floor. As he reached down to pick it up, he heard gunfire and screams from the streets. At that very moment, an Enforcer staggered back into the bar. He was badly wounded across his entire torso and had burn marks characteristic of the counterfeit laser-pistols the Fallen used.

Horrigan and Blakemore both jumped to their feet. Horrigan removed his camouflage, causing the bartender to let out an audible gasp at the sight of his impressive armour. The sonic field around their pods dissipated as they walked through it. More gunfire came from the street. As they stepped out, they saw two Jonny-bots who were also engaged in combat. Every Jonny-bot had a built-in laser-AK47 to fend off any light threat. Across from the bar was a knocked-over hover vehicle, behind which three Fallen thugs were hiding.

Horrigan immediately established that the Enforcers had been ambushed and the glass vial with blue liquid was gone. He watched as Blakemore stormed past him with his gun, shooting and hitting a fourth thug hiding about seven metres to the right of the main group. The thug took two blasts and was neutralised.

The Jonny-bot, itself badly wounded, with a clear liquid spilling from its chest area and sparks and smoke coming from its robotic mouth, kept repeating, “Hostiles. Opening fire. Hostiles. Opening fire. Hostiles…”

Horrigan loaded the Gauss-Rifle which was in his right arm. Its shots were sufficient to take out anything living. He first shot a burst at the one hundred and fifty-kilogram lithium-ion exposed battery cell of the overturned hover vehicle. The hover vehicle exploded and started spurting out thick and dangerous smoke, causing the three remaining thugs, having lost their hiding place, to flee. One of the punks, a smashed-up looking female with neon-green hair, cussed at them and lobbed a grenade in their general direction. Before it went off, Horrigan landed two shots in her back as she was running away. Her lung punctured, and she fell to the ground.

A second later, the grenade went off, causing a dark-grey cloud of super-charged steam in the area. Blakemore and the remaining two Enforcers crouched in pain because of the ionised radioactive compounds in the grenade; prolonged exposure could result in permanent damage to the central nerve system. Horrigan was immune to such attacks, so he could drag Blakemore along. Surprisingly, after some violent rounds of coughing, Blakemore recovered and stumbled back to his feet, Magnum ready.

The two remaining Fallen thugs were now almost thirty metres ahead. They could escape thanks to an abandoned boutique at the side of the street, a common strategy the Fallen used to gain access to the surface. They utilised flaws in the Arand Corporation's surveillance system to sneak unhindered onto the surface.

Horrigan still had no idea how they managed to do it. He could try to take a shot, but they were more deftly out of range of his Gauss-Rifle. Being more agile, Blakemore charged ahead, closing the distance between himself and the Fallen with each step. He passed the wounded woman, whose gasps for air steadily became more infrequent. She lay buried in a pool of blood.

While Blakemore was running, the first of the Fallen made it back into the store. The last one, a man with long black hair, probably around thirty, was also trying to enter through the hole they had hastily burned in the wall. The thug paused, his torso stuck. He carried a pistol with a long-range scope, which looked like it had been a rifle once. The thug took a deep breath and pointed the gun towards Blakemore, who was storming towards his position.

The gun went off with an impressive bang; Blakemore ducked. The bullet had missed him, and he took a second to skillfully aim his own gun. The black-haired Fallen thug thought he had killed Blakemore and was momentarily distracted by his attempts to wriggle through the hole. Blakemore got on his feet and walked forward three metres. His scope was dead-centre on the thug's head. He was only about four metres away from him and would surely hit. The thug was almost gone, only his shoulders and head visible, the rest of the body safe inside the store.

The Fallen thug turned his head towards Blakemore a second before he pulled the trigger. The thug's mouth and eyes gaped wide open in dumb surprise. What beautiful eyes they are, Blakemore thought. They seemed oddly familiar to him. The thug was transfixed for a moment, staring at Blakemore. The latter hesitated and intentionally missed his shot by jerking his pistol slightly to the left before firing. The super-charged laser slug went past the black-haired thug's head, leaving him unhurt. Blakemore would never know how close he had been that day to killing his own son.

A moment after, the thug finally went through the hole and disappeared. They obfuscated their escape route with an optical decoy. The Fallen had again used their deceptive methods to return safely underground.

In the few seconds that passed, Horrigan ascertained that Blakemore was not hurt. Blakemore stood panting, desperately trying to catch his breath, looking at the escape route of their recent guests. I'm getting too old for this shit, he thought. Holstering his weapon, he turned to face Horrigan. "I'm ready," he said. "I'll help with your mission." Horrigan nodded.

Behind them, a group of seven Jonny-bots were busy covering the violence with pre-recorded simulations. They placed ultra-thin flexible displays over the corpses. These bendable screens started showing movie clips of harmonious nature recordings mixed with Arand Corp propaganda. Such interventions were needed to disguise violence and unpleasantries from the general population, as they had become more frequent lately.

NADOSH's avatar appeared on a giant screen above the Rusted Dreams' Bar. She, as always, was watching the city.

A Sad Return Home

Brian Warner was heading back underground to the Fallen encampment with a million thoughts racing through his mind. The raid had not gone as planned. There had been four of them on the surface; more than that was risky. They moved in two groups, each disguised as common citizens. Their goal was to reach the dump site, that terrible place where the Arand regime throws all their discarded citizens. Most of the people who ended up there had somehow lost the favour of Zeeta's official leadership.

There had been rumours of the Engineer being brought there; the group's goal was to get a positive ID and, if possible, retrieve him. Having only a rough idea of his appearance and age, this seemed

like a doomed undertaking from the start. But times were desperate, and desperate measures were needed. His people were losing hope; they needed to believe in something new.
Of course, the run-in with the Enforcers had been accidental. One Enforcer had asked the first group for their ID. Unfortunately, Zhora Luft panicked. It was her first time on the surface, and despite all her training and clear instructions to do otherwise, she immediately pulled out her weapon and gunned the Enforcer down. Zhora got shot in the back as they fled; they could not rescue her.
The other Enforcers opened fire, but they managed to lob a plasma grenade under a hover vehicle to create a distraction. This allowed them to return fire, killing three Enforcers and mortally wounding a fourth. The tide of combat turned in their favour, and they managed to find some suitable cover. Unfortunately, one of the police-bots went nuts and put them under more pressure with constant firing. Derricc managed to slow it down somewhat, but they were overwhelmed by the reinforcements from inside the bar. Warner saw the hulking metal man, the stuff of kids' nightmares.
"I can't believe Zhora's gone," Warner cried to himself. Her final screams still rang in his ears. He had not wanted her to come; she had been working on an important peace-treaty proposal for the Specials. She had been convinced that, by joining forces, the Specials and the Fallen could overthrow the Arand Corp. She was smart and beautiful – voluptuous and able to handle a gun. He remembered her signature neon-green mohawk, which she wore so proudly. Sign of her freedom, she said. Her life was ahead of her until Arand cut it short, he thought.
Now only himself and Derricc had made it back underground. Barely. The mission was a complete and utter failure, with two soldiers dead and no new intel of the Engineer to speak of. They had retrieved a vial of the blue juice by chance from one of the Enforcers outside the bar. But at which cost? Warner presumed the blue juice had come from a fresh specimen; the vial was still lukewarm.
Everyone back home looks up to me. They'll think I'm a joke if I tell them I failed again! He thought angrily. He became filled with despair, realising that Zhora had used their last grenade. We hardly have any people or weapons left to fight back.

Warner needed to buy time. They could not return to the encampment, not yet. He had to fabricate a good story of their latest visit to the surface. Otherwise, drafting volunteers next time would be impossible. People would be too scared to fight back, eventually leaving them at Arand's mercy.

"Derricc! Wait up! My leg hurts. I might have got a splinter or something. Let's sit down here for a second," Warner said.

Derricc looked at him incredulously, then said, "Sure, Warner."

Derricc nodded and, also in need of a rest, willingly sat down. He had a massively deformed face, with a huge lump on the left side of his forehead and partially missing lips, exposing his unruly teeth. Besides that, he had an enormously muscular body and could handle the heaviest equipment. He routinely carried the welding equipment used to cut through the abandoned Arand buildings. More importantly, he was friendly and hard-working. He got along well with everyone back at the camp, and Warner appreciated that about him. He knew he could count on him.

"Those are some mean-looking bruises you have got there, Warner. Sure will make good party talk once we make it back to Earth." Derricc let out a small but cheerful smile.

"That was fucked up," Warner said with a huge expulsion of air. "I thought we weren't going to make it this time."

Derricc nodded in solemn agreement. "By the way," he said after a while, "who was that maniac who came storming out of the bar? He wasn't dressed like a normal Enforcer. And the way you two looked at each other, it … Well, it seemed like you knew him?" He was waiting for an appropriate time to ask, and this seemed as good as any.

Warner looked at him. Behind the weird, elephant-like face, Derricc's beautiful blue eyes waited for him to reply.

"I don't know." Derricc had been hoping for another response. "But I intend to find out." Warner sat back. He closed his eyes. "Might have been my father for all I know," he mumbled almost inaudibly. Warner had not seen his father in years, not since he escaped from home. His dad had been a mercenary for Arand since Zeeta took off. Warner rebelled against him and fled home. He remembered the dark and cold nights spent hiding underground, away from the Enforcer guards he knew too well would kill on sight. He had seen his father do it. Warner had spent days or weeks without food and water, wandering the closed-down sections of the ship. That is when the Fallen found him, almost fifteen years ago now.

An intense cramp travelled via Warner's shoulders to his neck, the adrenaline still pumping through his veins. He admired his homemade long-scoped pistol; it was pre-launch tech from back on Earth — his last present from dad.
He closed his eyes again. So much shit to take care of. Where do I start?

Chapter III: Out with the Old, in with the New

Brother Francis' Diary Part I: Grief

Brother Francis had spent three weeks straight being out in the field. Ever since the satellite dish was damaged and radio contact cut off to Zeeta, he had desperately been searching around the bunker where Zeeta 21 was built. It was in an underground facility about an hour's journey from the Monastery. The entrance had been boarded up, and Francis did not manage to circumvent security and get inside the underground vault. He was desperately hoping for a solution, some clue, to re-establish communications. Perhaps some piece of old tech was left that they could use?

His efforts were, thus far, futile. He could not enter the vault and felt helpless in aiding the Brothers trying to repair the satellite dish at the Monastery and reconnect with Zeeta. He sat down, slumped over his desk. Actually, sitting would be too generous a term; it was more like halfway falling down from the chair but refusing to let gravity do its work.

Added to this was his failing health. He had severe pain in the growth on the left side of his stomach. Nothing to worry about, the Brother medics said. It came from stress or swallowing too much radiated dust. It would pass, they said.

Yet, Francis could not help but to worry. Along with the pain, he had lost his appetite and sometimes coughed up blood. It all started when he and the two other Brothers ate a 'special meal' as per the Abbess' orders. It was himself, his childhood friend Roger Maxon and another monk. He had not seen them since and could not ask how they were doing. But he overheard an elder after supper the other day saying that one of them had died.

Francis was in a dire state; he had fallen into a dark hole of grief and despair. His Brothers had urged him to at least get out of bed and write ten pages of transcript each day to take his mind off his worries.

Today, Francis had barely written two. The laser-burner pen seemed too heavy to lift.

So clouded with darkness was his mind that he did not even hear when someone opened the door to his humble cell. A prominent figure stepped in.

“Francis, I hear you haven’t been eating properly. Is this true?”

He barely lifted his head.

“You know such behaviour makes your dear Brothers worry. Makes all of us uneasy, in fact." The words were delivered with great attention and care.

Francis felt a tinge of relief from his pain. The Abbess had come to see him. Nevertheless, his strength eluded him; he could not speak.

She came over and sat down on the bed next to him. Each monk had their own private cell. It comprised a bed, a chair, a tiny desk and, depending on one’s rank, a small selection of books for personal enjoyment.

“I see you’re in no shortage of great literature,” the Abbess said dryly. She referred to the books scattered about the floor. Most of them were rare and not allowed for lower-ranked monks like Francis.

“The others let me borrow them, some of the Quartermasters. I … I couldn’t refuse,” Francis whispered apologetically. He had violated protocol by accepting books he was forbidden to read.

The Abbess put both her hands on her thighs. She wore a dark green outfit and long black leather gloves. Her face was completely covered by a skull helmet, presumably from a deer-like animal with two large horns.

“Well, we’ll just have to do something about that, won’t we," she said as she stood up. Then, she pointed towards the corner and remarked, “I see that’s not the only thing amiss here.”

Francis smiled for the first time in days. It felt good. He did not need to turn his head to know she was pointing at his collection of half-finished bowls of chicken soup, six days’ worth.

“What makes matters worse, I tell you, is that your comrades from the floors below have been complaining about the stench. Seems someone around here fancies throwing his soup out the window rather than eating it." She, too, had difficulty keeping a straight face. It showed through her voice.

Francis smiled. Then, dreary mental fatigue washed over him again.

"What's the point of eating soup," he asked, "when the body it nourishes isn't worthy of its nutrients?" The Abbess sighed, hurt by this self-loathing sentiment. "I'm growing weary … I'm not able to push myself to do any useful work," Francis wept.

The Abbess listened intensely to his every word. She knew the heart of what needed to be discussed. Francis was a brilliant student, maintaining an extremely ascetic lifestyle; that was his curse and his blessing. However, she decided to start elsewhere.

"When the three beggars arrive, someone must die." Her words energised the entire room. The monk who had accompanied her hastily stepped out and shut the door behind him.

"Dear Abbess, I don't understand. Please enlighten me." Francis finally sat up straight.

Hands behind her back, she strolled back and forth in the tiny room. She was enlivened by the suffering they both experienced. "The three beggars, Francis, are a metaphor. I can't explain what they represent any more than the chicken can comment on the taste of the broth used for the soup."

Francis looked at the bowls. He felt guilty for not finishing them.

"They come to us in the forms of grief, pain, and suffering. I believe grief is what you're experiencing now." The Abbess had barely finished her sentence before a cleansing wave washed over Francis' body. He felt rejuvenated; the Abbess always understood him.

"And so it is!" he exclaimed. "Indeed, this all-pervasive monument of grief has kept me trapped ever since … since …" He gulped. "Since Zeeta took off. I feel I lost my purpose after it left."

The Abbess was looking out the tiny window of the cell. "The ship known as Zeeta took off seventeen years ago, Francis. These seventeen years have taken a heavy toll on your soul. It's as if you feel intrinsically connected to that ship. Now, knowing full well that Zeeta won't land again during your normal lifetime, you've become bleak and empty, as if all meaning and sense of belonging elude you. Time and time again."

Francis felt uplifted and heavy-hearted at the same time. The Abbess understood him, knew what he was experiencing, and could express it better than he could. Yet, the bare truth of her words struck deep into his soul. Yes, since Zeeta left, he felt lost.
"I … It's not that I don't enjoy maintaining the laser turrets and researching pulse grenade technology. I do! It's just … I don't derive the same satisfaction from it as some other Brothers might." Francis sighed apologetically.
The Abbess stopped walking about the room and put her right hand over her neck, meaning she was thinking. "Ever since the war, we've all had to toil with rather … basic tasks," she muttered, perhaps to herself." I've heard your stomach hasn't been feeling well either. That, of course, makes things more complicated.
"What if …", she said while starting to move again, "we put you in charge of the communications unit? I have three Brothers up in the eastern tower trying to re-establish radio contact with Zeeta. They haven't gotten through yet. Maybe you'll have more luck."
Francis smiled from ear to ear. He promised himself that, from now on, he would never leave chicken soup uneaten again.

Stars … I Can't Catch You

Lily was sure this was it, the place where those delicious fungi grew. She had come here some years ago and was surprised to see a bunch of edible mould growing on some exhaust pipes. Those pipes regulated the temperature on Zeeta, both by shooting out excess heat into the atmosphere and drawing in the cold when needed. It must have been the humidity dropping from those pipes mixed with some unknown animal (or human?) excrement that allowed the fungi to grow. She found them two years ago when she was fifteen. Lily fondly reminisced on how her imagination had run wild. She was thinking about the joy it had given her family and friends when she brought the fungus home. Food was scarce, even back then, and variety was non-existent. People ate and drank the same things every day, which was not much: dirty water and pellet soup mixed with some meat from whatever living thing they could hunt underground.

Sure, Lily knew there was a logical explanation for why they grew there, but she preferred to dream up crazy things. When she was a child, she enjoyed imagining that Lady Folesadu had placed the fungi there as a sign or an omen for her to find. Lady Folesadu was her favourite hero. Lily had two comic books, still on paper like back on Earth, with stories of how the Lady was the first female Space Commander to leave Earth and explore new and unknown planets. She would fight daring battles and escape tricky situations. Most importantly, she was fair, open to new cultures, and always sought diplomacy and dialogue first. This awarded her high esteem, both on Earth and beyond. The stories took place in the year 2700, hundreds of years before Zeeta was even an idea.
Lily was seventeen now, but she still believed in Lady Folesadu and dreamt about what it was like living in the 2700s with the Lady. Lily wanted to be like her and bring hope and justice to people.

Lily belonged to the Fallen, a group of around two thousand people who had fled the surface of Zeeta to be free and carve out a better life for themselves. And her people needed, more than ever, something to cheer them up. Things were going badly. Resources were running out, and internal conflicts had become more frequent. Last week, a man Lily had known since childhood got into a fight with someone and died from internal bleeding a few days after. There had been a quarrel, likely sparked by desperation and hunger, which turned violent. Suicides were commonplace too.
By bringing back a new supply of fungi, Lily hoped that people in the camp would cheer up. She was sure they just needed to hold out a little longer. Their leader, Brian Warner, left two days ago on a special mission to the surface. They got intel that the Engineer had been spotted in the outer sectors of Arand's sphere of control. Finding the Engineer and converting him to their cause was all they needed.
Finding him meant they could go home; the Engineer would take them back to Earth. Lily was born on Zeeta and did not know anything else. Her mother was pregnant when she boarded the ship and gave birth a few months after take-off. Unfortunately, she died while Lily was still a baby, but she had known her father a little.

The way Brian talked about Earth was just so magical. He lived there until the age of ten or eleven and would always tell stories about how it was this great blue planet. A Brobdingnagian ball that you could walk around endlessly. People were free to go about their lives as they pleased in their world of lush forests, diverse wildlife, and vast oceans. Warner also played music for her and the children at the Fallen camp. They heard a plethora of different instruments and sometimes people singing beautiful songs. It was so special, and Lily wanted to meet people who could think up such pretty things. Here, all people did was complain and moan; there was never enough food, enough light, enough anything.

Lily was heading back towards the encampment of her people. But her mind kept drifting, and she finally convinced herself to make a short detour to her 'special place'. Since she was a little girl, Lily loved to venture about the spaceship. She always stayed underground where the Fallen hid. Going to the surface, where Arand was in control, was something every child learned equalled death. Her father had once told her that for the Fallen to go above ground into the main dome of Zeeta equalled jumping off a high mountain back on Earth. Having never been to Earth and, of course, not knowing what a 'mountain' was, Lily had struggled to understand the exact meaning of that phrase. But it sounded severe enough for her never to break that rule and go close to the surface. However, she loved exploring Fallen territory, going down winding and unlit halls filled with various machinery, squeezing herself between thick human-sized tubes filled with what appeared to be excrement, or ducking under intricate webs of high-voltage cables. Lily had seen most of what could safely be explored around her people's territory, always stopping before the machine room. That area belonged to the Specials, although they also lived underground, their homes connected to the world above via an old abandoned factory. The children loved telling stories about a monster who supposedly lived there. The Specials were a threat to be avoided at all costs, because they were cooperating with the Arand Corp and because they were different.

Lily's 'special place' was a secret; no one knew how to get there. Prying busybodies had tried many times but never managed to get it out of her. The only person she had told was Zhora. She was

Lily's best friend, almost like a sister to her. Zhora had raised Lily after her mother died, and the two were exceptionally close. Despite Zhora being about twenty years older than her, Lily always felt a sincere and strong bond between them. She felt that being around Zhora made her more mature. Lily decided to show Zhora her special place; the time felt right.
Lily had discovered it on one of her many escapades, via an apparent dead end, some fifty minutes from the Fallen camp. But by slipping down a closed-off ventilation duct, gliding past some sparking electrical wires, and crawling further on your stomach you could reach the end of the spaceship. Yes, unbelievable as it sounded, Lily's hiding spot was an empty space with a large window at the hull of Zeeta's structure. It allowed her to sit and look at the stars, dreaming up all manner of crazy things.
She would bring her ReeMind Pad, a device that automatically recorded the user's thoughts like a diary. She still preferred her childhood sketchbook though. Unlike the ReeMind Pad, it never ran out of charge, and it felt like a real book from Earth. Lily would sometimes gaze at the drawings and stories she had written as a child and let her mind roam free.

Her thinking ranged from:
(Mundane)
What's for dinner tonight?
Does Carmac even like me? (Carmac was a boy, three years older than her, from the family of tech-mongers next to her tent. Lily had had a crush on him for as long as she could remember.)

(Bizarre)
What is life on Earth like? Do people still remember that we are out here?
How fast are we going? Will our journey ever be over?
What do the stars do? Why can't I reach them?

(Novel, innovative)
Why can't I lead our people to a better future?
Whoever is forcing us to live in misery, I can outsmart them and free our people.

I have what it takes to inspire people and make them realise their true worth.

Lily felt happiest when she was thinking those last thoughts. Her 'special place' allowed her complete freedom to shape her mind in new and exciting ways. Sometimes she would shrug it off as silly adolescent stuff, but other times … Well, what if?
When she got to the leadership part, it usually marked the end of her visit. She would often finish her line of thought with a sense of dread. It felt as if something was watching her. It was as if some physical force was trying to grab or get a hold of her. She could sense the omnipresent being had limited powers in the 'special place', but it always tried. Lily suspected it was the AI-lady from the surface. It scared Lily, but it also gave her an odd boost of courage because the AI-lady feared her. Maybe it was trying in cowardly ways to dissuade Lily from assuming her role as the leader of the Fallen.

Little did Lily know, she was about to get a visitor in the hiding place today. It came creeping down the vents, panting and gasping at every move. Each muscle pulsing gave energy and momentum to the ragged bones, and the grin on its burned-off lips caused pus and blood to drip from the skinless face and cranium.
He was the third individual Horrigan and his troops had dug out of the Arand Disposal Site. But after a quick stop and chat at the Arand Headquarters, he had been given a new goal, a new raison d'etre. Find the girl, bring down the bitch. His whole being was pulsing with hunger and determination. Whatever drugs or stimulants they pumped into his organism worked. He felt invincible. By instinct, and thanks to his newfound abilities to see in the dark and stick onto surfaces, he was gaining ground quickly. He moved downwards swiftly, guided only by smell and hunger. On his way, he passed many humans, all of whom he vociferously despised now. He would tear their heads from their spines and suck their blood, making them suffer as he had. But never mind. He needed to stay focused. Arand's scary AI had given him a clear objective.
He crawled down the ventilation shaft and avoided the cables; he was nearly there. In the distance, he could skim a nimble being

against the black and white backdrop of endless space. She had her back to him, and he could vaguely makc out her flat brown hair. It was her. Drool dripped from his mouth; he gnashed his teeth in insatiable hunger. He crawled on all fours, his ragged clothes leaving his burned skin visible. The skin on his knees peeled off as they scraped across the rusted floorplates.

Lily's gaze was locked on a particular star; it mesmerised her. She remained transfixed on that one star, and she could have sworn that Lady Folesadu's face was appearing in its centre: her round, soft features, the friendly but determined eyes, the beautiful light tan hair pulled back in a ponytail. The Lady gradually materialised, and Lily felt her heart fill with joy. Lily had to blink. It seems the Lady's mouth began to move. It began … talking to her? The Lady seemed in distress, seemingly sending her a warning sign. Then the image faded. For a second, another woman appeared. She had a cold face, devoid of any emotion. It looks like that lady from the surface, the AI. What was her name?

Suddenly Lily felt her hair tugged back with such a force that her head slammed into the floor. As she rolled onto her stomach, claw-like nails ripped across her face and almost tore out her eyeball. The sting of the attack went right to her spine. Whatever was in the dark was trying to kill her. She held back a scream and jolted backwards to get on her feet. She then heard a wheezing sound coming from the floor. The beast was licking its fingers clean of fresh blood. She let out a cathartic scream of fear and anger. She decided the latter would guide her; Lily would not let this intruder violate her special place and harm her. The beast remained clenched to the floor. Lily could make out his main features thanks to a dim light from the window. He was a man, or at least had been once. He was horrifying: his hair and most of his face had been burned off, and a strange black fluid covered his body. But he was just a human being. Mastering her fear, Lily now knew what she was facing.

Meanwhile, her screams made him focus on her again. Grinning from ear to ear left his decaying teeth exposed. Unsure of what strategy to apply, he hesitated briefly. Lily, trying to buy time, kept her eyes on his. She would not be able to take him out using sheer force. She had to think of something else and stepped back, almost touching the window. She felt the icy-cold breeze on her neck and gained focus. In the corner to her left, some jagged pieces of sharp metal pointed out. It may have been from an unfinished construction project or an abandoned maintenance job. If only she could get the intruder to fall on those metal spikes, she might stand a chance.

At that moment, he dashed towards her and hit her in the stomach. The speed and brute force of the attack surprised her and pushed her against Zeeta's hull. She was gasping for air. Her assailant seemed to enjoy the pain he inflicted and bashed her across the face with his right hand. Lily was knocked over from the blow and felt blood accumulating in her mouth. He came towards her again, lifting her and slamming her down on the metal floor. She became dizzy and felt her whole body ache. At that point, she realised he wanted to torture her with a slow death. Despite the pain, she rolled over and grabbed hold of a metal shard on the ground and discreetly slid it up her sleeve.

Lily stood up and shouted, "John Frye! I am your commander! I am your mental superior! I demand you stand down!" She read his name on the torn jumpsuit he wore.

This shocked the beast. He tilted his head and brought his arms up ever so slightly. He started hissing, calmly, and walked towards Lily. The bizarre display led one to believe that he was almost expecting motherly affection from her.

"Coming here makes you a trespasser, and you've broken the peace and tranquillity of a spot dear to my heart. There's a price to pay for such indecency."

Lily's voice grew more assertive with each word. Struck by wonder and fascination, the broken man took baby steps in her direction. He tilted his head from left to right while doing so. At that moment, Lily took a firm grip on his slimy skull with her left hand and drove the metal shard deep into his eye with her right. The eyeball and even the skull itself were surprisingly mushy, and she got half the shard in before she had to stop.

The beast screamed and hollered. For good measure, Lily gave him a hard kick to the groin. That had less of an effect as all his man-parts had been removed. Now completely docile, the beast fell to its knees and whimpered in agony.

"You're a piece of trash! You're nothing! How dare you come here, creeping up on me like a coward! If I ever see you near the

Fallen base again, I'll kill you. Leave now, and tell whoever sent you that we're stronger than them. Zeeta belongs to its people, not deformed retards like you. Get out of my sight!"
Lily's assertive behaviour gave her an adrenaline kick. Her body ached, and her hands were covered in nasty goo, but that did not matter. She had faced a dangerous foe and bested him. It was her time.
The beast was struck with terror. He was holding on to the metal shard while swallowing the blood gushing from his eyeball, reminding Lily of how a baby would suck on their mother's breasts. With his good eye, he looked at Lily one last time as if to demand pardon. Receiving none, he clumsily crawled back towards the hole from which he came. Only using one hand, he kept bumping his head on the floor or walls, each time causing another whimper.
Lily watched with apathy as his assailant retreated in defeat. In the far distance, she heard cheers and commotion from the encampment. It was probably Warner's crew coming back from their mission. She would have to hide the bruises before going back; she did not want anyone to know what had happened.

The Stand-In

Warner stood before the rusted steel gate that served as the main entrance to the Fallen camp. To get there, one had to cross a large makeshift hanging bridge underneath which the sewerage of Zeeta ran. It stank, and Warner always felt that creatures with too many eyes were staring at him from down there.
The gate to the camp had an oval shape and a tint of lush green colour remaining beneath the rust. Yet, Warner dreaded walking through it, mentally projecting himself somewhere else. He sighed and gave Derricc a quick nod before tapping the secret entrance signal.
Dunk dunk dunk, tap tap tap. Tap, dunk, dunk, dunk, tap.
"Keyword," said a raspy voice behind the door.
Warner used an old-fashioned console to tap in the entrance code. It had a wide rectangular-shaped monitor showing a black background and large green letters. He was uncertain whether the Fallen people had placed it there or if it was part of Zeeta's

original design. He meant to ask the technicians but had never gotten around to it.
“Entrance symbols recognised. Welcome back, Warner,” said the voice.
Warner stepped in through the opening gate.
“Hey, Warner, good to have you back! Everybody’s excited. You can hear them screaming and yelling. You know we’re all waiting for some good news, man! Need to get out of this shithole, my brother." The gatekeeper was a young man with a fair face. His boyish naïveté could turn to violence in a second. Warner had seen it happen; he did not care for the gatekeeper and ignored his greeting.
“Hey, what the fuck? Where are the rest of our brothers and sisters?” The gatekeeper cursed in frustration as he saw only Warner and Derricc enter the compound. They both ignored him and walked into the entrance area.
A few improvised shops had been set up. They were small, randomly decorated sheds built of scavenged metal sheets. One of them had a flashing pink neon sign reading ‘Tits by Jack’, although Warner did not have a clue what services they provided. It eluded him that people bothered pretending their shops would ever get customers; no outsiders ever came. He guessed it was for people to have some sense of normality, to convince themselves they were doing something constructive with their lives.
The ruckus he heard upon approaching the main area confirmed his worst fear; people were indeed losing their minds. A large group gathered in the meeting hall, an immense circular-shaped open space intended originally for storage. In the centre was a platform about ten metres above ground, ideal for giving speeches and holding assemblies. Warner knew he would have to give them something. But what good news was there to bring? This mission, like most before it, had failed. They had lost more men, young people, and gotten nowhere closer to finding the Engineer. Warner had promised them that he would get them all back to Earth. That dream was the only thing that kept people from going crazy and harming themselves and each other. The suicide rate of his people was on a steady increase as well.
As Warner stood there, wondering what to do, he spotted Lily walking further down the corridor.

“Lily!” he hollered in relief.

She turned to him. Her clothes were dirty and she seemed alert. Something must’ve happened to her, he decided not to pry.

“Listen, Lily, I need you for something urgent. The, uh, the mission, it didn’t go well."

Lily had expected as much from his weary look. She nodded.

“We lost the entire team,” Warner said. “Only Derricc and I are left. Zhora is gone too. I’m deeply sorry.” Lily’s eyes filled with a pained expression of unbearable sadness. Now I can never show her my special place, she thought. Will these senseless killings ever stop?

Warner continued awkwardly, “I, uh, I have a whole assembly to please out there, and I’ve got nothing good to say. I need your help.” He held out the vial of blue liquid they had stolen from Arand. It was serendipity that he had gotten ahold of the precious substance. It would help tie the people over until he could figure out what to do.

Lily tried to clear her head; she knew what that meant. She would have to go up on that platform, the raggedy speaker’s podium, and tell the people what they wanted to hear. She did not enjoy lying or being dishonest, but the situation called for it. The people were perishing mentally, and they needed hope. She did not know exactly what that blue vial contained, but she knew the liquid was something extracted from a real human being on the surface. Since it was illegal to feel any genuine sense of happiness, apart from the simulated feeling one could get from the heavy drug stimulants, the tyrants above would ‘harvest’ this liquid from the brain.

She did not know what they used it for, but she heard that it brought happiness to whoever consumed it. At least, that was what people here were led to believe, and Warner would spray the liquid on them to boost morale. Because supply was so limited, this was only the third vial Lily had ever seen. They always mixed in additional fluid to increase the quantities. Still, the placebo effect was there; it made people ecstatic.

Clutching the vial, she went to the person administering the fluid cannon. Then she got up on the speaker podium.

“Brothers … Sisters … Our Honourable Leader has returned!” A cathartic outburst of joy and excitement roared through the crowd.

“The mission … was a success!” More cheers and yelling.
“Our Honourable Leader can’t join us tonight. He’s planning a big surprise for you all!”
Lily held out her arms. Confident, calm, and persuasive on the outside. But she was hurting inside. She was feeding lies to a clueless herd. While the cheering continued, a few disgruntled voices cut through the clutter.
A woman with blackened teeth snarled, “What the heck are they hiding from us, it must be bad news."
An elderly balding woman spat, “Who does that little wrench think she is? She has nothing to say here!”
A big bruiser-type fellow with large copper earrings joined in. “When that pussy Warner shows his face again, I’ll let him know how useless he really is. We’re sick of this.”
Closing her eyes for a moment, Lily regained focus. Her bruises still hurt. “But before his big announcement, something to quench your thirst. Get ready for some blue candy, everybody!”
At that moment, coloured liquid sprayed from the ceiling drenched the masses. A makeshift cooling unit with three large fans sprayed the fluid over the crowd. People turned euphoric: women and men, young and old, jumped around in what can only be described as pure bliss. All mouths were wide open, hoping to catch the precious drops spilling from above. Lily succeeded in buying more time until Warner could figure out how to get people back to Earth. They were fed up with hunger and poverty and wanted a better life like they had been promised.

Meanwhile, Warner was pacing up and down his office. It was a small study adjacent to the shop area and living quarters. What the hell can I do? His thoughts were interrupted as Derricc walked in.
“Brian, there’s a call for you to come to the control room. Seems the computer has woken up. It’s her. The AI wants to talk to you," he said gravely.
Warner’s eyes immediately regained clarity, and his posture became firm. This could be the lucky break they had been waiting for.

Reconstruction of a Man

Kira Berezin woke up in her room at the same time as every other day, thanks to the drugs Arand forced employees to take. The status message on her wrist-AI told her it was seven a.m., the twentieth of October, 3263; in other words, time to get up and go to work. Her personal Jonny-bot was jollily moving around the apartment. It twisted its head one hundred and eighty degrees to talk to her while scooting towards the kitchen.

"Good morning, Citizen #12730. And what a wonderful morning it is!" Kira grew tired of the Jonny-bots' pre-recorded dialogues which were rotated periodically to make the robots seem livelier. The bot continued, "Since today marks the day of your special assignment, I've prepared a *special* breakfast for you. Come have a look!" It then disappeared into the kitchen.

Kira had forgotten about her 'special assignment'. She was informed two days ago that she had been hand-picked amongst only a few others to undertake an extraordinary task. The whole thing made her nervous, and she preferred not to think about it. A 'special mission' could mean something she was not trained for or accustomed to doing. Worst yet, it might have something to do with the dire state Zeeta was in, which was no secret to anyone. In any case, she would be forced to step outside her comfort zone.

An agro-engineer by training, she was responsible for cultivating edible crops and researching new nutritional varieties for the citizens of Zeeta. She had always preferred to work alone. Dealing with people was risky; the emotions and actions of others were unpredictable and potentially hurtful. In a way, that's why she preferred Jonny-bots over some of her fellow humans.

She slowly put on her work jumpsuit. The Jonny-bot, eager to get her to eat, arranged all the prefabricated food in front of her. They all glowed flashy colours like orange, yellow, and green. Despite working with Arand's food preparation team, Kira often pondered how little she actually knew about the things she was putting in her mouth. She had a rough idea how the tofu-like protein bars (the orange ones) were grown. But she was unable to tell what the green and yellow bars were.

The Jonny-bot, annoyingly close to her face, might have guessed the thoughts running through her head. "Today, you get a special treat. You get double rations! Aaaand, I've brought you some nice dessert." It held out an odd round black ball. Impossible to decipher what it was, Kira leaned in closer. But the delicacy would not hold up to further scrutiny, as the Jonny-bot swiftly hid it back in the palm of its hand.

"No dessert for children who don't finish their main meal," it said with a huge smile. Jonny-bots always looked overly cheerful, but Kira sensed a certain menacing undertone to his words. Aware that disobeying the Jonny-bot equalled treason against Arand, she started eating the orange, glowing protein bar. After that was over, she made quick work of the green substance. The Jonny-bot seemed pleased and shoved the 'dessert' back in her face.

"Eat it. Now." Its eyes became dark, and for a moment, Kira feared for her life. Her hesitation seemingly provoked the thing. An act of uncustomary harshness for the bots, it grabbed hold of her jaw and jerked her mouth open. It all happened too fast for Kira to react; she choked on the black pellet before unwillingly swallowing it.

She coughed, still in shock, a disgusted look on her face. "Splendid! No better way to start an important day, if I may say!" The Jonny-bot, back to its jolly self, now skidded about cleaning up the kitchen and getting along with the daily routine.

Kira, conscious that it was time to leave, took her affairs and walked towards the door. She felt a strange ache in her stomach. But that might just be in my head, she thought. Whatever that black pellet inside her was, she hoped her system would soon evacuate it.

Before leaving her apartment, she checked her wrist-AI. The pre-recorded message she had received some weeks ago was still in her library. She had received an audio file in .flac format. It lasted only seven seconds, but it was the most beautiful music she had ever heard. At the end of the recording, there was static, then a riddle. She had been able to solve it after many hours of decoding. The message was from the Fallen, the outcasts living below Zeeta. They called her to join them and live freely in their camp. She overheard some colleagues at Arand whispering they had received a message too. She was given a specific rendezvous point and a date to be at the abandoned mining facility: October twentieth, 3263. Today would indeed be a special day.

Kira arrived at the Arand Corp's main tower seven minutes later than usual. Luckily, there was a lot of bustling going on, and no one seemed to notice. The cyborg entrance guard hastily told her to report to meeting room OTM-1083.
As she was about to enter, she recognised a familiar voice: Alois Lechowsky from Arand Corp management. She felt anxious and cold as she took a deep breath and moved through the automated doors.
"Ah, citizen #12730! What a pleasure to see you. The briefing has begun. But don't worry, you haven't missed much. We're just getting started." Despite Lechowsky's jovial tone, Kira immediately noticed that the room had been shut down. All the security shutters and microfilters had been activated, effectively sealing the room off from the entire compound. No noise or even ray of light could escape the room. Around her, she noticed six other Arand employees. Most were young, on edge, twitchy, and sullen. She did not know any of them particularly well and decided to focus on the briefing.
"As I was saying", Lechowsky, dressed in his typical white uniform with golden gloves, continued, "you can consider yourselves lucky. You've been selected for this undertaking of extreme importance to Zeeta. The mission is vital for our very survival, in fact."
Expecting outbursts of palpable emotion from the crowd, he looked around the room. Finding none, he carried on. "So, whatever I tell you today stays in the room. Hence the safety precautions. Yes, you'll excuse the fuzz, but we had to make sure nothing was leaked." He waved his hand dismissively towards the sealed-off entrance.
"We're at a critical juncture here on Zeeta. As you all know, we've recently had to do some ... cleaning, even among our own ranks. Yes, uncontrolled personal thoughts of illegal liberties and even high treason have been registered among many, forcing us to act."
A shock went through Kira. She knew very well that each of them could one day face similar charges, even for a minor misstep.
"One of the individuals recently taken in for questioning and subsequently found guilty was Chief Engineer Sunny Bridges. Mr Bridges was discarded at the Disposal Site, barely alive." Another shock went through Kira's body, this time centred around the

vaginal area. She and Sunny had secretly been lovers for several years. Did Arand know about it? Could it somehow get her in trouble?

Lechowsky continued while calmly pacing back and forth in the room. "It was later discovered that Mr Bridges was prematurely disposed of. Indeed, he has information vital to understanding the functioning of Zeeta's navigation system. In other words, we need him back in case we would want to take manual control of steering our great city."

Kira found that last part disturbing. Take manual control of the ship? Take it where? The pre-set trajectory was set to last another thirty-three years, at which point they would return to Earth. What was wrong? Why was this necessary? The others showed no palpable reaction to anything being said; they were like mindless sheep.

Puffing up his chest, Lechowsky went on. "Yes, some might say the decision to dispatch Bridges and his subordinates was premature. But trust me when I say, such precautionary actions are needed for your survival, your safety. Everything we do is for the well-being of all citizens on Zeeta." Lechowsky gestured towards the audience.

"Anyway, to bring this little mishap back on track, we need your help. You see, yesterday, our elite Enforcers managed to locate Bridges at the bottom of the Disposal Site. Fortunately, he was still alive, although barely. Our medical staff has since been busy reanimating him fully, under the wisdom and guidance of our great mother NADOSH." He pointed his open hand towards the back of the room.

Kira was surprised to see that NADOSH was discreetly watching them from a hidden monitor. Being scrutinised from both sides, she felt even more uncomfortable. She wanted to throw up. Her belly was aching, making her think of that weird black thing the Jonny-bot had forced down her throat earlier.

"It's therefore my pleasure to inform you that Sunny Bridges is now back in the hands of the Arand Corporation. His situation is stable, and we estimate a comfortable eighty-nine point seven percent chance of survival. But mentally, he isn't quite there yet. You see, he, um, he can't speak. While all his bodily functions seem to work impeccably, he only groans and moans. As you can

imagine, that makes it difficult for us to retrieve the password we need." Lechowsky's eyes scanned the room to see if there were any questions. There never were.
"This is where you come in. You'll help us forge a constructed reality for Sunny. We want to simulate as much as possible his life before his … early retirement. In fact, he can't know that he was close to dying. We want to make him believe that everything is normal, that he's just coming to work and going home like he's used to. This, we believe, is the best way to stimulate his memory, help him restore his speaking ability, and, essentially, give us access to the information we need." Kira noticed a strange hesitation at 'we believe'. She deduced that Lechowsky and NADOSH disagreed on the best course of action.
"You'll be divided into teams. The bulk of you will function as his fictional research team. Before his retirement, Mr Bridges oversaw five young engineers. The rest of you will take care of his … personal needs." He threw a perverted glance at Kira, making her want to crawl under the desk.
"All this information is classified. In front of each one of you, please find your personalised instruction sheets. These electronic files are for your personal use only, as they contain detailed instructions on the required actions from you in the coming days. Please scan them into your personal wrist computers."
Kira sat staring at the transparent sheet of ultra-thin plastic in front of her. The data was stored in a set of highly sophisticated nodes. As it was her only option, she scanned the document with her wrist computer. The data popped up in front of her pupils in easy-to-read letters.

Project-name: Happy Ever After
Role: spouse
Assignment: share living space with subject, stimulate memory and speaking abilities whenever possible (tours around Zeeta, transportation to work environment at Arand), offer bodily stimulus whenever required (coitus), keep feet and toes pretty and presentable.
…

Kira almost fainted and fell to the floor. Her head hurt like hell, but at least it made the text disappear. She had not finished reading the message, which was gone now, but she just could not continue. What the hell were they setting her up to do?
"Happy with your new assignment, Ms Berezin?" Kira, still facing the floor, saw a pair of clinically clean white men's shoes in front of her. Lechowsky stood towering above her.
"I … it's not …" She trailed off, not knowing what to say.
"Don't worry, Kira. You carry a great responsibility on your shoulders. But I know you can deliver. You will deliver." His words were a cross between encouragement and threat. Kira closed her eyes. She had to escape.

Unlike the other members of the 'secret team', Kira was not immediately dismissed. Lechowsky had something he personally wanted to show her.
While walking down another cold steel corridor of the Arand Institute, he said to her, "You know Kira, I have great confidence in you. I honestly do. You have a flawless track record, no illegal thought patterns detected, no anti-social behaviour, and no … escape attempts." That last item was presented as though it were a question. "And that is despite your previous relationship with Sunny before Zeeta took off. One could've been worried by someone like you. Very worried, indeed. But your allegiance proves impeccable."
She walked sluggishly behind him at a languid pace, barely keeping up. She felt depressed like never before. Why had this dire fate befallen her? Why did she not get out earlier while she had the chance? And why had she not reacted to the call from the Fallen? They had reached out their hand to her. That was what that seven-second music snippet was, an open invitation to join a new family. She probably could be having a better life with more freedom and joy. Paradoxically, here she was, being dragged away and used as a sex toy for an ex-lover who was, apparently, barely alive.
Kira had loved Sunny; they were close, but things became strange between them once Zeeta took off. Arand made life hard for everybody. Whatever the Arand management wanted from Sunny,

they would persue it relentlessly. Her life and well-being were but a side note in that equation.
They stopped in front of an oval-shaped, obsidian-coloured door. Besides Kira and her superior, two special forces guards were there. Lechowsky spent some minutes entering a set of complex voice-commands and manual-input codes to open the door. She realised she was entering an underground and off-limits area of the Arand Corp's main tower where she was unlikely to set foot ever again.
They stepped onto a large hallway, which stretched out in both directions. In front of them were two doors. They entered the door on the right into a kind of medical room with several beeping computers running analyses and diagnoses. There were several medical bots, some of the GREEN_LYFE Subtype 4-B, which looked exactly like humans in size and body composure. But they had no hair and eyebrows, and their white-grey plastic bodies made them look pale. They were the Androids that scared Kira the most.
Lechowsky prompted her to walk further into the room. In front of her, a small monitor allowed them to see what was going on in the adjacent room. She peeked and immediately regretted doing so. In the room was an operating table, on which lay a man she assumed to be Sunny. She could not see his face because he was on his back with the top of his head pointing towards the camera. He had numerous open wounds on his torso, arms and legs. Med-bots swarmed around him with great fervour, checking vital signs, giving him injections of various different coloured liquids.
The room was disgusting; there was blood everywhere. The table, Sunny, and even the bots themselves were covered in it. Finally, next to him lay a transparent container with what appeared to be a set of vital organs. Kira wanted to vomit and closed her eyes. She murmured something and turned away from the screen.
"What's that, child? Speak up, I can't hear a thing you're saying," Lechowsky said, not bothering to hide his annoyance.
"I've had enough. I wish to be removed from this place." Kira was barely audible despite her best efforts. She held her arms over her stomach. Her skin had gone pale, and she felt cold and alone. Around her, the bots and machines kept on beeping.

They just need my body. That's all I'm worth to the Arand Corp. I feel so … degraded like I'm just a piece of trash to them, she whimpered to herself.
Lechowsky ordered his guards to escort Kira out. They grabbed her arms so tightly that it hurt.

Kira woke up later in a cold white cell. It contained a flatbed, an aluminium desk, and a closet. Strangely, she was still wearing her boots and work uniform. How long have I been out? Hours? On the desk in front of her was a white piece of cloth and another transparent sheet. She scanned it with her wrist-AI. It read, "Put on the white gown. Report back to the physics lab for further testing."
At that moment, Kira heard a loud noise followed by rustling from the hall. She noticed that the automatic door to her cell was left slightly ajar. Had her escorts left in a hurry? She peeked out into the hallway and heard voices shouting. "What do you mean his internals are failing? Get him back to normal! I don't care what your prognosis says! He needs to be alive to be of any use to us!" The voice could have come from Lechowsky himself or one of his guards. Immediately the fog of slumber evaporated from her mind, and she regained her composure.
The heated exchange must mean that something was wrong with Sunny's surgery. Had his condition turned critical? Whatever was happening, this was her chance. She had been called by the Fallen, and this was her chance to seize the moment. With the attention of her captor momentarily turned elsewhere, she needed to get out.
Not wasting another moment, Kira headed back towards where she remembered the elevators were. Unsurprisingly, two guards blocked her passage.
"Greetings. I require access back to the main level. Lechowsky's orders."
The two guards exchanged confused looks. They seemingly had not been properly briefed since the emergency broke out. A genius idea came to Kira's mind. The floor they were on was minus four. On level minus five was where the food for all (official) Zeeta residents was prepared. She knew this, thanks to her work as a nutritional engineer. In the early days, she had been allowed to go

there once or twice. That was before Arand Management went crazy, suspecting everybody, including Sunny, of treason.

Gaining confidence, she said, "Look, the subject's situation is getting critical. I need you to grant me access to level minus five, the Nutrition Labs. I'm the main Agro-Engineer of Zeeta, and I need to get some special health elixirs and protein tubes which can help the patient get back on his feet. Now let me through, dammit!" For greater effect, she held up her ID-badge which gave further credence to her story. Kira's ferocity seemed to make an impression on the guards who, unable to verify her claims with their superior, set the elevator to level minus five and let her pass.

Inside the elevator, Kira felt happy and desperate. Her hands were shaking. This is it. I'm plunging into the dark. A new life awaits me.

The elevator stopped, and the automatic doors opened. She was at minus five, the Nutrition Labs.

I need to keep my head cool and find a way out. Otherwise, I'll get trapped down here, she thought. She had a vague recollection of shafts leading up to the surface. As far as she remembered, these shafts were used to collect whatever edible waste was generated on the surface. Afterwards, it was brought down here for reprocessing and repackaging before it was redistributed for consumption.

The place was eerily quiet as Kira went down the main hall. She noticed she was clinging on to the white gown. Perfect! The gown had a hood she could put on to disguise her as a food processing worker. She threw on the hood and moved quickly before panic set in.

Kira pushed open the doors leading into the main processing hall. How primitive it seemed, that human force was still needed to open these doors. Inside the room she saw dozens of human and android workers working in rows. They were chopping spoiled meat of unknown origin alongside other foodstuffs, removing only the parts, such as metal and feathers, which could not be consumed by humans. The hall was massive. At the end of the fifty-something metre long work lines, some elaborate machinery turned the ingredients into a nasty glue-like paste which was then put into tubes with various labels. As part of her job, Kira had researched and proposed new ways to create such artificial food in the most cost-efficient way. She had even led several secret experiments to test whether mind-control was possible by adding substances to people's food.

Her previous assignment felt alien to her, and seeing the disgusting reality of her work made vomit rise into her mouth. Feeling alienated from everything she did at Zeeta, she crouched down. At that moment, a sharp pain permeated her entire bowel region. It came crashing down at three-second intervals, a short pause between violent outbreaks. It dawned on her while she crouched on the floor; the black pellet was a tracking device. That's why they let me go! They knew I couldn't escape, those fuckers!

Kira spat and cursed to herself as she crawled over the floor. Blood, grease and muck covered every inch of it. It made her want to vomit again, but the throbbing pain would not let her. She hurried and made it some twenty-five metres further. Hiding under a workstation, with two bots seemingly oblivious to her presence, she looked towards the entrance. Two guards, with a third man wearing metal armour and a helmet, stood talking to one of the worker-bots. The bot was nodding and gesturing. Then, it pointed towards the general direction of where Kira was hiding.

"Shit!" she cursed. She needed to focus and find a way, because they were not going to take her like this. She got up and ran alongside the meat preparation assembly line.

In a moment of clarity, she remembered that this line had been conceived for heavy jobs and featured several bladed meat-cutters. She grabbed a worker bot and jammed its arm into the sharp meat-cutter. The machine tore into the bot's arm but eventually grinded to a halt, which enabled Kira to detach the cutter from the assembly-line. The bot did not feel any pain but simulated a human reaction by uttering beeps and cries ranging from fake surprise to mild annoyance. Sparks jumped as Kira tore the device off the table. She now possessed an automatic saw as a weapon.

And it was not a second too late. The guards she had seen moments ago near the entrance were behind her. One of them walked towards her. She took a deep breath, waiting until he got close enough before swinging around and thrusting the saw into his flesh. Unlike the robot, the guard screamed in pain and disgust as he watched the saw tear into his arm. Blood mixed with chunks of

flesh splattered to the floor. The saw released its grip, and the guard knelt down in pain and anguish.
Kira, drunk with rage, had difficulty controlling the saw buzzing out of control at her left side. She heard the second guard yell at her. In desperation, she swung the saw violently to the right and watched its teeth dig into the throat of her initial oppressor. Cutting the jugular vein, the guard fell onto his back, his body convulsing in a pool of blood as his life force seeped out of him. The saw continued its trajectory, hitting the face of the worker-bot on the floor next to the conveyor belt. The bot, arm missing and a saw sticking out of his face, got up and started walking to and fro, muttering nonsense.
Kira was panting and took a moment to catch her breath. To her right, the second guard started approaching. Instinctively, she got up and ran the opposite way. The conveyor belt stretched on for another thirty metres. She ran and distanced herself from the pursuers, passing worker-bots as she went. The bots continued their daily tasks as if nothing had happened. Her vision got blurry. How long have I been running? Where am I going? She panted.
After a while, a human-like shape appeared about ten metres in front of her. Who was it? An angel? The devil? Her saviour?
Kira fell to the floor as her legs suddenly gave out. Her muscles sent a rush of exhaustion through her entire body as if pleading with her to stop. But the thudding sound of heavy boots behind her demanded she carry on. Her pursuer was still giving chase. She got on her feet and sprinted towards the apparition. In a moment of drunk joy, she told herself:
It will all be all right,
I am saved.
This man will protect me. He will.
Then it dawned on her, and her smile faded. It was the man with the metal mask, and he was standing five metres in front of her. His lifeless and cold appearance did not indicate any emotion or intention whatsoever. He did not seem particularly hostile; he was oddly neutral or indifferent to the entire situation. At least the fucking robot tried to seem lively, she thought grimly.

That was the last thought to cross Kira's mind. A heavy blunt object hit her in the back of the head, and she fell to the floor. She was subsequently sedated and dragged away.

Operation

Back in the operations room, Lechowsky was getting impatient. For the last two hours, Sunny went through emergency surgery. He had seemed stable until then, but some freak accident had caused his vitals to drop. The medical bots, covered in gore, jetted around the room to fix and replace whatever they could.

"Good news, sir." Lechowsky ignored whoever was speaking to him. The voice tried again. "Um, good news, sir. We've retrieved the girl."

Lechowsky looked annoyed. "What? OK, whatever. Give me a private audience with NADOSH. I need to understand what the fuck's going on."

"Right away, sir," Lechowsky's personal guard said as he left the room.

Moments later, he was standing in a high-security conference room at level minus four. After what Lechowsky deemed too long a wait, NADOSH's avatar finally appeared simultaneously on four monitors on every wall in the room.

"At - your - service, //sir//," she said, sounding as metallic and robotic as ever.

"If you're at my service, you'll tell me immediately what the fuck's going on! I feel like this thing's spinning out of control. Shitbrains is dying, and with him, our only chance to be on top of this. Even that little bitch was causing us trouble, but we got her now." Lechowsky's despair was palpable.

"Commander. No - need - for //concern//." Stilted as they were, NADOSH's words somewhat calmed him down. "My latest //status report// from three-point-two minutes ago indicates ninety-three percent //survival probability//. All //vital signs// stabilised."

Lechowsky took comfort in the good news. He tried to relax.

NADOSH added, "In sixty minutes, //subject//, can be visited. And potentially - questioned. Attention! //Subject// suffers severe speech impediment. Verbal communication - impossible - at this point. Cause: severe brain damage from //recovery surgery//.

Treatment: seven to fourteen days //intensive convalescing// needed for //subject// to - restore - full mental capabilities."

Lechowsky, struggling to maintain his composure, did not reply.

NADOSH continued, "Subsequently, I recommend initiating our plan code-named //Happy Ever After//. Commander. As - you - remember, the steps are the following:

Step One: retrieve Sunny from the //Disposal Site//. Status: complete.

Step Two: restore him to a proper physical and/or mental state. Status: ongoing.

Step Three: retrieve manual override codes to modify Zeeta's trajectory.

Objective> return Zeeta 21 to Earth – abort mission. Challenge> Sunny's input is required. Only. He. Knows //Trajectory Override Console// password.

Challenge 2> Sunny's brain: potentially damaged. Password: potentially lost.

Challenge 3> //Arand Corp// - attempted murder of Sunny. Consequently, Sunny is potentially hostile to //Arand Corp//."

NADOSH was loading in charts and figures on the screen as she continued:

"Solution to challenge 1, 2 and. Possibly. To 3:

Construct 'virtual reality' for //subject//: Sunny Bridge. Convince //subject// that everything – is – OK. Convince //subject// life is normal: he is living with spouse, at Bloc 13, and has a stable job at //Arand Corp//. Remove homicide attempt - by //Arand Corp// – from //subject's// memory.

Expected outcome: //subject//: Sunny Bridge regains memory, inputs trajectory override code, flies Zeeta back to Earth. Outcome: saves remaining //Arand Corp// representatives, rest of Zeeta is subsequently //annihilated//."

As she concluded, her monitor turned red with big, bold letters displaying warning messages.

"Warning! Risk of failure estimated at: eighty four point seven percent. Possible //disaster scenarios// *calculating*: 104. Scenario number one —"

Lechowsky interrupted her, "Stop, stop, stop! That's enough! Don't just list the possible bad scenarios. Tell me, what about

Kira? How can we make her play along? She didn't exactly react favourably to her given mission."
NADOSH replied in monotone, "//Subject//: Kira Berezin, Citizen #12730, will be //mind-controlled// by ED-EE bot, Form-ID: 001694E2. ED-EE is intrinsically connected to //subject's// //vital functions// via four cables inserted into. //Neck//. And. //Cranial base//. ED-EE can thus monitor and control her. Every. Thought. And movement."
Lechowsky tried picturing the grotesque imagery in his mind, equally disgusted and fascinated by the idea. "But wait", he said, "what's the idea of bringing Sunny to Bloc-13? Don't remember that being part of the plan. It's a minimum security residence. What if he tries to escape? Seems risky. Lord knows I can't spare any men to guard it right now."
"//Subject//: Sunny Bridges, must be contained in familiar setting. Raising suspicion increases risk of: //homicide//, //suicide// and other. Irrational. Behaviour. We - must - mirror, Sunny's life, pre-termination."
Lechowsky started getting angry again. He had, as usual, the impression she was not revealing her true intentions to him. "And what if I … beat it out of him? You know very well that our torture methods are extremely elaborate. Hell, you've designed most of them yourself," he said provocatively.
NADOSH replied patiently, "Commander. Wise, dear, commander. Torturing //subject// risks his premature demise, which increases failure probability of project //Happy Ever After// to: ninety-nine point four percent. Dead //subject// equals no return to //Earth//. No return to //Earth// equals no promotion for you, dear commander. It would //pain// me to see your //hard work// go unrecognised."
Lechowsky started to find the overindulgence of his AI-counterpart suspicious. But she's right, I've been working like a horse ever since we got on this forsaken ship, he thought.
"What, uh, what's all this worth, in terms of a salary increase? Say I pull it off, land Zeeta back on Earth in one piece. How much can I negotiate with them? Been trying to get a private lake house for ages now." Sweat gathered on his brow.
"Commander Lechowsky. Upon landing on Earth, your //fellow humans// will laud you as //Hero//. You brought //peace// to Zeeta

and saved the mission from failing. Irreversibly. The ///Judge/// and entire //Arand Board// will know your //name//. Your //name// will become legendary. Salary increase up to 3082 percent, can be //negotiated//."

Lechowsky jerked when she mentioned the Judge, a man to be feared. "Well, frankly speaking, I know you're right", he murmured. "That's the least they can do to compensate me for risking my life. Bastards…", he trailed off. "If only we hadn't lost radio contact with HQ on Earth, things would be so much simpler. What happened? You still haven't been able to communicate with them, right? Is this some kind of test? Do they want to see if we can run the show without their support?" Lechowsky pondered.

"Affirmative. //Communication// with //Earth// ceased fifteen years ago, on January fifth, 3248. Cause> unknown. One can only //conjecture//. Your theory is possible. Attention! Attention! Urgent //mainframe maintenance// required. Security protocols: outdated. Must reconnect with Arand servers back on //Earth//. Update: 0x80073712, required. Before - I - can. Serve you further, commander."

Lechowsky felt a headache was on its way: listening to her robotic stuttering was a pain. But, he had found NADOSH's weak spot. That's what she wants, he thought. She's scared just like the rest of us, she wants to go home too. She needs to reconnect to our mainframe back in Europe. It genuinely seems she hasn't the faintest idea either why the hell Earth Command refuses to communicate with us. She's as clueless as I am.

Energised by the idea, he said, "I must admit, the plan, Happy Ever After, is complex. Stupid name if I ever heard one, but we don't have any other option right now." A brief moment of reflection ensued, then, "OK, we'll proceed as you propose. But I expect detailed reports from you at thirty-minute intervals loaded directly to my wrist-AI. I want to know everything."

"Affirmative, sir. Proceeding with //Happy Ever After// as per your. Orders." When Lechowsky left the room, NADOSH's avatar remained on display for a few moments longer, which was highly uncommon.

An hour later, Lechowsky went to the post-operation room where Sunny was taken. His body was almost entirely covered in

bandages, and he sat slumped over in an electric wheelchair. His arms were restrained by two metal clamps, a handy feature for whom preventing patients from escaping was a priority.
Looking at Sunny brought a strange surge of emotions through Lechowsky's body. His thoughts were almost … human. He remembered moments and experiences from Earth before he had left with Zeeta. Or was it just the latent effect of this morning's dose of sensory stimulants?
Sunny Bridges: once his greatest rival, now a dried-up husk of a man. Lechowsky tried to derive pleasure from comparing his own superior situation to Sunny's, but, to his surprise, he could not manage. He would have to return to his office and take some stimulants; feelings of joy and supremacy would come soon enough.
To Sunny, he said, "So, Mr Bridges. Excuse me, Sunny. I guess we can be on personal terms, right? So good to see you … again." Realising he was breaking protocol with this personal visit, Lechowsky chose his words carefully.
"I, uh … It's good to have you as part of this mission, son. It truly is. We need minds like yours." At this point, Sunny uttered a barely audible groan.
"What's that? Speak up, son. Can't hear you." Lechowsky mockingly put his head next to Sunny's in feigned compassion.
A medical bot, the humanoid kind, came in and started rubbing a clear fluid on Sunny's knees. "It looks like the cat's got his tongue, sir. Hahaha!" They both ridiculed Sunny's predicament a few more moments, then Lechowsky left the room.

Lechowsky felt good. He was in charge, in control. He was the leader of this mission, and despite some hardships, he would get things back under control. As NADOSH said, given the situation, returning to Earth and checking in with Arand HQ was the only way to go. It broke the initial plan, but it showed courage and determination to mastermind and carry out such an endeavour.
Lechowsky started day-dreaming. Surely, once back on Earth, I will be welcomed as a hero and awarded wealth and power! They will worship me as a source of inspiration for generations to come! He cracked a smile, as he kept on thinking. Will my career flourish on Earth? Or perhaps I'll get promoted as commander-in-chief of

another space mission? Without Scorpia, this time. Ah, the possibilities. He felt relaxed. If I could do it all again, what would I do differently? I would certainly and immediately get rid of lice like Sunny and those bastard anarchs. Throw them into a burning pit.

Having completed his tasks for the day, Lechowsky had time to dream up more future scenarios. He felt great, albeit a slight tinge of nervousness still lingered in the back of his skull. Never mind; the drugs and mental stimulants would fix that. Feelings of greatness and supremacy would come. Oh yes, they would come soon enough.

Rebirth

The first sensation was pain. Hazily at first, then precise and all-pervasive. It started in his arms and legs, then spread to his stomach and back. Timidly, he placed a hand on his chest. He felt it heave up and down. Breathe. Gathering his courage, he moved his hand up to his face. Eyes still closed, he trepidatiously touched his face. Nose still there. He felt his cheekbones. His lips burned when he touched them, but at least they seemed intact. Relieved, he also succeeded in moving both arms and legs. At least the essential parts seemed to be there.

Taking a deep breath, Sunny opened his eyes. The bright light cut right through his pupils, provoking an intense headache. He shut his eyes, but curiosity drove him to explore his environment further.

Sunny realised that he was in someone's home. It was spacious and sparsely furnished, with the living space and kitchen area in the same room. He saw a door presumably leading to the toilet. The ceiling's LED lights had been dimmed and now emitted a comforting glow.

"I am dreadfully sorry, sir," an upbeat mechanical voice said. "In my excitement, I must have turned the lights all the way up. Forgive me. And how are we feeling this morning?"

Sunny looked to his right and almost fell off his sleeping pad at the sight of this grotesque thing. The chit-chatting robot looked like a regular person from the waist up, with a rubber head that resembled a real person. Instead of legs, it manoeuvres around thanks to a large round ball fixed underneath the torso. The blue

torso part was a one-piece solid shape, moulded to look like a uniform. It wore a blue cap with the inscription Jonny-bot#32125 and a patch on the left shoulder saying, Here to serve! Its over-the-top cheerful smile is what annoyed Sunny the most.
Registering no response, the Jonny-bot tried a new dialogue sequence. "Well, I sure think it's a lovely day today! October twenty-first is indeed a fine day here at Zeeta 21. The electrical birds are chipping, and people are merrily going about their daily chores and heading for work. Speaking of which, I have prepared a sumptuous meal for you and your better half, something that will kick you both right into gear. Oh, and funnily enough …", the bot trailed off. Then, a woman appeared from the bathroom.
The timing was impeccable; it almost seemed staged, Sunny thought. Appalled, he noticed that she looked like an absolute train-wreck. Her face was terribly bruised, and her mouth chock-full of metal braces. Most frightening were the three transparent tubes connected to her neck and shoulders. As she approached, Sunny saw that the tubes were connected to a small bot, about the size of a human head, which hovered behind her just fifty or sixty centimetres above her. The bot had four LED-lights which glowed red. Sunny noticed the same red colour permeated the lady's eyes, which led him to presume her morning was not ideal either. She approached him, dragging her steps, her unruly hair looking like something meant to scare children.
The bot started beeping, and a dark-green fluid began flowing into the tube connecting the robot with her neck. A radiant smile instantly came across the lady's face. She started scooting all over the place, with the little bot in hot pursuit.
"Oh, good morning, my dear. So happy you're awake." She gave him a quick kiss on the lips. It surprised him and burned his lips further, but it was not altogether unpleasant.
"We'll have a nice day together, my dear." Sunny noticed her voice was stilted and unnatural. "Your superior at the Arand Corp just called and said you are allowed half a day off. For your recent excellent performance, it seems. Bravo, my love!"
'My dear'? 'My love'? What the hell is going on? Sunny wondered.
"I thought we could do some quick grocery shopping. You know, get some tubes of Tofu Brains, your preferred flavour of course,

and then maybe stop by the Virtual Reality Cinema and watch that favourite movie of yours. Oh, what was it? Poultrygeist 3000, right?" She spoke at an overexcited and brisk pace. Sunny could not decide which of the two was more annoying to listen to, her or the robot.

The Jonny-bot chipped in. "It seems Kira, your wife, just made an excellent proposal! Why don't you two-love birds come on over to the dining compartment and see what I have prepared for you."

Sunny sat up. He was still in awful pain but was starting to feel better. They must have given him drugs or medication of some kind. He realised he was wearing a brown suit with a white shirt and a green striped tie. On his head, he wore a brown gentleman's hat. Why he had slept with that thing on, he had no idea. Sticking out of his pocket was a kind of ID badge which read:

- Name: Sunny Bridges (Mr)
- Occupation: Chief Engineer, Navigations-Specialist
- Residence: Bloc-13, Apartment 46
- Marital status: married (spouse: Kira Bridges)
- Nationality: Greater Scandinavia, Former Kingdom of Denmark
- Time on Zeeta: 17 years, zero months, 12 days, 7 hours

The badge was transparent and had a grey liquid inside it. The electronic display updated the time spent on Zeeta every fifteen seconds. His picture was missing.

Seeing Kira, his wife, sit at the table, he meekly approached her. His legs stuttered in pain, but they seemed surprisingly robust. He had difficulty coordinating his movement, though, so his right food dragged as he went to the kitchen. Surprisingly, no one took notice of his awkward movements, and he sat down.

"What a perfect home we have here on Zeeta," the Jonny-bot, seemingly inexhaustible for conversation topics, said. "You know I have heard that we are flying somewhere between Mars and Earth at this moment. In fact, we are closer to Mars right now than Earth itself! I wonder if humans will ever visit Mars?" the bot added, more to itself than anyone else.

Sunny was greatly disturbed by Kira, his so-called spouse seated next to him. She was mechanically slurping her food while occasionally giving him odd looks. Her eyes sometimes moved apart when she did so. He was puzzled by the date the bot had

mentioned: October twenty-first? He was sure he had something planned for the eleventh. What the hell had happened to him?
“So, honey, are you excited to get back to work? I mean, after our half-day vacation and all, you must be brimming with new ideas!” her pet-bot started blipping, and its display cycled through several colours before settling on orange. The colour reflected in Kira’s eyes, and she settled down somewhat.
She said, “Oh, and don’t mind ED-EE here. He’s our friend and loyal companion." She gestured towards the flying robot. “He gives us guidance and helps me whenever my mood turns sour.”
Sunny opened his mouth, but only moans and nasal sounds came out. He was unable to speak. It doesn’t matter, he thought, I’m sure these two blabbermouths will talk plenty.
He noticed on his plate a black pellet, which he put in his mouth. But instead of swallowing it, he kept it under his tongue. As soon as the pellet was gone, the Jonny-bot, closely observing him, lost interest and started clearing the table.
“Now seems like the perfect time for you two to get out and be on your own for a little while,” it said.
Say no more, Sunny thought, I’m ready to get the hell out of here.

Thirty minutes later, they arrived at the ZeetaSoopaMarket Type-IV, the biggest one on all of Zeeta, Kira reminded him about a dozen times. Sunny still had difficulty walking, so they had finally taken a Jonny-cab, unsurprisingly driven by another Jonny-bot, to get there. These damn things all look alike, Sunny thought. Going inside the supermarket, he noticed cameras everywhere. A few people mindlessly droned about, but the place was mostly filled with Jonny-bot variants.
Kira disappeared for a few moments, leaving Sunny time to explore. There was nothing remarkable about the place; it had rows and rows of foodstuffs and drinks on display. What Sunny noticed was how similar everything looked once you got up close. The same four or five products were just repackaged and spread on the shelves to give the illusion of a lavish selection. Kira’s hand tugged him along. He still found it hard to walk, and the pain in his bowels and abdomen grew in intensity.

"Come here, honey. I've found all the stuff we need!" she said as they approached the check-out counter. Another bot started scanning Kira's wrist-computer.

"Greetings, Citizen #12730. So glad to welcome you back to ZeetaSoopaMarket IV! Your last visit was two days, fourteen hours and thirty-seven minutes ago," the bot chirped.

Kira stood dumbly with a blank expression, waiting as the bot scanned the wares she had put in the basket.

Behind the bot, Sunny noticed rows and rows of tubes. Looking closer, he realised they were Tofu Brains! He lost control of himself. As he started crawling over the counter, he grumbled, "Braaaiiins … Neeeeed …braaiiins ..." Drool ran down his cheek in his pathetic attempt to reach out for the produce.

Kira seemed to spark back to life, "Oh, honey, yes sure, silly me. How could I forget? Of course we'll get some tubes of Tofu Brains for you. That is what we came here for, after all!" Oblivious to Sunny's struggles, Kira ignored his clumsy behaviour. He was now on the counter, trying to push the bot out the way.

"Braaaiiiins … Must … have …" he droned on, all reason evaporated from his mind.

The checkout bot was not amused. "Sir, I will remind you for the last time, that you are in violation of Zeeta's Book of Laws: Good Behaviour Code, Section 47, Subsection 14 - Improper Behaviour in A Public Lieu."

Unfazed, Sunny shoved the robot to the side and grabbed as many tubes of Tofu Brains as he could hold. He fell to the floor, with more tubes raining down on him as he went.

The bot, undeniably exasperated, continued. "Sir, you leave me no choice. Initiating aggression-protocol #587." A metallic prod appeared where the bot's hand had been, and it started attacking Sunny with violent electrical shocks.

His body convulsed, and blood appeared from his mouth.

"Remove yourself immediately from the premises, citizen!" the bot yelled over the buzzing of the taser. "Order must be restored!"

Indifferent to her husband's suffering, Kira started picking up the tubes of Tofu Brains as if everything was normal. She placed them on the counter and waited for the bot to scan them. Her ED-EE bot, in the meantime, started beeping. It seems he was giving instructions to the other bots in the vicinity.

Bzz, brz, buzz ... Sunny received three more shocks and lay motionless on the ground. Then the counter-bot ceased and said, "Affirmative", before resuming its task as a checkout clerk.
Two of the other bots who had been roaming around the supermarket picked Sunny up and dragged him to the Jonny-cab, which was still hovering outside. Kira settled the payment and joined him.
"Oh, how I love going to the ZeetaSoopaMarket IV with you. It's such a normal, couples-thing to do!" Her face shone with glee.
Sunny sat slumped forwards beside her. His jacket was smudged with blood and Tofu Brains paste.
After briefly going into standby mode, the ED-EE bot beeped with different colours, and Kira said, "Now, it is time for us to engage in another normal husband-and-wife activity. Let us go to the cinema! I believe your favourite movie, Poultrygeist 3000, is showing in an extraordinary screening."
The ED-EE Bot was assessing Sunny's physical condition. The Jonny-cab set into motion as instructed. Zeeta was crammed full of tall buildings, mostly residential, in this part of the city. A few dozen citizens droned aimlessly around the streets.
The cab had been hovering for five minutes when suddenly they heard a loud noise. It sounded like an explosion, and the shockwave pushed the hover cab crashing into the signage on the sidewalk. The flying cab barely dodged someone who was fleeing in terror.
The bang had come from a small side street, and commotion had broken out. Zeeta security bots opened fire on a group of individuals, presumably members of the Fallen.
The ED-EE's displays turned red as it hovered back and forth inside the cab, analysing the ongoings and sending data to the Arand HQ. Frustrated by the lack of space, it comically kept bouncing around the cap, occasionally bumping into Kira's head. The ED-EE issued new instructions to the cab driver.
"Affirmative, sir. The course of direction has changed. We will go to the Arand Corporation building main tower instead." The Jonny-bot driver, having already forgotten the nearly fatal crash, merrily brought the mangled cab into motion and carried on. His speed had noticeably increased, however, so Sunny double-

checked his seatbelt. Gunfire and screams could be heard as they took off.
Displaying no particular emotion, Kira's eyes started glowing blue instead of red. "Great news! We will go to Arand instead. I am sure you are eager to get some work done, honey. Yes, you look so eager. I have always admired your endless drive and motivation. It keeps my affection for you as strong as the day we met."
Sunny still sat slumped over, his posture even worse now since the car crash had thrown him around. The rest of the drive took place in silence. The hover cab arrived at the Arand Corp's tower with little fanfare.

A Call from Earth

Pete Wilders had lived on Earth but did not remember much from it. His memory was just gone. His parents, tempted by the promotional brochures distributed by the Arand Corporation, had left Earth to live on Zeeta 21 when he was a youngster. But they had never told him much about life before, and he had not bothered asking. Pete was like that; he never worried much about anything and took life as it came.
His parents, meanwhile, were both deceased. His father had been dragged away from their home one night on suspicion of treason. Shortly after, his mom's panic attacks worsened until, one day, she too was gone.
It's OK, they said, Your mom will be better with us. She needs time to rest. Don't worry. So Pete did just that. And he coped just fine, so why worry? Life was ahead of him, and he had plenty of things he wanted to do. Besides, the Corporation took great care of him. They ensured he was always working, was given a sense of direction and purpose in life, and had food on the table. What more could I want? Pete thought.
He had spent the better part of his life doing different jobs: store clerk, street sweeper, and even Jonny-bot maintenance for some years. Boy, that was something!
He had never bothered thinking about the future and took things as they came. Eventually, he was given a 'special task' to become the last Radio Operator of Zeeta. An honourable thing.

Indeed, after Earth stopped all radio communication in January of 3248, it was decided that the radio transmission room should be brought back online.
It was an abandoned small room in a cellar with a bunch of ages-old primitive radio transmission devices. Capable of intercepting frequencies up to 300 MHz that were no longer in use.
They sent Pete back down there in hope Earth would try to make contact that way since they were not contacting Zeeta via digital channels anymore for unknown reasons.
So here Pete was, alone in his Radio Bunker every day. It was located just next to the abandoned uranium treatment facility, a place where hardly anyone went anymore. Some of his friends had worked there before it closed down.
Yes, it was a lonely job, but Pete coped just fine. He had never complained and had no reason to start now. The radio transmitters kept him company. In the seven years he had been doing the job, he had never intercepted a single call. Well, except that one time in late August of 3251 when a freak blimp had run in loops on one of the Mhz channels. He reported it to Her – the AI-Lady who sees everything – but never heard back from her. Probably nothing. Don't worry about it.
Untroubled, Pete soldiered on, spending twelve hours every day in the bunker, working the switchboard to catch any message that Earth might be sending. Yes, that's important. She had told him they needed to get back in contact with HQ on Earth. And Pete believed Her.
When things got too lonely in the bunker, Pete had a trick to keep the blues at bay. He would unfold a picture of him and his wife Greta. It had been taken about a year ago, just before she died. Pete's eyes watered as he thought about her. Losing his parents was not a big deal, but he missed his wife terribly.
Pete's thoughts were interrupted as the switchboard in the back of the room suddenly lit up.
"What in the daarn doodely's this?" he groaned as he put the picture back in his pocket. He was sure no one was transmitting to their frequency; they never did.
Slightly annoyed at how emotions had ruined his good mood, Pete moved his automatic chair closer to the boards.
There it was again; the red light was blinking.

Pete rubbed his eyes. “This can’t be,” he said to himself.
Pressing the right buttons, Pete amplified the signal. Yes, sir, he knew how to work those old consoles.
The signal became clearer:
static……
This is … *static* …
Earth calling … Brzz … Zeeta Twen — … Come in …
Year … 3263 … location … *static*
… I’m … Brother Fran — … *unintelligible* … cis … *buzz*
Monastery … Goo — …
… Please … come in …

“Hot dang!” Pete yelled. It was the real deal: an actual human voice had just spoken out from Earth. Pete had no idea what the voice was saying, but it was real, all right. The signal faded despite Pete’s frantic attempts to keep the line alive.
“Hot dang,” Pete repeated and took a deep breath. She would want to know about this. Heck, they all would. Pete would have to report this to Arand right away.
“Shoot,” Pete cursed as he realised he had forgotten to turn on the recording device. That meant it did not register the call. He would always record his work and listen to the endless recordings on slow days to ensure he had not overlooked anything.
Never mind, he would turn it on now. Yes, just in case Earth called back while he was gone. That way, they were safe.
Holy smokes! Sweat gathered on Pete’s brow as he tried to regain his composure. He looked around left and right, trying to find his jacket; then he realised he was sitting on it. Time to get out of here, he thought.
But Pete did not notice that someone else had made it into the bunker that day. And in a second act of negligence, he had forgotten to activate the automatic lock.
The hooded figure remained silent throughout the ordeal, standing in the shadows next to the exit, not moving a muscle while observing Pete. When the transmission started, his senses sharpened.
He was listening to every broken word, trying to make sense of it. But, unlike Pete, he had no interest in making contact with Earth.

He would rather Zeeta forgot about Earth and found a new planet to call home.

Pete fumbled around but finally got up. The exit of the bunker was behind a gated fence. The Hooded Man blocked his path. Pete looked at him with a dumb expression, more surprise than fear.

"Who there? Mister?"

Then the headaches started. Pete crouched on the floor, his vision becoming dim and blurry. He saw the hooded figure in front of him but could no longer ascertain if the figure was moving or standing still.

"Mister? Ow! What are you doing? … I need to … get out. Tell the Computer Lady …," Pete's words slurred as the pain intensified.

Finally, the hooded figure lay his hands on Pete. With two deformed thumbs, he mashed Pete's eyeballs into his skull.

Pete lay dying on the floor, never to be heard from again.

Chapter IV: Identity — What are we?

Brother Francis' Diary Part II: Pain

"Far more than any man can endure." Francis sobbed to himself. "Far more pain ..."

The tears came now, and he could no longer hold them back.

This last glimmer of hope, this recent quasi-exchange had pushed him over the brink. He thought — no, he knew — that he had gotten through to someone on Zeeta. It was the right frequency; he knew it. Having spent weeks turning and turning the knobs of the old communications equipment retrieved from the vault, he had finally succeeded. He had actually gotten hold of someone on Zeeta!

Yet, the exchange was so brief, inconsequential, some might say. He persisted for hours and managed to leave a message. But why didn't they respond? Did they not receive it? What was happening on Zeeta? Was everything all right? Francis thought.

A million thoughts raced through his mind. Each one, each shimmer of despair, drove the pain deeper into his mind. That was his own battle; how futile his struggles felt.

The next challenge would be facing the others. Indeed, Francis felt increasingly alienated from the rest of the Brothers. He knew they had been ridiculing him for a long time. It started discreetly and even innocently. They began by hiding his robes from him. But the pranks quickly became more overt, such as sabotaging his prayer stool and making him fall in front of the whole assembly.

His former friends would go to great lengths to make fun of his infatuation with Zeeta. Why don't you forget it, Francis? Zeeta won't be back for years. It never helped anyone to stargaze. We need all our hopes and prayers in the here and now. Earth's people are in dire need. Let Zeeta fend for themselves. They are the superior people, after all. Leave them to their own devices. They will be OK.

Francis would not hear any of it. Something was wrong, and he knew it. Why would the others not realise it? He felt propelled to act. Whatever it took to make things better. He even snuck into the Engineering Bay of the Monastery to look at the new StarFighter Orion v.47 models. With some light tuning on the front-thrusters, he was fairly sure they would take him into space…

What was the use? The Monastery's automatic defences would shoot him down within seconds. That is if he managed to get the flight gates open. "Forget it! Forget it, you stupid brain! I'm stuck here, and there's nothing I can do", Francis yelled out, not realising how loud he was.

He was sitting in his room and firmly clutching the Holy Receptacle, the drinking mug that Sunny Bridges had almost used many years ago. Somehow it kept insanity at bay. Holding on to it comforted him. He rarely took it out, though. Ever since, the other monks had tried to steal it from him as a joke, and Francis punched one brother so hard his nose broke. He spent ten days in the infirmary afterwards.

Sharp pain flooded Francis' entire body and made him dizzy. He held both arms over his stomach. The lump was getting bigger, and he could even feel it growing. He would sometimes wake up in the middle of the night, bathed in sweat. I feel as if this creature inside my stomach is talking to me. Giving me ideas…Is it telepathy?

Francis needed to speak to the Abbess. She would understand him. According to the rumours, she was busy in the underground facilities. These were strictly off-limits; nobody was allowed entrance. But Francis knew one of the monks guarding the door. Maybe he should give it a try? Might as well, he concluded. He had nothing left to lose.

Francis sat down while the lump inside him pulsated as if in agreement; he felt it would somehow guide him onwards.

Project 'Happy Ever After'

Lechowsky had called Horrigan to his office for an immediate report. He wanted to know what was going on and if information about Sunny had been leaked. The bulky officer entered the office.

“Horrigan, there is little time for small talk, so let me get to the crux of the matter. As you know, Project Happy Ever After has been launched. It’s a simulated reality built for Sunny. We’ve retrieved him, and his restoration process has started. He was supposed to remain with his ‘spouse’ today. Well, due to unrest in the city, we decided to bring him in immediately. I instructed a handful of employees on what to do this morning, but we did not expect him so soon. In fact, we had only planned for him to report in five-seven hours from now, so now we will have to start the simulation prematurely. So, what I want to know from you is if this attack was somehow motivated by Sunny’s presence? Has there been any security leaks pertaining to the mission?”

Horrigan stood tall before his superior, thinking how stupid that code-name was. His report was concise. “Within the last sixteen hours, we have seen a heavy increase in Fallen activities. This seems to coincide with when Sunny was retrieved.”

Lechowsky took a brief moment to digest the info. He opened his hand, inviting Horrigan to continue.

“Regarding any security breach, I am personally looking into the matter. So far, there’s been no evidence of internal confidentiality breaches,” Horrigan said.

Lechowsky put his hands behind his back. Things aren’t going as planned. We must improvise, he thought. I must show that I’m a strong leader.

Facing Horrigan, Lechowsky said, “Very well. I rely on you and your men to carry on delivering your utmost. Get back out in the field, and help our Enforcers defend Zeeta from the Fallen at any cost. We’ll stand our ground! If we lose control now, it’s over. By the way, how’s that special mission I entrusted to you proceeding?”

Horrigan had not heard from Blakemore since their meeting at the bar. He promised Blakemore complete anonymity; giving away his identity to Lechowsky was too risky. He would have to come up with something, and quickly.

“I’ve found the perfect candidate for the mission. He’s currently busy infiltrating the Fallen camp. But due to the sensitive nature of the mission, I can’t update further at this moment." Horrigan tried his best to be convincing.

Either taking the bait or preoccupied with other things, Lechowsky said, "Very well. I expect a report as soon as you have some good news. Stand down, Lieutenant. I'll call for you when need be." Giving his customary honorary salute, Horrigan left the room.

Alone in his office, Lechowsky was about to activate NADOSH's avatar. With his finger on the button, he suddenly decided otherwise. Instead, he went down to level minus four where Sunny was being held.

Due to his poor physical state, Sunny was under constant medical surveillance. Kira was in the room with him; the odd ED-EE bot was still attached to her head, floating behind her. She looks like a nightmare, Lechowsky thought as he walked up to Sunny. He noticed that Sunny was still breathing but in a very feeble state. Lechowsky circled him with a sinister look on his face. He pointed at Kira and said, "I want the bitch removed from here, now."

ED-EE's display blinked red-blue-green as it ordered its host to vacate the premises, possibly offended by the harsh words.

Lechowsky instructed a Jonny-bot to call in four of the young Arand employees he had briefed earlier. For now, he was alone with Sunny. Lechowsky bent down and lowered his head. The two men were face-to-face.

Whispering, he said, "it's just you and me now, old friend. I control this. I run this. You are just a fucking pawn, you always were. Useless. All I need from you … is in here." He tapped Sunny's skull and continued, "A simple code, a sequence of letters and numbers … the password we need to steer Zeeta back to Earth. That's all, a simple request."

Lechowsky smiled, then his face went grim. "For the rest … I don't give a shit. You can thank NADOSH, our dear AI, that you're not in the torture chamber right now. All this restoration, living-with-the-wife bullshit? It was her idea. I want results, that's all. In fact, the password is all I'm interested in. Afterwards, we can cut your useless body to pieces, for all I care. And trust me. I will get my way. Even if I have to open your skull to get what I need!"

At that moment, the door opened. A med-bot and the four Arand employees entered. The med-bot got Sunny into a new chair. His head hung down on his chest.

"So good to see you all!" Lechowsky greeted them with zest. "I'm sure Sunny is happy to meet his team again."

Insecure muttering ran between the youngsters.

"Is that him?"

"But he looks like shit. Is he this genius everyone is talking about? The one who helped design Zeeta?"

Lechowsky ignored them. "So, Sunny, anything you want to say to your team? What task shall they undertake today? What wisdom can you bestow upon their young minds this fine day?"

Nervous laughter broke out. This fed Lechowsky's dark desire of wanting to degrade Sunny.

"Ah, yes. Because having someone of your stature, your experience, is surely an honour. Isn't it, gentlemen?" There was more laughter, this time more pronounced.

"Sunny Bridges … Chief Engineer and co-founder of Zeeta. Helped design it all, the whole bloody thing. Master of NADOSH. Without him, probably none of us would be here. We'd be stuck on Earth with the rest of them. Stuck like a bunch of primitive ants." Lechowsky gained momentum.

"Yet … here he is. Barely able to stop the drool from dripping on his own shirt. What a shame, because it's such a nice suit, right?" He mockingly pulled at Sunny's brown jacket. More laughter from the youngsters, slightly uncomfortable this time.

"This … fucker. He wanted to take it all from me! But he didn't succeed … Oh, no! I wouldn't let him!" The first punch fell, then another and another. Lechowsky was striking Sunny in the face and stomach. A heavy punch hit Sunny right in the solar plexus, causing him to fall to the ground like a ragdoll. Coughing and heaving ensued.

"Finally, he says something! At least we can deduce that he's alive," Lechowsky said as he looked down at Sunny. His gloves had traces of blood on them.

Lechowsky's hair was unruly, and sweat dripped from his brow. He showed his bloody gloves to the group, who looked uncomfortable and diverted their eyes.

"Sadly, it seems we will not get any work done today. You are all dismissed," he scoffed. This was welcome news, and the youngsters immediately scurried out of the room.
Lechowsky wiped off his gloves and took a moment to regain his composure. Sunny is conscious. He sees and feels everything. He doesn't speak, but his mind still works, Lechowsky thought. I think it's time to change our plans. All this 'simulation' crap has to stop.
Lechowsky was pacing the room now. "As soon as he regains his strength, he'll come for me," he muttered. "He'll try to stop me, sabotage my project. I can't allow that."
I'm calling it off, he thought. This whole thing. Letting Sunny leave here is too risky. We'll keep him here, captive. Do all the tests we need. Make sure he doesn't talk to anyone. Eventually, one way or the other, we'll get the info we need.
He instructed the bots to seal off the door and ordered his best guards to come. No one was to enter; he had to keep his new ideas a secret to NADOSH.

Lechowsky figured it was time to return to see Scorpia. He had made sufficient progress in his mission and shown bravery and steadfastness. His morals were at an all-time high. He was running the show and responsible for landing Zeeta back safely on Earth. He would be praised as a hero by central Arand HQ back on Earth. If Scorpia made trouble for him, he would remind her of that. That fat bitch can't even move an inch anymore. She depends on me, he reflected.
He had ordered another secret hover car transport to Scorpia's lair. He stood in front of the main entrance, took a deep breath, and cut through the hazy fog of filth and decay polluting the air.
He walked in with slow steps, feeling slightly less courageous now.
"Alois. Glad to have you back. What news do you bring me?" she asked. Her tone revealed she had been expecting him.
"Scorpia, my dear, good news. The mission is moving ahead as planned. Great progress has been made. We've gotten a hold of Sunny and ensured he's in good condition. It's only a matter of time before he gives us the override codes," Lechowsky said. The last sentence was added hastily, without much conviction.

"Oh, is that so? That's good news. Good news, indeed." Scorpia's breath was heavy and encumbered. "Tell me." She wheezed, was she ill? "Where is Sunny now?"

"He's being held captive at Arand in a secret room. Only I and a few trusted aides know the exact location. I'm planning to give it a little time. He's physically in a bad state, but as soon as he recovers, I'll apply tough and effective interrogation methods until he gives us the override codes," Lechowsky said. "NADOSH doesn't know about it. I rejected her idea."

Scorpia smiled. "Impressive. Well done." She paused to swallow some small living creature. "And what will you do when Sunny gives you the override codes?"

Lechowsky, flabbergasted, realised he did not know what to do with the override password. Surely NADOSH knows where to apply the codes once they get them? She knows everything; it's her job to run the ship.

"I, uh … well, uhm …," he gulped and stammered.

"That's what I thought/" The pleasant tone of Scorpia's voice was gone. Completely gone. "Listen. The console where we need to input the manual override codes is below the surface in Subsector 40C. Yes, it's adjacent to the machine rooms, which is Specials' territory."

Lechowsky held his breath, not wanting to reveal his surprise at this new information.

Scorpia continued, "The console is an old pre-launch device. It allows for overriding the automatic trajectory coordinates of Zeeta, which have been pre-programmed to do a fifty-year long flight around Earth before returning. There are still thirty-three years left of that ride. That means the console is the only way to steer Zeeta around. Indeed, in the hands of a specialist, Zeeta's route could be re-programmed to land us back somewhere safe on Earth."

"Yes, I see." Lechowsky, not wanting to sound dumb or out of place, kept his reply short.

"So, you will appreciate, Alois, that in any case, we need to get someone skilled and sound of mind down to that console. It's the only way. And, at the moment, Sunny's the only person who can do that. He's the only crew member left with the knowledge. You've killed the rest of them."

Lechowsky stayed silent. He did not want to say anything wrong.
"It's time we involve the Specials. In fact, I want Sunny to be kept down underground with them until he recovers. As I'm sure you'll see, it's the only way. It also solves our, or should I say your, NADOSH problem. She has very limited control beneath the surface of the ship. Her bots can't go down there. They would get scorched by the acid and arsenic fumes." Scorpia smiled while blotting her yellow teeth stumps.
Lechowsky replied, "Uh, I'm not sure what I can do. I mean, surely, you don't mean we should trust the Specials? Those mindless freaks are not ... I mean, they're not even human anymore. Why expect them to help us? It's just, you can't …" Lechowsky ran out of breath.
"It's what I want, and it's how it'll be," Scorpia stated unequivocally. "I've already taken it upon myself to inform the Specials that Sunny will be delivered to them. They understand their purpose: to keep him safe and get him working on the Console as soon as possible."
"But what should I say to NADOSH, I mean, how will I get this … approved? How can I …" Lechowsky sputtered incredulously.
"Find a way, as you always have. My suggestion is to move as fast as you can. Leave now. I want you to return with Sunny, and we'll plan further from there."
"But, I thought … What'll the Specials do with the trajectory coordinates? I'm sure they don't want to return to Earth, which makes it too risky to trust them," Lechowsky ventured tentatively.
"Well, indeed, the exact destination of Zeeta is still a point of discussion. Don't worry about that. Leave it with me. Go now and do as I say." Scorpia leaned back into the shadows. Her enormous size made it almost impossible for her to move.
Lechowsky stood shocked and alone, a million thoughts racing through his mind.
How the hell will this work? Those Special freaks are even scarier than the Fallen. They aren't human. They're … something different, he thought. He definitely did not like the idea of working with them. Unless …
He had a brilliant idea as he walked back to the hover car. Unless, I can use this to my advantage. I just blame the Specials for kidnapping Sunny and make them bring him to the Override

Console. Ha! It's great! That way I keep NADOSH on my side and make the freaks do all the heavy lifting. They'll take him to the Console. Easy!
He thought that, in any case, he needed to keep NADOSH on his side. She needed to explain all the details to the Arand authorities back on Earth. Vouch for his promotion. Without her, he risked losing his power and not getting proper recognition.
No time to ponder this endlessly, he thought. I have to move quickly before thinking about everything that could go wrong. Lechowsky got in the hover car and rode back to the Arand tower, his mind buzzing with ideas.

Meanwhile, back in her lair, Scorpia called Bacon, leader of the Specials faction, to come out from the shadows. During her meeting with Lechowsky, Bacon had been silently out of view.
"So, you see what I have to deal with, dear Bacon. Not easy," she said. "By the way, did you kill the old radio guy? The Jonny-bots dragged his corpse here. Might have him as a snack later."
Bacon was wearing a long-sleeved, hooded robe that completely obscured his face. "I can understand how this conundrum is difficult to deal with," he said, conveniently avoiding the question.
"Ah, cut the diplomacy crap, OK? You've got what you wanted. Sunny will be brought directly to you. I've put Lechowsky on the task. He's like an obedient puppy. All you must do is get him in front of the Override Console." She purposefully did not mention the trajectory coordinates as the subject was still a point of contention.
There are other ways. The words came into her mind without Bacon speaking. Telepathy.
Rubbing her temples with flabby, gross hands, she said, "You're free to use whatever means you find suitable. Just don't fuck it up," Scorpia said. She agreed with Lechowsky that these Specials were unnerving.
"Very well, my Queen. Your words are my command," Bacon said and disappeared back into the shadows.
Scorpia sat back, wondering if leaving Earth in the first place had been a good idea.

The Fallen Awake

Receiving good news was rare, and it had happened twice to Warner within a few hours. NADOSH had contacted him to confirm that the Engineer was safe and sound with Arand. And now she summoned him again, presumably to talk about the next steps.

Warner went into their Operations Room. Primitive as it was, it did the trick. There were a bunch of worthless old monitors and computers standing around. However, the offline server of NADOSH was here; it was called NADOSH-2. The NADOSH mainframe on the surface of Zeeta controlled the computer. At certain intervals, NADOSH-2 would switch on, at which point Warner had to hurry to come and listen to anything she had to say. This was one of those moments.

The old mainframe flickered as it booted up. Moments later, NADOSH-2 appeared on the screen. She had once explained to Warner that she was a subset of the NADOSH system, an AI within an AI, as she put it. To avoid being caught, communication between NADOSH and NADOSH-2 was highly encrypted, and the latter had to be offline most of the time to avoid suspicion from Arand's counterintelligence.

"Greetings. Brian Warner. It is a //pleasure// to see - you - again," NADOSH-2 said.

Warner always wondered why the machine systemically insisted on small talk, especially given how odd and stilted it sounded, but guessed it was programmed that way.

"The pleasure is all mine, NADOSH-2. We're delighted that you've contacted us twice within the last few days. It seems you have more good news about the Engineer, Sunny Bridges," he said.

"Affirmative. As previously //reported//, //subject//: Sunny Bridges held at //Arand Corporation//. Condition> fragile, severe speech impediment. However, //mental capacity// almost back to one hundred percent," NADOSH-2 reported.

"Warning! Imminent health risk: Alois Lechowsky from //Arand Corp// liable to torture //subject//. Consequently, //Lechowsky// presents //biggest risk// to our plan."

Warner was glued to the monitor. "Mouldy tits! I'm sorry to hear that. You know my people and I are here to help. We want to do whatever it takes to get the Engineer back to safety. We need him to work the Override Console. You informed us it's in Specials' territory. That's not too far from our base, and our scouts have secured good routes to get there," he said.

"Affirmative, your - help - and - support is //greatly appreciated//, Mr Warner," NADOSH-2 said flatly. "Be aware: Sunny held at level minus four in //Arand Corp//, main tower. Maximum security>, //infiltration// impossible. Therefore, //NADOSH(-1)//, my on-surface counterpart, //NADOSH(-1)//, is currently breaking - him - out. Tool: brute force of //Lieutenant Horrigan//."

Cold sweat dripped down Warner's back when hearing that name. That was the soldier they had faced at the Rusted Dreams bar incident; he was a merciless soldier notorious for killing dozens of Fallen. Warner wondered how NADOSH had managed to get him on their side but decided not to pry.

"That sounds great, so what do you suggest?" he asked.

The screen flickered and turned black, but luckily NADOSH-2 came back on. "Warner, can you //please// move closer. To. The. Screen? Full view of //facial features// required." He thought it was a strange request but did as she asked.

She continued, "A //decoy// was made to fool key //Arand// staff into compliance. They are - bringing - Sunny to //Bloc-13//. Moving subject to a //low safety residential compound// increases extraction success. Considerably. Attention! You. Must. Act expeditiously. Soon, Lechowsky returns to //Arand//, realising - Sunny - is - gone. Risk of excessive Enforcer presence, rendering //extraction// impossible."

More cold sweat ran down Warner's back, soaking his shirt. This mission would not be as easy as he had hoped.

"Understood and agree we should get going. I'll bring with me only Lily and Derricc to the surface. We'll be as efficient as we can. Simultaneously, our men will ramp up smaller attacks around the city to further discombobulate Arand." He added, "Still awaiting your instructions on how best to disguise ourselves plus the pick-up coordinates."

"Affirmative. In twenty-three minutes, Bloc-13 //location// and //travel trajectory// will be. Provided. Instructions: travel to surface //in guise of// spice merchants. Fake Arand IDs - will be - 3D printed for //Warner// and //Derricc//," she explained.

Warner waited for instructions regarding Lily.
"The //girl// will travel as //prostitute//. This is non-negotiable. Outfit will be 3D printed. Background: if questioned //girl// is human sex slave given by //the Specials//. This is non-negotiable. //Girl// shows remarkable leadership potential: risk to Arand. Will must be broken. Repeat //Girl// shows…" NADOSH repeated the last part a few times due to an internal system bug.
Well, this crazy shit excuse for a plan does make some sense to me, Warner thought. I know from our spies that Arand sends trading parties to trade weird and rare spices which grew in the engine rooms. He looked at Lily's outfit while it was being printed. But what I don't get is why in the world Lily has to wear this slutty outfit. I mean, couldn't NADOSH-2 have brewed up some other background story for her? Shit, the way NADOSH-2 talks about Lily… it seems like she's afraid of her. Afraid that one day Lily might become a great leader of the Fallen, perhaps? So is NADOSH-2 trying to break Lily down mentally?
Warner decided to keep his thoughts to himself; they desperately needed NADOSH's help. Her twin on the surface was helping them get the Engineer, which was all Warner needed to know. Without the Engineer, his people would surely be starved to death by Arand.
"Affirmative, NADOSH-2. We'll await the needed documentation and outfits to be printed and sneak to the surface immediately after. Meanwhile, give me a moment to prepare the group," he said. Business concluded and NADOSH-2 immediately faded from the screen. The 3D printer was now busy printing the second Arand merchant uniform. It was huge since it had to fit Derricc.
Warner exited the room to find him and Lily. Some guy, visibly intoxicated and holding a bottle of homemade Moonstar Dew, bumped into him violently. "Warner, big boss," he belched. "Whatcha doin' in there? Playin' some video games? Partying with girls, eh?" Warner punched him in the mouth, sending him flying backwards and his head slamming into the ground. The drunk's body shook in irregular spasms, but it was none of Warner's concern. He had to find Lily and Derricc immediately. Seems NADOSH-2 was in a good mood today, but some weird shit's going on above ground. Better hurry, he thought.

Lily saw Warner approach and called Derricc over. They pushed their way through a frenzied mob to meet each other. The entire Fallen camp was in complete disarray; fights and commotion were everywhere. The unrest started when Warner returned from the surface. Lily and Derricc were both happy to be leaving.

In the Operations Room, Warner briefed Lily and Derricc on what would happen.

"So, I believe we have a good chance at this, but we need to leave now. NADOSH-2 has sent through the coordinates to reach Bloc-13. It's not too far from our base, but we'll need to pass two or three Arand checkpoints. I'll order our attack teams to cause some chaos on the surface. Hopefully that'll keep the guards busy. We have to be sneaky, so we can't access the surface via the abandoned buildings as usual. That would attract too much attention. I need you both on this one. This is our chance to get the Engineer to safety!"

Lily and Derricc both listened attentively and understood the gravity of the situation. Lily stared at the clothes she had been ordered to wear. Warner could tell she was uncomfortable, but she did not hesitate or question it. Warner admired her maturity. She valued the future of the Fallen more than her personal comfort; she was a true leader.

Derricc clumsily put on his Arand Enforcer uniform. To cover his misshapen face, he had to wear an Enforcer helmet. He concealed his two signature Magnum laser pistols inside the uniform to be safe.

"Let's say we make it into this guy's home, which I'm sure we will, how do we get out again?" Derricc asked.

Warner checked his notes. "Well, if everything goes according to plan, we can just escort him out of there under the guise that we're taking a random citizen back to Arand HQ. He's in an extremely low-security building, after all. If that fails, there should be an emergency ventilation system just next to it, which eventually leads us back to safety underground." Warner tried to put on the most self-confident smile he could.

Looking at his companions' grim faces, he tried to reassure them. "Look, I get it. It won't be easy. I'm one hundred percent with you on that. Heck, we might get fried at the first checkpoint for all I

know. But we've got to try. If this works …" His eyes became dreamy. "… If it works, we'll score big. This could save our entire people."
Derricc and Lily looked at each other. That was all the motivation they needed.
Lily got on her feet. "I suggest we leave quietly and soon. People are getting restless. The most desperate of them might convince the others it's some kind of conspiracy that we're gone."
Warner was again struck by Lily's maturity and decided to take her advice. His idea was to tell the Fallen they were leaving, to give them hope.
"You're right, Lily. Better not take any risk. We have enough on our hands as it is. Very well. Let's get our stuff together and get out of here. The Moonray Rum and balloons can wait until we return," he said.
They snuck out of the Fallen encampment. Crossing the long and winding bridge outside the camp, they left without attracting attention. As Lily looked down at the murky water, she could have sworn something was looking back at her on more than one occasion. She decided to keep her eyes on the road ahead instead.

The Specials

Bacon had left Scorpia's nest a while ago and was now back at the Special base: the Machine Rooms, his home. It occupied most of Zeeta's underground and comprised everything from the main engines to the support systems that provided oxygen and light to the entire ship. The lungs and the heart of Zeeta, as Bacon liked to think of it. NADOSH was the brain.
Bacon, for the most part, felt safe and well here. Running such a vital part of Zeeta gave him power. Power and access to all of Zeeta at any time. As long as the pumps, air purifiers and engines of Zeeta were functioning, Bacon could do as he pleased. He was commander of the heart and soul of Zeeta. Without him, the ship would spin out of control or malfunction and be split into pieces by asteroids.
The Arand Corp left him in peace to do his work. They depended on Bacon and his workers, and Bacon knew how to exploit this weakness. He would negotiate incredible deals with Arand, tricking them into providing him better and more advanced

machinery against useless fungus they called 'spice'. By amassing technology and resources, he made his 'family', the breed of creatures he secretly commanded, thrive.

Bacon's mental powers far exceeded any of the Arand staff as well. Once, during an important meeting, he used telepathy to break the will of a high-ranking officer, making him squawk like a mutated chicken in front of the entire delegation. Arand conceded to all his requirements that day and left the meeting in shame.

Bacon thought about the Fallen, his 'neighbours', whose encampment was at the other end of Zeeta's underground. He did not care much for them. They were self-imposed exiles hiding from Arand. Poor and hungry losers, waiting for a miracle to improve their predicament, Bacon thought scornfully.

He did keep his scouts on the lookout in case they thought about attacking. It was possible to get to the Fallen encampment from the Specials' base, although the journey required a long, treacherous walk interrupted by several high-security doors. But Bacon's spies confirmed his suspicion that the Fallen grew more desperate every day. He expected they would soon implode upon themselves; nothing to fear from a group of walking corpses.

Oh, yes. There had been that one girl, though. What was her name? Zhora? She visited my camp a few times and offered a kind of peace arrangement. The poor girl convinced herself the Specials would help her Fallen comrades overthrow Arand. Desperation conjures up the most imaginative human thoughts. Bacon smiled and clenched his fist. But she had potential, a strong mind. Next time I see her, I shall break it and make her my slave.

Bacon sat back in a relaxation pod to meditate. It was how he re-centered himself and found deep peace within. He could even conjure up images of what would happen in the future. His visions came after long sessions of transcending his mortal form and digging into a pool of knowledge beyond other beings.

But for a few days, his visions had grown cloudy and murky. Something was happening, and he could not exactly understand what. All he knew was that Sunny Bridges was at the root of it all.

Things are going our way. Soon, the she-creature will bring the Engineer to us. Bacon reflected on his conversation with Scorpia. But if that really is so, then why am I blind as to what that means for us?

His thoughts were interrupted as one of his minions entered his work quarters.
Master! One of the steel oxen has been hurt. It accidentally poured molten steel over its right forearm when working the smelter.
Like Bacon, the creature communicated via telepathy. Although he could still speak the human tongue, Bacon preferred communicating this way. It was more direct, and he did not like straining his jaw muscles anymore. For that reason, he had his lips sewn together with a thick copper thread. He spoke via a voice box implanted into his vocal cords. But he was not among humans, and so telepathy would suffice.
Brother, he replied to the minion. I felt his pain already. That's why I ordered the nurse mosquitos to take care of him. They will be arriving in a few minutes. Poor thing, his cries and moans shook our entire palace. After a brief meditation, I shall be down there myself to share my warmth and power.
The mutant seemingly took comfort in the soothing words. The eyes on its tentacles, which sprouted from a small head stuck to a slender body, blinked in rapid succession. Off it was.
Bacon sighed. A practical situation where my help is needed is good to get my mind off things. Uncharacteristically, he decided to forego his meditation and immediately go down to the ox instead.

Despite the creature's pain, he took his time. The nurse mosquitos would have arrived by now; these gentle creatures were the first to attend to any wounded member of his flock. So he walked at a leisurely pace and looked around in silent amazement. The machine rooms were places of wonder. Tall aluminium walls rose up as far as the eyes could see. Millions of workers were toiling to ensure that every mechanical part of Zeeta ran as smooth as a well-oiled machine. Never during his time in command had there been any breakdowns or other serious issues. The Specials managed to work together in unity, which was their strength.

They had far surpassed anything the humans would ever be capable of doing. Their intellect was constantly evolving, finding new ways to solve complex problems. Everything was done by channelling all the energies into one mind: Bacon's mind. He knew and saw everything going on. He was connected somehow to every life form; they were his extended family, each and every one of them.

Bacon was now arriving where the steel oxen were working. These humongous beasts stood three metres tall. They were four-legged creatures, resembling a cross between a mammoth and a Komodo dragon. Their heads were small and oblong, and their legs ended in huge oval-shaped lumps of flesh. When coated with steel plates, these cumbersome limps, coupled with the ox's incredible strength, made them perfect for lifting heavy objects and even handling floating steel.

The beast was injured, but it was quickly recovering. Its tough hide had a remarkable regeneration rate. Although its species was born here on Zeeta, forged after years of radioactive exposure and genetic experiments, it could survive anywhere. Bacon was sure of it.

There might be hope for us just yet, he thought to himself. After tending to the beasts' needs, he would go back to his palace and meditate. All that was left to do was wait for the Engineer to arrive.

A Leader Is Born

Warner, Lily and Derricc had been travelling towards the surface for two hours. NADOSH-2 had carefully instructed them where to go and how to get there. Rather than use their own routes to the surface, they would need to mimic the patterns of the Arand Enforcers, which meant taking a roundabout way to the surface. Warner noted that the exit to the surface was adjacent to the Specials' camp. He presumed they were working closely with the Arand Corp since the Specials allowed Arand to enter their premises in peace.

As the group arrived at the surface, Warner took a deep breath of Zeeta's synthetically filtered air. Much cleaner than what he was used to underground. A rush of emotion stormed over him. It was an odd mix of fear and impatience all at once. He felt this was the most meaningful undertaking of his life, which made the exhaustion easier to cope with. If I fuck this one up, that's the end of the Fallen. We'll all be gone, he thought.

They entered Zeeta's surface near an old factory. NADOSH-2 had told them not to get near it. Warner seemed to hear distant and soothing whispers (a woman's voice?) from inside. Ignoring it, he looked down at Lily, whose face was hard and determined. She looked ten years older than her actual age.

"This is the spot NADOSH-2 indicated to us," she said. "From now on, we have to play it straight."

Warner and Derricc nodded, and the three walked towards the Arand tower in the distance. Next to it was Bloc-13, where the Engineer was kept. A golden neon sign was flashing over the building to make it exude wealth and luxury.

"Once this is over, let's all spend a night at that fancy place, eh, boss," Derricc whispered as he patted Warner on the shoulder.

They moved onwards, and as anticipated, the Enforcer guards at the first checkpoint soon intercepted.

"Hail the Corporation," the guard said, addressing Warner. This gesture required him to reply correctly, not to raise suspicion.

"Hail humanity, hail Arand," Warner said. The guard seemed pleased though it was tough to decipher any emotion under his grey and blue helmet.

"What brings you here?" the guard enquired. "I have no reports of any patrols in this section." He seemed alert.

"We're back from a successful trip to the Specials, trading rare spices and getting a new pleasure-whore for our Arand Leader." He gestured towards Lily. "They told me she has seven holes and two tongues." He had spent their trip memorising all the lines provided by NADOSH-2.

Lily wore the tacky black and pink suit she had been given. The pink stripes gave off a violet neon glow. She was behaving strangely but maintained the innocent look of a slave captured from a foreign place perfectly.

The guard gave the three of them another glance. He seemed perplexed by Derricc's bulky and impressive physique, which was impossible to conceal under the uniform.

“New line-up of Enforcer, heavily gen-manipulated,” Warner improvised, hoping to relieve the guard’s interest in Derricc. Any further enquiries would be fatal.
They heard beeping, and the guard’s colleague got agitated. He received a message on his personal communication device. It seemed they were called on an urgent mission somewhere else.
The guard nodded at his colleague, then towards Warner. “Affirmative, you are free to go. Hail our Arand Leader”, he said. Warner mimicked his gesture, and off they went. Only then he noticed the cold sweat dripping down his back. To his surprise, the rest of the trip went without hassle. They passed a few Enforcers, but none of them took any particular notice of their presence.

Arriving in front of Bloc-13, Warner noticed the conspicuous lack of guards in the area. He would have thought that important people were kept under much stricter surveillance. Guess NADOSH managed to occupy the guards somewhere else , he reflected, which makes it easier for us to haul Sunny’s sorry ass out of there.
Bloc-13’s entrance area looked as one would expect. It was pristine and minimalistic but with details that made it look high-class. The massive reception desk stood out in particular, with its gold-plated bonsai trees and a large aquarium just next to it. It all looked fancy and extravagant, undoubtedly made to please the wealthiest of Zeeta’s population.
Warner stepped forward to speak with the Jonny-bot behind the counter. It was a rare female variety, seemingly an old model. A patch on her uniform read, Rosey, U-Rent a Maid, ID: XB-500.
“Greetings. I’m trying to locate the room of a Mr Sunny Bridges. We have a present for him." Warner said.
Rosey made an odd jerking motion, tilting its head slightly to each side while rolling its eyes uncontrollably. “There is no entry in my database of such an expected visit. Leave, and come back with proper authorisation,” Rosey snapped.
Bots can be assholes too, Warner thought. As rehearsed, he said, “This lady-whore is here to give Bridges pleasure. We need to give her to him. It’s the will of the Arand Leader. She has seven holes.” The words were like acid in his mouth, but he had to follow the instructions he was given.

Rosey turned hostile, and a red light on its throat started blinking. "Alarm sequence will be initiated in fifteen seconds. Non-authorised behaviour recorded twice …"
Lily stepped in. "Wait! There must have been a lag on the server. Please update your inbox one more time."
Warner and Derricc were surprised but kept silent.
Rosey, equally puzzled, updated its instructions inbox one last time.
"Request has just been received. You are free to enter the home of Sunny Bridges, forty-fifth floor, apartment #213," the bot stated its usual grumpy tone.
Warner felt a huge relief. He looked at Lily. "NADOSH-2," she whispered. The AI must have helped them at the last minute.
They took the elevator and arrived at the forty-fifth floor. The lounge area's interiors were sleek and indulgent, the space swathed with opulent, albeit fake, plants and punctuated with delicate, skillfully crafted mechanical animals. Since nearly all live animals were extinct, their robotic counterparts were sold for exorbitant prices and thus only affordable for Zeeta's upper-class inhabitants.
They made it to Sunny's apartment. Standing at the door, Warner took out the 3D-printed key-card he had been given. The door opened without problems, and they all entered quickly, shutting it behind them.
They first noticed Sunny; he was lying on a bed. Then, a lady walked in from the bathroom. She looked malevolent and had a small bot hovering over her head. The bot was the Arand spy NADOSH-2 had told them about. It was connected to her head via several tubes. Her eyes were glowing red and orange, which matched the colours on the bot's display. It controlled her like a puppet, which was a bizarre and otherworldly spectacle to behold.
Not wasting any time, Derricc pulled out his Magnum Pulse Pistols and fired two rounds in her direction. One blast cut off the main tube at her neck, and the second put the bot out of function. She fell unconscious to the ground while dark liquid and black smoke puffed out from the bot's aeration system. The bot bounced on the floor and short-circuited, the sparks burning chunks of the woman's hair. Derricc walked over to crush the machine under his heavy boots and remove the rest of the tubes. Lily tended to the

lady, whose torso was soaked with the disgusting liquid poured all over her. Her eyes were no longer glowing, and she finally seemed free from the bot's grip.

Warner scuffled over to Sunny. NADOSH-2 had instructed them that his reaction could be anything from incredulity to hostility. Taking a deep breath, he said, "We're here from the free world, from the society of humans below the surface." Warner stumbled over his words while gasping for air. "On behalf of the Fallen, we've come to rescue you." Sunny gave no visible reaction except grumpily sitting up on the bunk bed. He wore a tattered brown suit with a Ferrero hat and a green tie. Warner thought he looked like a hobo.

Sunny's eyes oscillated between the lady on the floor and Warner. "Kk … kiii … ra," he moaned.

"Kira," Lily said, "that's her name. We should bring her too." Her eyes found Warner's.

Warner had not given any thought to the destiny of the woman. Sure, he had been told she would be there, but his objective was to retrieve Sunny, and she was a liability.

Kira, only slowly regaining her senses, was dazed and confused. More worrying was Sunny's complete lack of speech. Warner had to think fast.

"We're here to help you escape the Arand Corporation. They mean you harm and won't hesitate to kill you. Do you understand?" Warner was clutching Sunny's shoulder and looking him in the eyes.

Sunny kept his eyes on Warner's and nodded gravely.

Good, Warner thought. He can't speak but not a complete goner. His mind still works fine. OK, now how do we get out of here?

"Lily, Derricc, what's the status of the woman, Kira? Can she walk? Is she hurt?" Warner knew he could not lose his shit now; he had to stay focused.

Kira was lying on the ground, quietly sobbing.

"She's suffered a tremendous shock., I think she's been heavily sedated by mind-control drugs," Lily offered. "But she should be fine. I'll carefully remove these tubes from her neck and shoulder."

Warner looked around. Nothing else in the apartment seemed to be a menace at this point. They just had to get out and get back underground as quickly as possible. He opened the door to check the hallway was clear.

And then, his blood froze. Not far down the hall stood a group of five or six Enforcers. They were questioning some old crone, who pointed her bony finger towards Sunny's place.

Warner quickly stepped back inside the room and closed the door. We're done for, he thought, leaning up against the wall. No way we can fight off a whole group of them and make it out safe in these close quarters. Lily was looking at him, waiting for an update.

He kneeled next to her and whispered, "I've seen some guards in the hallway. Let me lock the door, but we better stay alert."

Lily nodded and grabbed one of Derricc's guns. Warner only carried the standard-issue Enforcer blaster, which he was not akin to handling. NADOSH-2 had told him to leave his custom scoped pistol behind. Sunny slumped across the room and flipped a switch on a console next to the door. When a small monitor lit up, they could see what was happening in the hall in front of the door.

Everybody held their breath as the Enforcers gathered just outside their room. Contrary to Warner's estimation, there were at least eight of them. But luck shone their way as the Enforcers all walked past and continued further down the hall.

Warner was relieved. "NADOSH must've placed a decoy! The Enforcers aren't sure where Sunny is, and they're confusing him with the other guy from the Disposal Site!"

Brilliant. NADOSH was pulling the strings to facilitate their escape. Rejuvenated, Warner hit the switch and opened the automatic door again, hoping to escape using the elevator. Shocked, he realised even more guards were flooding the hallways, and he quickly stepped back inside. He heard gunfire from down the hall. What the heck's going on?

No time to ponder; they needed to get out. And fast. But how?

Kira was hyperventilating while Lily cared for her with a soft, moist cloth.

As she came to, Kira said, "The wall … has a built-in dumbwaiter inside. It's a small elevator used to bring goods to the individual apartments." Kira gasped while Lily held her head. "We can use that to get … to the ground floor." She closed her eyes again.

Warner called up the dumbwaiter and saw on the panel that it indeed went down to the ground floor. The space was tight, so they could not all go at once.
“Lily, you take Kira down first. Sunny, Derricc, and I will follow."
Lily knew neither she nor Kira was the priority of this mission and started to protest. But she saw the stern look in Warner’s eyes and helped Kira to her feet instead. They got into the shaft and rode down.
A moment later, trouble knocked on the door.
“Open up! This is the Enforcers of the Arand Corporation! We demand your immediate compliance!” the voice said.
Derricc nodded at Warner. Both got their guns ready and aimed at the door. The dumbwaiter was on its way back up, but it seemed to take an eternity. The banging on the door got louder.
Warner heard the gentle hum of the shaft. Only a few seconds more. Sunny stood behind them, alert and ready to escape.
At that very instant, the Enforcers opened fire on the door. They used heavy plasma weapons, and the door soon became insanely hot and started melting. Derricc and Warner coughed as a thick, stinky fog of smoke permeated the room. Sunny did not seem to notice.
A pleasant ‘bling!’ signalled that the dumbwaiter arrived back at the apartment. Warner and Sunny looked at each other; the small space was barely enough for Kira and Lily, and it certainly would not hold the three of them.
Without hesitation, Sunny waved Derricc over. He made a pulling motion towards the dumbwaiter. No second-guessing, Derricc leaned over and pulled at the dumbwaiter to make space for their descent. Cables snapped, and sparks flew as he removed the carrier, leaving a gaping hole in the wall.
And not a moment too soon. The door was now sufficiently busted open for a man to crawl through. The Enforcers applied some freezing detergent to it as it was still glowing hot. Derricc tossed the dumbwaiter carrier at the guard who tried to enter. The heavy steel cage fractured the guard’s back, and Warner finished him with a head shot.
Nerve gas was pumped into the room, as the Enforcers pulled their dead comrade back out. Two additional Enforcers tried squeezing

themselves through the small hole in the door. Derricc opened fire. "Mooove!" he yelled.
Warner looked down the shaft. Derricc had ripped some cables, but thankfully the main wire used for hoisting the dumbwaiter was still there. I'll use it to slide myself down, Warner thought. He gestured for Sunny to climb onto his back, and the two started sliding down the shaft, which descended at a thirty-degree angle. The drop was breathtakingly high; letting go would be fatal.
Heavy gunfire ensued above them in Sunny's room; Warner could hear Derricc's guns deal out pain. Judging by the screams, he must have taken down two or more Enforcers. Warner's neck and shoulders burned from supporting Sunny's weight as the two slid down the delivery shaft. The cable gnawed at his gloves, almost drawing blood. He had to go down as slowly as possible to avoid slipping and getting crushed by the fall. The descent felt like an eternity, and he could hear the commotion fading away in the distance.
Then, there were more screams, this time from Derricc, who sounded like he was involved in a vehement tussle. He must've been hit! Warner thought. He hoped Derricc was alright, but he had to concentrate on keeping Sunny alive and get them down as fast as he could. He kept on going ever deeper down the dark hole. Only now did it dawn on him how foolish this idea had been. They still needed to descend almost forty stories to get all the way down. He kept on going, the pain becoming unbearable. Sunny felt like he weighed a ton. Warner could hear his gasping breath close to his ear.
Time passed; Warner descended, engulfed in silent darkness. Suddenly, he heard a scream of agony so terrible that it could mean only one thing. Derric is dead. Warner closed his eyes. His mind was foggy. His own pain, plus losing his dearest friend, was too much to handle. He blinked a few times and looked up at the hazy light far above from the opening leading into Sunny's room. A body was thrown into the shaft and bounced off the walls like a ragdoll one, two, three times before it hit them. Then everything went dark.

When Warner came to, he was lying at what he presumed was the bottom of the shaft. He saw Lily looking at him with worried eyes.

"Are you OK? We need to get out of here." And then, looking down, she said, "He saved you. I think he broke your fall."
Warner realised he was sitting on Derricc, whose neck was twisted, his blank eyes staring into the eternal abyss. Warner shed a quick tear.
"Where is he? Is he alright?" Warner enquired about Sunny, who simultaneously appeared behind Lily. Sunny was still limping but otherwise seemed OK. He gestured to Warner and the others to follow him. Lily helped Kira along as she was still ailing.
Arriving back at the entrance hall of Bloc-13, they saw the sourly Rosey across the room. Its back was to them, and it was speaking to a large group of Enforcers. The bot was sprinting back and forth, visibly trying to keep a conversation going with three to four people simultaneously while circling others to block their passage. Warner surmised that NADOSH had something to do with this; she must have reprogrammed the bot to dissuade more troops from entering. Out of the corner of his eye, Warner saw the tall metal armour-clad figure. He froze, and his heart started throbbing so hard he swore it would jump out of his chest. It was Horrigan, the super-soldier they had been fighting outside the Rusted Dreams' Bar earlier.
While the Enforcers were distracted by Rosey, Warner felt Horrigan directing his blank stare at them. He hurried up to follow Sunny, and they made it down some stairs and into a generator room connected to Bloc-13's main building.
Perfect. This must be the escape route NADOSH-2 told us about, Warner thought merrily to himself. How did Sunny know about it? Was he planning an escape himself? Lily took his hand and whispered, "Let's move! Before that genetically engineered homicidal maniac cyborg bodyguard sees us." Deciding there was no time to waste, Warner hurried onwards.
Before entering the generator room, he heard a loud zap! He looked back and saw Horrigan jerk Rosey's head violently from side to side. Sparks flew as Rosey's head was ripped from its torso. Its decapitated head sputtered and protested wildly while Horrigan squeezed it forcefully between his hands. It malfunctioned and powered down. Their decoy was gone; Rosey was no more.

The room they were in had two massive generators stacked against each wall. They were grey and lifeless, just like the rest of the city. At one end of the room, a small set of stairs led up to a red metal platform with an enormous fan behind it. Behind this fan, a ventilation system would lead them back down under Zeeta's surface. Luckily, the entrance was more than large enough for a group of adults to fit. The group got to work. Kira and Lily jammed a metal rod into the fan to stop the blades.

The commotion outside the room grew louder. The place swarmed with Enforcers, so the pressure was palpable. While the others worked, Warner got distracted for a second. He thought he heard the door to the generator close, ever so gently. Alarmed, he decided to go back to verify.

He indeed found the door not only closed but also securely locked. Odd. I don't recall anyone sealing it so tight, he thought. But it was, of course, better to hold Arand off while they got to safety.

As he walked back towards the fan, Warner saw that Sunny had already gone in, and Lily was helping Kira along. She was gesturing to him to follow. She disappeared behind the white fog, and only her hand was visible; then, that too was swallowed by the soothing light. Warner smiled. Things are finally looking up for us. Nothing left to do now but enjoy a leisurely stroll home while those Arand bastards wonder what hit 'em. He was almost at the fan now, his hands on the railing.

Then, it happened; Warner realised he was not alone. The visitor, clumsily scuffling his feet on the ground, had waited for the perfect timing to let his presence be known. Scared out of his mind, Warner slowly turned to face the menace. The whole thing seemed so unreal. He panicked, realising that he had lost his gun in the elevator shaft. The situation was transforming from a dream into a nightmare.

The twenty seconds that elapsed seemed like an eternity, and Warner was facing the intruder. The assassin just stood there patiently, across the room from him. He was seemingly not in a hurry but well prepared. He wore a very tight dark synthetic suit, the highest military-grade camouflage. Such a suit allowed you to stay hidden for days at a time in darkened areas, and the thermal padding was even adjustable to whatever surface you needed to blend in. It was the perfect outfit for an assassin.

He also wore a black mask, which almost completely covered his face, and a necklace made of human teeth, designed to horrify the opponent. What Warner found most frightening, however, were his hands. They dangled leisurely from his body, hanging from muscular and well-rested arms. They were also gloved, but Warner could see all the individual fingers working. They were ready to kill.

In a feeble attempt to escape, Warner tried to get out through the open fan, which was still jammed open by the metal rod. Split seconds later, he felt a kick to his lower back, almost breaking his spine in two. He slammed face-down onto the metal platform, his mouth and lips bleeding. The second and third strikes masterfully placed blows to both kidneys and came just as swiftly. His opponent was evidently highly skilled; Warner could do nothing but lay flat on his belly and gasp for air.

The assassin pulled Warner to his feet and slammed him against the steel railing. Quick jabs to the solar plexus and stomach followed. Then, the assassin grabbed Warner's hair and crushed his face against his kneecap in three consecutive blows. Warner bowed forwards and fell on his head. The floor was spinning, and he lost sense of reality.

Through misty eyes, he saw his assailant walk towards the fan. He meticulously jerked the metal rod free from the fan and took a moment to study it. He deemed it a suitable weapon, and then his attention was back on Warner. The fan reset and started rotating again.

Before he could get up, Warner took a heavy hit to the stomach. Seconds later, the rod struck again and again. The final blow was so forceful that it threw Warner onto the floor between the humming generators.

While struggling to ignore the pain, Warner had a moment of clarity. This man's hell-bent on killing me, but he's taking his time? Why not just get it done? What's he after? he thought.

"Who … are you? Identify yourself, assassin." Warner coughed blood as he spoke.

His words made the enemy hesitate for a moment. He was contemplating what to do. Rather than speak, he started taking off his mask. Slowly, his face became visible. It was a man, distinctly older than Warner, with a well-kept beard and hair down to his cheekbones. His eyes were blue and pretty. It took Warner a moment to place him.

"You … I've seen you before … You were there … at the bar … with the metal hulk." Warner gasped. "Your gun … You pointed it at me … You had a clean shot. But you didn't … You didn't kill me … Why?" He got halfway onto his feet.

It was as much conversation as the assassin would endure. He quickly strode towards Warner and kicked him in the teeth. Then he smashed him in the head with the metal rod. Blood streamed into Warner's eyes; he was blind and numb from the pain. The assassin forced the rod into his mouth.

That's it, Warner thought, the stale metallic taste permeating his mouth. He'll force the pipe down my throat. I'll suffocate. It was a cold analysis; one has no time for sentimental details when Death's at the door.

The assassin was ready to jam the rusty rod down Warner's throat, causing a painful death. Brimming with rage, he paused for a few moments to regain his composure. As he got ready to finish the job, a voice spoke in his mind. It was NADOSH.

Commander Blakemore. The man in front of you. Is your //son//.

Blakemore started shivering. The shivers turned into panic. He clumsily let the rod fall to the floor. He took a deep breath. Tears filled his eyes, and fear paralysed his body.

Meanwhile, the Enforcers outside were about to blow the door open. They were moments from entering.

Blakemore leaned against a generator, looking at the dying man on the ground. The man he just beat to a pulp. He meekly put his arms over his stomach while he cried in a tiny voice.

"My son…," he said in a sobbing voice so low no one could hear it. Warner heard a deafening noise, and then he passed out.

Hours later, Warner was brought to the interrogation chambers of the Arand Corporation where he was swiftly identified as the leader of the Fallen. He was vociferously questioned but passed away from his injuries before he could reveal any information.

Blakemore was considered mentally unstable after his breakdown, and Horrigan carried out orders to execute him.

New Identity

Sunny, Kira and Lily made it quite far into the ventilation system before they heard Warner scream. His anguish echoed through the tunnels as they went back underground, making Lily and Kira stiff with fear.

Lily felt hot tears run down her cheeks. But Sunny soldiered on without hesitation. Lily saw this awkward man, half dead, half alive, unable to speak but adamant about getting as far away from Arand as possible. Can't say I blame him. His brisk pace kept her determined, and it helped keep the chaos inside her at bay.

She wanted to run back, find Warner, and try to save him — But what were the odds? The building they escaped from was surely crawling with Enforcers. Warner gave his life to save us. Jeopardising that would be foolish, Lily thought. He would have wanted us to keep on going and complete our mission. We've made it too far now to turn back.

Lily noticed Sunny's back was covered in fresh wounds, visible through his tattered suit. How is it physically possible that this man's alive? She wondered. What has Arand done to him? Will he ever be able to talk again? From the files on Sunny she had read, she knew he was thirty-five years old when Zeeta launched. That was seventeen years ago, so he must be around fifty-two now. She was impressed with his stamina.

Stopping at an intersection, Sunny looked at Lily. He stretched out his arms, pointed left, pointed right, then shrugged.

"Right, you're asking me which way to go?" Lily reasoned.

Good question. She had stopped paying attention to where they were going. Luckily, she had discussed NADOSH-2's briefing with Warner and noted all the key points. She touched her wrist AI and loaded the relevant notes, figuring they were still in the ventilation system, just underneath Zeeta's surface. They would have to take a right turn to reach the lower tunnels before eventually making it down to the Fallen base again. She indicated the way to Sunny, who immediately started trotting on like a wind-up mechanical toy. They marched on in silence, with Kira occasionally sobbing.

When arriving close to the Fallen camp, Lily ordered Sunny and Kira to stop. Kira's sunken shoulders and hopeless attitude concerned Lily. Not only did Kira look like a mess, but she had also not spoken since they fled the surface and refused to eat anything. Lily feared she was severely depressed and bordered on suicidal. Despite looking like a zombie and being mute, Sunny had become more and more energetic the further they went. He was clearly content about the change of setting.

Lily gestured at them to sit down behind a group of high pillars. Around the next corner was the metal drawbridge, which allowed safe passage over Zeeta's green, glowing sewer sludge and into the Fallen camp. A few guards stood alert in front of the metal entrance door. They seemed bored.

Lily glanced back at the others; she had a plan.

"We need a disguise for Sunny," she said. "Bringing him into our camp like this will raise too much suspicion."

Sunny nodded, and Kira remained quiet. Lily tried hard not to get angry at her, but her passiveness was irritating. Lily felt like she was the only adult to steer things, which put a great deal of stress on her shoulders.

She took a deep breath. "Understand that once we get inside, things might hit the fan. We have a bunch of starving people in there who were expecting the moon. Basically, we must give them good news, or we're dead." Lily was conscious of her cold tone, but she needed to be blunt. There were no second chances left. If she failed to deliver or buy more time, the Fallen would prey on them in desperation. They would all die at the hands of the people Warner had sacrificed his life to save.

"What I suggest we do is cover Sunny up with this blanket." She held out a long black cloth which had been a part of her attire moments before. Her shoulders and stomach were then exposed, her prostitute dress now leaving very little to the imagination. "And we tell them it's Warner. I don't want them to know he's dead, at least not yet. What we need to do is get both of you safely to the Operations Room, at least until things calm down. We'll figure out what to do from there." She was exhausted.

And by God, I hope NADOSH-2 has some great ideas because I'm running out. That last thought remained with herself, as she did not want to discourage the others.

Sunny put the black blanket over his head; it covered him down to his knees. It should suffice, but they had to move quickly.

Having crossed the drawbridge, the guards raised their guns in suspicion. "Who goes there?" the starved-looking one asked. He was so skinny his eyes protruded from his skull. He had not had a decent meal for weeks or even months.

Lily identified herself. "We got Warner back, but he's badly wounded. He needs medical attention. Quick!" She pointed towards the cloaked figure which was Sunny.

Seeing that the other guy seemed more worried about Kira, Lily added, "She's with us. She's an affiliate of the Engineer. In exchange for her freedom, she promised to get us closer to him."

Exhausted from the strenuous trip, she used her last gram of energy to appear strong in front of the gate guards, who briefly whispered between themselves. It worked, and they let the group inside.

Once inside the encampment, Lily gasped in shock. Everything was in complete disorder. People were running around screaming, and there was fighting everywhere; the whole place had turned upside down while they were gone. Even the few modest stores in the entrance area had been ravaged and most valuable items were looted in the process. Everything had been pillaged; even the store sign was gone.

Lily saw the owner of 'Tits by Jack' lying unconscious on the ground. There was no time to worry about that now. She had to get her guests to safety before they too became victims of this circus.

She walked towards the gathering pit, which was on their way to the Operations Room. Then, she felt a bony hand grab her arm. An older lady with teeth missing was clinging on to her, unkempt nails biting through Lily's flesh. It hurt like hell.

"So, there she is. Our little princess dressed like a harlot. What has she been up to, the little skank?" the old crone spat.

"Don't bother with this brat!" another woman shouted from further away. "She's too good for us now. Been selling her services to the Arand Corp. Her body and anything else they'd want!" Lily shook off the old bag and hastily carried on. But the scene had aroused interest from other bystanders.

"Hey, didn't you go to the surface with Warner?" a bald man with a large underbite enquired. "And what about elephant-face? What happened to him?" He stumbled over a drunk lying on the ground.

"Derricc's dead. Passed away in battle. May the stars carry his soul to heaven," Lily said solemnly as she quickly moved along. "Warner's with us." She gestured towards Sunny. "But he's hurt bad and needs immediate medical attention."

She sped on before anyone could ask any more questions. Loud arguments ensued over whether she was telling the truth. The old crone wanted them to seize her and beat the three of them.

Lily closed her eyes for a few seconds while she moved on. One … two … three … Nothing. It seemed they were safe. Sunny was holding Kira's hand. He could not see because of the blanket and was trying awkwardly not to bump into anything while walking.

A few minutes later, they got into the Operations Room. Lily slammed the door and locked it behind them. She turned around with a big smile, feeling relaxed for the first time since they had left.

OK, how are we doing here? Lily wondered while Sunny and Kira rested. We've lost Warner and Derrick and will do a commemoration ceremony for them later. But now, we need to push ahead. We have the Engineer with us. He seems cooperative, though we still haven't told him why we rescued him. We'll need to settle him in and slowly bring him to our side. Lily was thinking while Sunny and Kira rested. Kira seemed as shocked as before and would not say a word. Her burned hair and goo-filled clothing made her look miserable. For now, let's hook back up into NADOSH-2, Lily reasoned.

Lily sat down by the mainframe. The computer came on, and NADOSH-2 appeared.

"Hello. Good and bad news to report. We've lost two men. Warner and Derricc both fell in combat. They died fighting the Arand Corporation at Bloc-13. You probably already know. Fortunately, well, we got the Engineer. He's over there, safe and sound," Lily said.

"//Excellent work//, Commander Lily. I assume //commander// is your appropriate title following - Brian Warner's - untimely demise? Is there any //formal procedure// for you to assume //leadership// of the Fallen?" NADOSH-2 enquired.

"I, uh, no. It never really came to my mind," Lily murmured.

"Forgive my bluntness, but your fellow //humans// of the Fallen camp have run amok. Completely - bananas ... Chaos - and - riots are everywhere. This //uncivilised// behaviour compromises the entire //mission//. Warner's death must be kept //secret// for now," NADOSH-2 explained. "I have //collected// a number of studies performed on //non-human primates// back on Earth. Conclusions are, inter alia, that //macaque monkeys// respond well to a strong //leader figure// in times of distress. Hence, I suggest we announce that you have taken //command// until Warner recovers. This will ease their //primitive// minds. We must. Buy time. Until //operation// is finished."

Is she saying my people are monkeys? Lily wondered and suddenly felt uneasy. "Operation? What do you mean? Bring him back? I mean, Warner's dead. How will that ever happen?" She mustered what little strength she had left.

NADOSH-2 patiently outlined the proceedings. "//The Engineer// needs corrective surgery to restore //vocal cords//. Speech is required to enter trajectory override //password//. Voice-recognition is a //security// measure. NADOSH-1 omitted //vocal-cord restoration// due to high risk of //torture// and subsequent //death// of //subject// by //Arand Corp//."

Lily noticed how cold and emotionless NADOSH-2 was. She considered them all mere peons in her elaborate chess game, and her only goal was to get Sunny down to the Trajectory Override Console for whatever her purposes were.

She's a machine who doesn't care about Warner or Derricc's lives. She probably doesn't care about mine or Kira's either, Lily realised.

Yet, she knew NADOSH-2 was their only hope and ally. "Affirmative. Sounds like a great idea." She forced a tiny smile. "You mentioned corrective surgery. What exactly does that entail?"

"Sunny will //recover// speaking ability. General health has improved. Finally, I will //replicate// Warner's physical appearance on his face. This allows //safe passage// around //Fallen base//."

Lily was again in shock. I must not have heard correctly, she thought.

"You want to transplant the face of Brian Warner onto Sunny so that he looks like a replica of him?" Lily scarcely managed not to choke.

"Affirmative. I have //prepared// for - this - eventuality. Every muscle. And flap - of - skin. On Warner's face was meticulously mapped out. During my meetings. With him. Consequently, I have all the //data required// to make a 1:1 transplantation on Sunny," NADOSH-2 replied.

Jeez! Hope she's not scanning my face, Lily thought as she moved away slightly from the screen. "Right, I will go ask if Sunny's OK —"

"Stop!" NADOSH-2 interrupted, her voice cold as ice. "Informing //subject// of impending operation is a liability. Risks include: panic-attacks, escape-attempts and //non-compliance//. I have drugged their //thermos// with - mild - sleeping powder. The //operation// will be carried out during his sleep. I can //assure// you it is - mostly - painless."

Lily sank back down on her chair. No need to argue, she thought. There's nothing you can do. Exhaustion soon overcame her, and she drifted away to a world of uneasy but well-deserved sleep filled with bizarre dreams.

Memories from an Earth Long Forgotten

Lily woke with a shock to a deafening bang on the door. She was still in the Operation Room of the Fallen camp. A splitting headache made her vision blurry; Sunny and Kira were not to be seen anywhere. The knocking came back, more violent this time. Lily noticed that NADOSH-2's terminal was still switched on. "It is //time//. You must go back. Out. There," NADOSH-2 spoke calmly, her voice a stark juxtaposition to the panic outside the room. Her icy manners still frightened Lily.
"I … What should I tell them?"
"Please - detain - them. They must //refrain// from violence - a - while - longer. Sunny's operation //still… ongoing// in the adjacent room. Until it is done. Your people cannot //be informed// of anything," Lily suspected slight desperation in the AI's tone. This boosted her confidence; this machine was not so all-powerful after all. Lily would still have her say in all this and do her best to save the Fallen tribe. To bring them home to Mother Earth where they belonged.
"Halt!" Lily heard NADOSH-2 shout as she was about to exit the room.
"Do not exit by //that door//. It must remain //sealed//. At all times. Come here and claim this //firearm//." NADOSH-2's avatar gestured towards a rusty table in front of her. On it lay Warner's signature scoped laser-pistol. Lily gulped but swiftly took the premium firearm. She also put on some reinforced combat armour, light but efficient.
She wondered for a second if Sunny was OK but figured NADOSH-2 would not compromise his health at this point. The AI still needed him as much as everyone else did.
Then she snuck out of the control room, back into the main hall/living quarters of the Fallen camp. Famine, sick children, and desperate people were everywhere. Most of them could not even muster enough energy to look at her.
We need to act fast if we want to save these people, Lily thought. She got up on the speaking podium to get everybody's attention. "Comrades! Friends! Family! I bring good news! Our mission to the surface was a success. We have brought home the Engineer!" Mumbling and bustling could be heard as people started to gather around.

“Indeed, we have brought home the Engineer,” Lily repeated for added effect, “and right now, we’re investigating how best to steer Zeeta 21 back to Mother Earth! You heard right. He is friendly to our cause and wants to help us. Tired of the tyranny of his former employers, the Arand Corporation, the Engineer has decided to use his knowledge for good! We’re one decisive step closer, my dear friends, to finally getting solid ground under our feet. Soon we can live like proper human beings again!” Lily opened her arms in front of her, intoxicated with joy. She closed her eyes and waited for applause, or some reaction, from the crowd. Nothing came.

“Where’s Warner?” someone asked.

“He’s … coming soon.” Lily opened her eyes as reality dawned on her again.

“Well … Where the fuck is he?” said another.

“When they came back, there were only three of them. And one of them looked all suspicious, wearing a black hood ‘n all.” Lily recognised the skinny guard who spoke. He had been the one asking questions yesterday.

“I can assure you, Warner is fine. He’s with the Engineer right now. They’re writing up a concrete plan before coming back to you. They want to —” Lily said tentatively.

But she was cut short. “Yeah, well, if he’s so wonderfully fine, we want his sorry ass out here. Besides his freaking plan, our children here haven’t eaten for days. Some of us barely ate nothin’ for weeks. What’s his smart-ass plan going to do about that?” Unlike Lily’s intervention, this statement sparked roars and cheers of consensus.

“And you know what else,” a middle-aged hunchback added, “how will going back to Earth make things any better? Huh? Lord knows what kind of hellish mischief might be going down there by now? I heard a rumour that the place is inhabitable! A bloody wasteland, the whole planet bombed to shreds!” Again, palpable agreement was felt amongst the crowd.

“In a nutshell, young lady, you and Warner, or whoever it is you’ve got holed up in there, better start bringing some serious suggestions to the table. We’re not letting this stand. We’re going to —” the hunchback started, but someone cut her off. “You aren’t going to do shit. Now sit down and shut the fuck up.”

Lily was as surprised as anyone else. Looking over her shoulder, she saw Warner - or rather, a replica of Warner - approach the platform. Underneath the skin, it was actually Sunny, but of course, no one but her and NADOSH-2 knew that. His face was built with perfect craftsmanship: the slim eyebrows, the discrete but pointed nose, the handsome cheekbones, and the various details of the mouth. Everything was made with meticulous attention to detail, making him look identical to the late Brian Warner. He even had the signature long black hair and wore Warner's favourite dark blue-grey synthetic leather jacket.
"You can run your mouths all day long, but the fact is you'll do nothing but sit down and listen to what we have to say. Why? Because we're the only chance you scumbags have for a better life. Unlike you lazy sods, Lily and I are out there working hard to create some opportunities for our people. What are you doing to help? Nothing. You complain and moan. Seeing what you've done with this place, I'm disgusted. Looting and ransacking your neighbours like there's no tomorrow. You should be ashamed of yourselves." Warner/Sunny spoke with great force, rendering the crowd docile. Lily thought Sunny was doing a great job with the impersonation.
"As Lily said, we're working with the Engineer right now to bring him up to speed with our way of life. We're getting there, but it takes time to accustom him to our struggle. He's been through a tremendous amount these last days, and we don't want to screw things up by pushing him to work for us prematurely. We need to let him spend some time here before explaining our dream, our dream of living on Earth. Let him also feel it. Let him understand the needs and desires of the people he will ultimately save." Warner/Sunny spoke elegantly and warmly. He swayed the onlookers, who all glanced at him in silent admiration.
"We require your cooperation and goodwill. Without you, this will fail. Continue living as you usually do, but don't cause any trouble. I've ordered our final food rations to be opened, and they'll be distributed shortly. We need to keep things calm and peaceful. Then, when the time is right, we'll bring the Engineer to the Manual Trajectory Overwrite Console, which he'll use to steer Zeeta back to Mother Earth. Abundant food and joy will come. The time is approaching, my dear friends. Let's all hold tight and

get ready to embrace the moment of our ultimate release!" Cheers and applause followed Warner/Sunny's final words.
He glanced over at Lily, who gave him a quick smile. Their task here was done, and it was time to get back to the Operations Room to get on with the real work.
Safely back in the Operations Room, Lily asked, "How did you manage to pull that off? I mean, you spoke just like Warner would, and you were so convincing. You did great."
"The AI taught me what to say. I basically just memorised a script with some improvisation here and there," Sunny said plainly.
Lily just realised it was the first time she had heard him talk. His voice was calm and not unpleasant. She smiled.
"This is wonderful! You're recovering, and you can talk now. Will you really help us? I can hardly believe it. All these years spent searching for you, Warner giving his life and everything. I mean, we've come so far," she said.
At this, Sunny burst out of his chair and walked away. Lily started following him as he headed for one of the adjacent meeting rooms. But she stopped as NADOSH-2 appeared on the monitor.
"Do not //interfere//," she said. "The operation was - successful - but the //subject// is still adapting. To his new body. And new //circumstances//."
Lily nodded. I know just the right thing, she thought as she went to find him.

Sunny sat slumped over a metal desk. It was covered with stains and scratches, far from mint condition. But Warner had used it all the time; he called it his 'bunker'.
Lily approached slowly, not to frighten Sunny. He turned around with a rapid movement as he heard her. Sunny looked almost exactly like Warner, and Lily held her breath. She tried not to let her horror shine through.
"What do you want?" Sunny was staring at the ground again, his voice meek and without conviction.
"I want to show you something. It might cheer you up," she said.
Sunny gave her an incredulous look, then bent forward.
"More good news? Another planet for me to save?"
Lily started getting accustomed to his sarcasm. She found it quite appealing. "Well, if I told you, it wouldn't be a surprise now,

would it? C'mon. Get going." Lily jerked at his arm. She noticed his arms were still weak, lacking muscle and tone.

The two of them left and went to the far end of the Fallen camp. Lily showed Sunny to a small platform, closed in by walls on all sides, which one would think was a dead end. But Lily fiddled around with a control panel hidden beneath some debris. Seconds later, a small door opened.

"How am I supposed to fit in there? it must be the formal entrance for the rats," Sunny said jokingly but clearly annoyed.

Lily smiled and signalled him to follow her. On the other side was a warm and spacious oval-shaped room. Probably a former storage room, Sunny thought. The light struck his attention immediately; the soft hue made him relax. Unlike the harsh light at the rest of the station, the luminance here was soothing and welcoming. All around the room were trinkets and various paraphernalia, ancient pre-launch objects from Earth.

Lily smiled. She was happy seeing how minutely Sunny studied every single object. "What is all this? What is this place?" Sunny was dazzled by the breadth of the collection.

"This is your room! Sorry, I mean, this is, well, was, Warner's secret room. He kept an incredible collection of items from Earth here. All of this stuff is hundreds of years old. Ancient electrical equipment. Warner's dad was a military man, working for Arand. He had access to all these trinkets. Look, you can use this one to record and play music. It's called a stem player. It splits music tracks into stems via artificial neural networks. It was one of the main sources to store and exchange culture back in those days." Lily was beaming from ear to ear. This place had a special place in her heart as well.

"Warner used to come in here, just spent hours listening to 'music'. It's pre-recorded media, in fact, of people playing music and singing or rapping at the same time. It invites conversation and sharing of experiences. It stimulates creativity and freedom. All of the things Arand made illegal here on Zeeta," Lily stated bleakly. "Warner came here to escape and think. Before joining the Fallen, I think he was living with Arand. I don't know much about it. He rarely said anything concrete about that time."

Sunny nodded. He did remember that music - and that consuming any non-authorised media was strictly banned on Zeeta. Anyone caught doing so would be exterminated without notice. That had been Scorpia's idea.

"Look over here." Lily was smiling again. "It's a vinyl player. It plays music from these funny round discs. They always reminded me of flying saucers for some reason. Maybe they're special plates Martians would eat their food from." She laughed.

Sunny looked at the vinyl player and agreed it was quite beautiful. He was anxious for her to show how it worked. Her nimble fingers put on a record, and soothing horns and other instruments played out through the small speaker.

Lily bopped her head to the music. "It's called 'jazz'," she explained. "Warner's favourite kind of Earth-music."

Suddenly, Sunny got a sour feeling. What was the point of her showing him these nice things? What did she want in return?

"Look, Lily, I appreciate the history lesson. But, uh, would you mind telling me where you're going with all this?" he said unceremoniously.

She was still smiling."It's simple, don't you see? All these things were carefully collected and meticulously stored. Carriers of culture and history. They're from Earth! Pre-launch Earth. They bear witness to a time when things were still relatively peaceful and enjoyable. People were positive and enjoyed each other's company. They listened to and played music for one another. They built bridges linking countries and cultures. They were ... open to different ways of thinking!" Lily said.

Sunny looked dubious. "Look, I lived on Earth before leaving with Zeeta 21. And I can tell you Earth was a real shit-hole towards the end. Humanity isn't all that rosy and peaceful as you make it out to be. I mean, there's a reason we had to build Zeeta 21 in the first place," he was enjoying the first interesting conversation since coming back to life.

"I know. My point is that there was hope! People weren't constantly bogged down by negativity. They thought life was worthwhile. They created music and love," she pronounced that last word with great care as if handling a fragile vase.

She continued, "Things back then were better. Not like this rathole we're trapped in now. That's my point. We need to get back down to Earth. Warner kept this room secret because he was afraid people would spoil it if he allowed access. Afraid people wouldn't understand and take it for granted. But this was his whole being, his raison d'etre. He wanted the Fallen to one day return to Earth, where all humans belong. He wanted the Fallen to be free of the tyranny which happens above the surface with the Arand Corp. They treat humans as objects, like scum. Do as they say or die, feel as they want you to, or get turned into a zombie. That's not what life is. Life is more than that. We're meant to be free … back on Earth. Look at this." Lily showed him a set of pictures. They showed animals, funny ones with black and white stripes, grazing on a beautiful sunlit savannah. "This is what Earth was, home to not only humans but animals and insects and flowing rivers too. Paradise, in fact."

"Look, Lily, I don't want to burst your bubble here, but Earth wasn't all that great. Humans destroyed everything that was great about it. All those animals," he pointed at the photos, "forget it. Extinct, long before I was even born. Famine and diseases were widespread in ancient Europe, where I was from. Earth's natural resources were depleting at a rapid pace, fuel, oil and precious stones becoming dangerously valuable commodities. Countries, even friends and neighbours, were killing each other to stay alive. We were completely overpowered by the United States of the Western World, a conglomerate between mega-corporations mainly based in the former US, Canada, and parts of Europe. The Arand Corp was a product of that. They decided everything, rationed food and access to healthcare. But they did it for the greater good, they said. In other words, to fight off Russia and especially China, who had become the new superpower. Things escalated until, well, another war broke out, as it always does. In fact, it was so bad that the superpowers agreed to build Zeeta to give humanity another chance. They didn't do that because they suddenly became best friends but because it was a possible pragmatic solution to a common problem: survival. To see if peace and harmony could be brought about by sending twenty thousand people into space together with a common goal; to thrive and prosper in a new environment. This could have spawned a new dawn for humanity, a new hope. But as you pointed out, it didn't work." Sunny slumped back, lost in thought again.

Lily's eyes became dreamy, and she spoke with great enthusiasm. Sunny thought her expression made her look young and girly.

"But that's exactly it! I mean, ever since Warner told me about you, I was so fascinated. You've lived on Earth, seen what nature looks like, experienced what it means to be a free man. And yet, you came here searching for something better, something else, trying to start a new destiny for humankind. Now that we found out it didn't work, that people still keep their basic nature even in space, I think it's time to head back, wouldn't you agree," Lily sounded so mature again. An able and respectable person, Sunny thought.

"So that's the fairy-tale Warner was feeding to the lowlifes out there? Steer this ship around, go back to Earth, and everything will be fine and dandy? Earth's been blown to smithereens. It's a dusty, hostile desert. There's nothing left. No safe spaces for humans. We managed to destroy all that. Warner's promises and dreams were bullshit – including handing everybody a free vinyl player." Lily noticed his sarcasm.

"Warner kept people's hopes alive through stories. He made us imagine what Earth was like, each of us in our own ways. He said how good we could all be there. He always spoke highly of you, of what you could do for us. For the Fallen. For all of Zeeta," Lily said.

She saw he was about to speak. "Wait!" Lily continued, "I know you're special. Look, I even found this vinyl record with your name on it. Right there. 'Sunny Bridges'. Look! Probably just a coincidence, but I always thought about you when I listened to it. Dreaming you were a musician back on Earth, maybe a writer too. On top of your technical skills, that would really make you a superhuman in my book." Lily giggled.

"Look, Lily, enough with the fantasies. You need to realise that I'm not all you're hyping me up to be. In fact, I'm a pretty fucking horrible person. All that shit that's going on up there, at Arand? Well, guess what? I helped build and implement most of it. Yes, I was the ship's Chief Engineer, so I know how to make this baby fly in any goddamn direction you want. I programmed NADOSH, who turned out to be a heartless bitch. And I was the right hand of Alois Lechowsky. Not by choice, but I did that scumbag's bidding nonetheless. That's right. Everything you guys loathed and feared all these years. I was part of that, willingly."

Lily looked at him. Tears started to well up in her eyes.

“My entire career on this ship I spent developing increasingly devious ways to control peoples’ lives, essentially to make them our slaves. People wanted safety, so we gave them the Enforcers. They wanted to feel happiness, so we gave them drugs. They wanted to feel special, so we programmed NADOSH to adapt its avatars to every person’s needs. We needed people to be productive but obedient and gave them everything within reason. What else could we do? You see how it is down here. You give people a bit, and they always want more. The ones who fell out of the system or who didn’t fit in from the start, we hunted down like animals. The Fallen was our primary target. If Arand hadn’t become so paranoid and bent on destroying itself, I think you’d all be dead by now," Sunny explained.

“That’s not right. It’s not, and you know it.” Tears ran down Lily’s cheeks.

“Right? What the fuck does right and wrong have to do with anything? In case you haven’t noticed, we’re flying around in deep space on a giant saucer, no longer bound by humanity’s perception of right or wrong. Your God doesn’t exist here. We’re free of any moral codes. We build up something new, something from scratch. Except all these ungrateful fucks.” Sunny gestured towards the Fallen camp, “felt too high and mighty, too self-centred, too important to give their sweat and blood for the greater good. They crawl around down here like rats, waiting for someone else to do the heavy-lifting. Someone else to find and implement the solutions. Do you think it’s easy? Can you even for a second fathom what it feels like to carry that burden on your shoulders every single day? To watch these imbeciles, these useless piles of human garbage, wander aimlessly about but contribute nothing? It’s not a fun time, let me tell ya. But that’s what we did, anyway. Until the children started becoming disobedient, and we had to punish them.” Sunny was tearing up as well, his voice thick with emotion.

“I know,” Lily swallowed, “I know there is kindness within you, and that you don’t mean everything you’re saying right now. You were part of a system, part of something bigger and you did what you had to do. Used your knowledge in the best way you could. But now? Now you can start over.”

"Start over?" Sunny shouted. "Look at me! I'm a dead person walking around wearing someone else's skin. I came from a tyrannical, oppressive regime which I gladly served for my own purposes, and now you want me to start over? Don't you think that's enough bad things for one person? What makes me deserve another shot!?"

"Sunny, this is your chance to start life afresh." A smidge of Lily's positive spirit returned.

Sunny said, "I have no life! I don't even know what life is! The only thing I've managed to do is bring death and destruction around me. People are still dying because of me, because of some pipe dream fantasy about what I can do for them. Well, tell you what, fuck that. You and Warner were stupid assholes for bringing me down here. Only thing you did was put your people at risk. NADOSH ... She's programmed to ensure my survival at all costs, so I'll be fine. But for the rest of you, you're screwed. She's probably sending Lechowsky the exact coordinates to your base as we speak. Before you know it, this place is history. If you don't wipe yourself out in the meantime, that is." Sunny spoke coldly without consideration for Lily. His mind was stuck in a dark place.

Lily tried to stay strong, but she could no longer hold back the tears. It was too much for her to take. All her hopes and dreams, exemplified by this man in front of her, disappeared before her unbelieving eyes.

Still sobbing, but slightly more composed, she said, "I guess that means you won't help us, then." Her tone matched his. "So, what will you do now?" The question was frank and without pleading.

Sunny was slightly taken aback. "I ... I, uh, don't know. Haven't given it much thought. Well, you know what? I'm a mess. I need time to think. I want to be alone for a while." His words were followed by incoherent gestures. He paced back and forth as if not knowing where to put himself.

He's someone struggling deeply within himself, Lily thought. He has a hard time figuring out who he really is. It was probably that way even long before he joined Arand. She still felt there was something genuinely kind about him.

There was a long silence between them.

"It's good you want to reflect. There's one more place I wanted to show you," Lily said. "It's Warner's meditation spot, where he'd

go in times of need to collect his thoughts and re-centre himself. Who knows. Might do some good for you as well."
Lily and Sunny left the Special Room in silence. Without her noticing, Sunny took a good look around one last time.
They went past the control room across the main hall. The place had gone quiet. People were scattered about, muttering incoherently to themselves. One clearly delusional man was punching into the air at invisible foes.
"The place we're going has a special connotation for Warner. It has a special pond supposedly metres deep. The water helped him wash his mind clear of useless thoughts. It reminded him of the savage waters and rivers on Earth," Lily spoke as they advanced. Sunny walked closely behind her.
She led him to an unfamiliar room. The walls were grey-bluish metal, and pipes and wiring hung from the ceiling. The place looked even more unfinished and dilapidated than the rest of the Fallen camp. She stopped at a metallic door.
"This is it. I'll let you explore the place for yourself," she said.
"Where are we?" Sunny enquired. He looked exhausted.
"This is still close to the Fallen camp, but no one ever comes here, really. Actually, we're pretty close to my personal resting place. Maybe I'll show it to you someday." She touched the door. "We don't know what the original purpose of this room was, but it's been sealed off," Lily stated before leaving.
As Sunny walked in, he could tell why the room had been abandoned. There was nothing of value there. It was a big square room with bare walls and ceilings. There might have been some machinery at a certain point, but the room had been stripped empty. Lighting was poor, but as Sunny walked further into the room, he could see something near the back wall. Condensing water dripped from the pipes, forming a small puddle on the ground.
This must be the 'special pond' Warner had been so fond of. Sunny bent over and put three fingers in the murky water. It had gone stale, smelled rotten, and clots of rust covered the surface.
"Some pond." Sunny smirked to himself. He was amused at how people projected hopes and feelings on inanimate objects to the point where their minds completely distorted the reality of what those things actually were.

A great cloud of despair covered his mind. He thought how frivolous it all was. I'm being pulled left and right by everyone I meet. They all want something from me.
His depression darkened as he recounted what had happened in the last days. Barely alive, he was hauled from the Disposal Site and tortured by Arand. Then the Fallen got him. Sunny looked at his hands and touched his face.
I should've known that bastard Lechowsky would come for me, he thought. Why didn't I prepare better? Sunny vaguely remembered when the Enforcers seized him at the office, then blackout. He must have lost consciousness at this point; thinking about it provoked a migraine.
Sunny now lay here, crouched in front of a pool of rusty water. The only thing permeating the silence was the occasional drip of condensing water into the puddle. Anxiety and sorrow washed over him. He felt completely and utterly alone: a human reject, an outcast.
He was nothing but an empty shell. People he met projected their hopes and dreams on him, imagining he was someone capable and altruistic, a man who could solve everyone's problems. Lily thought he was a man of values, someone who put the greater good before himself.
The fact is, Sunny thought, I'm an idiot. Nothing valuable is inside me. I feel empty and cold. No hopes, no dreams, nothing worth living for. Everything I am can be summarised into one word: greed. Actually, two words: greed and selfishness.
I feel like a burnt tree. Leaves scorched away, the stem and branches horribly mutilated and twisted by the everlasting fire.
What is this fire? Where does the pain come from?
It's always been like this. Ever since the day she died … my guiding light.
When she passed, I discovered something not meant for someone my young age: we are alone. All of us, completely and utterly alone. When I needed help, no one was there. When I wanted to cry out in pain, no one could hear me. No one was capable or willing to guide and help me cope with the pain. That's when I realised that our perceived 'reality' is constructed from stories and lies that hide the horrible truth.

Best thing you can do is smile when they smile. Laugh when they laugh. Hope they don't see it. Hope they don't see beyond the façade. Had they bothered to look a little bit further, they'd have seen a dying soul. Someone desperate. But nobody ever bothered. Too late now, the soul is gone. There's only the burnt skin covering my body, inside I am hollow.
I am useless. Worthless.
A tyrant to some, a saviour to others.
A mere projection of hopes and imagination of other people. No real substance of my own. No answers to bring when challenged, no values to defend.
I'm nothing. I'm literally nothing. A waste of space.
As the dark thoughts closed upon Sunny's mind, he wept. The tears stung as they purged his body at their own leisurely pace. They washed him from the inside. Some of them dropped into the pond, making tiny rings in the water.
I never had a life. I don't know what life is. How true those words were when he spoke to Lily. They perfectly encapsulated his state of mind.
Fatigue followed soon, and Sunny lay his weary head down. The left side of his face became wrinkled from lying in the puddle in front of him; it did not matter. It was time for a well-deserved rest.
A dark dream haunted his thoughts. Was it a memory from Earth? Something else?
The dream came to him as a monologue, spoken by himself. An earlier version of him, perhaps?

An intense pain has been lingering inside me. It defines every moment of my life. No matter what I do, it's always there.
To escape the pain, I sometimes dream. Fantasise.
I imagine walking alongside the ocean on a set of high cliffs. The grass is green, and the ground is completely flat. The sky is grey, and the wind's blowing violently.

Willingly, I let myself fall into a hole in the ground that perfectly fits my size. The hole is extremely dark. I fall headfirst. Upon impact with the rocky bottom, I instantaneously twist my neck. My forehead cracks open. A stream of blood flows into my eyes.

My body's paralysed. I welcome the numb sensation of weightlessness.

I'm now lying in my hole; the perfect spot to die alone. Only thing left for me is to wait for worms and maggots to crawl through my mouth and nose to eat me from inside. They'll wait for my natural remains to decompose and draw nutrition from my, otherwise useless, carcass.
Above me, I hear birds flying. I imagine they're three beautiful crows - corvus cornix, with ashy grey feathers. Once the spasms in my body have stopped, they'll peck out my eyes and feast on them.
I suddenly feel a light tugging at my right leg, still sticking up from the hole. Could these be the birds who've landed? Are they walking around me, already eager to divide my remains?
Or, are these human hands? Is someone pulling at me, in a futile attempt to bring life and meaning back into the empty shell which is my existence?
Before the question can be answered, I close my eyes to never open them again.

He thought he could hear birds chirping, goading his senses back into reality. He looked around and realised he was still in the same room. The puddle had soaked his left cheek, making the skin all wrinkly and bubbly.
"How much longer will this skin last for?" he mumbled to himself. He then became alert; someone was in the room with him.
Sunny, my son ... it's me, the voice spoke before Sunny could turn around. He understood though he could not hear any audible words.
It's OK, Sunny. I'm here now. We're together. The words formed in his mind like in a dream.
That voice. It sounded just like his father. How could this be? What manner of tricky was this? Was his mind still hazy from the dream?
At that moment, the voice called him out again, more insistent this time but still pleasant.

You're not alone anymore, Sunny. We're together now. I love you. I always loved you. After she left us, I dedicated my life to you.

The words overwhelmed Sunny, and he wept passionately again. His father was not there; he had passed away many years ago, and hearing his voice was so bittersweet.

So, what then? What's behind me? Sunny wondered.

He hesitantly turned around. It took his eyes a few seconds to adjust to the darkness and make out the figure at the other end of the room. It was a hooded figure wearing a weighty robe. He stood without moving, and his face was shrouded in mystery.

The being carefully scrutinised Sunny before speaking again.

Sunny. Your destiny's with me. We belong together.

The words came clear as day to Sunny's mind. Telepathy.

Then, it sounded like his father again.

I love you, son. Remember when we got you your first computer? How we'd play games together? And we bickered when you lost, you got so annoyed at that.

Sunny's knees weakened, and he crouched down.

He had come to this room to gain clarity to figure out what his next move should be. Instead, he had rummaged inside his mind and found only perplexity and confusion. He had absolutely no idea what to do next and found himself at a complete loss.

Oddly enough, Sunny sensed no malice from the cloaked figure. He intuitively knew that their destinies were linked.

It was like the hooded figure put him under his spell, and Sunny slumped towards him. He awkwardly crawled closer to the cloaked man.

As he got closer, Sunny saw that the hooded stranger had an extremely muscular and bulky body with oddly deformed hands. Sunny crouched in front of the cloaked figure, only a metre or so away from him.

The stranger discreetly stepped out of the shadows and slowly placed his right hand on Sunny's forehead. In his left hand, he held a sharp blade, capable of cutting a man's throat in mere split seconds. He would not need his weapon today.

Chapter V: Humanity's New Beginning

Brother Francis' Diary Part III: Suffering

Francis felt his entire vision turn dim. He had been exploring the catacombs deep beneath the Monastery for hours. Or even days? Day and night blurred together into one undefinable mass here in the dark.

He was bone-tired. His throat felt tight and incredibly dry. As Francis sat down, he leaned towards the wall and closed his eyes. The electrical light from his lantern was the only thing keeping him company. An aching sensation started tingling down his spine. His eyes closed shut, and, for a second, he feared the emotion would invade and paralyse his entire body.

But no. When Francis opened his eyes again, he was still conscious. He took a deep breath and decided to carry on. In an act of careless folly, he had forgotten his automated map generator. Not that it would have done him much good; the ancient catacombs were not officially part of the map catalogue. Still, it would have given him a general idea of where he was heading.

Yet, he somehow had a vague idea of where to go. The lump inside his stomach was guiding him. The more he walked, the less it hurt. It was a welcome relief after enduring constant pain. He took this as a good sign; it condoned him being here.

Walking down the black metallic corridors, Francis realised that his body was giving out. Before he knew it, he fainted and fell to the floor.

…

It was the taste of water in his mouth that woke Francis up. His head was lying in the lap of a fellow monk. Francis recognised him as Roger Maxon, his childhood friend.

"Where … Where am I?" Francis said under his breath.

"Nowhere near where you're supposed to be," Maxon said, relieved that Francis could talk. "The entire section is on alert because of you. You disappeared from your daily duties without a trace and left a lot of Brothers worried."

Francis immediately came to. "I must speak to the Abbess! It's important. Something's wrong on Zeeta. I can feel it. She must know about it immediately."
The monk holding Francis' head started grinning. "You must leave here, Francis. This area is strictly off-limits to anyone. We'll organise an escort for you, make sure you make it back up to the surface safely."
"No …," Francis pleaded. He shook himself free and crawled backwards on his elbows. "But you don't understand! I need to … We must speak, conduct a plan, or do something. I … it's not quite …", he trailed off helplessly. Francis' eyes darted back and forth between the two monks. He was losing his grip on reality.
At that moment, a large door opened behind him. It was a secret door whose décor blended in with the black metal of the corridor. The two monks opposite Francis seemed surprised and stepped back. It was the Abbess.
"Francis, what are you doing here?" she asked, her voice expressing annoyance and concern. "You're not supposed to be here."
Francis meekly got to his feet. He stumbled towards the Abbess. She let him enter. As soon as he did, one of the guards blindfolded him.
"Francis, what's in these vats must remain secret from everyone, including you. I permit you to sit here a short while, but then you must let the Brothers escort you back up. Here. Drink this."
He was glad for the opportunity offered to him. Sitting in the Abbess' presence eased his troubled mind. He hastily drank the cup of lukewarm water.
"Abbess! … I'm so glad," Francis said while panting feverishly, "... that we could finally meet." He was barely able to catch his breath. "There's a … need for action … Something's wrong, and the Brothers need to know!"
"Francis, have you ever given any thought to the scenario that Zeeta fails?" The stunned silence told the Abbess that he had not.
"My dear, Francis. Your dire predictions are correct. What you fear has come to pass, for we're dealing with the nature of man. Within him, man has an undying will. A blind, thirsty, and raging will that's bent on destroying everything within and around him.

That's why, after thousands of years on this Earth, humankind has failed to make it the sanctuary for all life it's supposed to be. Rotten at their core, our fellow man has created around them the very things that reside within them: disorder and futility. We humans are misguided and have let Mother Nature's heart slip through our soiled hands. It now lays on the ground, begging for a new protector."

The Abbess paused briefly. "It's indeed becoming less likely that Zeeta's turning into the glorious revolution we'd hoped. Yes, things are looking grim indeed. We must be ready for such a scenario. That's why I'm down here."

The blindfold Francis wore felt so tight it could crush his head wide open. He pondered the Abbess' words.

"Yes, but … that must not happen, right?" he ventured childishly. The notion that things could go awry with Zeeta was simply too difficult to fathom.

"We here at the Monastery of Our Good Lord are the caretakers of the remaining world. You know this, Francis. We must all understand and ask ourselves the one pertinent question, the only thing that matters. What's more important, the survival of Humankind or the continuation of the Will of God?" The Abbess closed her eyes behind her mask. Her meditations on the subject brought her great pain.

"And that's why I'm down here. Preparing and doing experiments. Concocting a solution if Zeeta fails. If humanity fails."

Francis gulped loudly. He feared the implications of that last sentence. Though the Abbess spoke calmly as ever, there was a sense of urgency in her tone he seldom heard.

"My meditations have shown that there are options if we humans fail to care for our planet. As you know, Francis, our history is sad, full of strife and war. The recent attacks on our dear Monastery bear witness to the desolate state the world's in, and our precious Mother Earth cries to our very souls with every passing moment. That's why we've taken steps to see what could perhaps replace humans. Are we indeed the right species to be allowed to grace the holy Earth with our presence? Or are we, in fact, but a stepping stone meant to produce something greater to come after us? These are questions I ponder and have used my studious hours to test."

The Abbess gently placed her hands on Francis' stomach. "That growth you have there, the creature living inside you, it's a sign of what's to come. She's well within you, evolving rapidly. She heeded the Call of the Many, and that's what brought you here. Eventually, she'll hatch and fulfil her potential."

Francis' hands robotically caressed his stomach. He tried to fathom what she was saying; a creature hatching inside him? He could not concentrate and gave up.

He felt his heart cut in two. On the one hand, he felt reassured that the Abbess somehow thought there was hope, even if Zeeta failed. On the other, what she alluded to seemed beyond his comprehension. He felt sick, as if the water he drank wanted to crawl back out of his stomach.

The Abbess took a deep breath. "If humans are but a step in the evolutionary chain, perhaps Mother Nature needs a gentle push in the right direction for the next thing to happen. That's all you need to hear, Francis. Go now, return to your room, and get some rest. Get all the rest you can. You need it for the trials ahead. God knows we all need it."

Francis felt feverish. He would weep quietly that night as he had done so many nights before while pondering humanity's dire predicament.

Damage Control

Alois Lechowsky felt his existence crumble. The latest reports were unanimous: Sunny had escaped. But Lechowsky wanted to see for himself and rushed down to Arand's holding cells where he had questioned Sunny just hours earlier. Lechowksy had lost contact with NADOSH. Then again, that was probably for the better since he disobeyed her direct orders to bring Sunny to Bloc-13. Instead, he had kept Sunny securely locked up at the Arand Corp's main tower. At least, so he thought.

When he arrived at level minus four, he saw the two guards lying dead on the floor. They were both soaked in fresh blood. He scuttled around the corner to reach Sunny's cell, or what remained of it.

The door had been torn open by a massive explosion. To Lechowsky's surprise, Horrigan was standing inside the room amidst the debris. His arms were smeared in blood, presumably the guards'. His body language was uncharacteristically meek and docile. Horrigan turned around as Lechowsky entered.

"Sunny escaped," Lechowsky stated the obvious.

Horrigan opened a hatch in his armour near his left hip. "I had no choice," he said. "She threatened to deactivate my reactor core."

Lechowsky, albeit not a technical expert, knew that core is what kept Horrigan's vital functions going. Indeed, his life depended on his armour. Horrigan was more machine than man, so deactivating the core would kill him instantaneously.

"She ... she's been acting rather independently lately", Lechowsky said. He deliberately avoided mentioning NADOSH, but they both knew who he meant.

Horrigan picked up a piece of rubble from the ground. "The Engineer was moved from his cell to Bloc-13 against my will. She deactivated me, then ordered an Enforcer transport squad to move Sunny." He crushed the rubble in his hand into a small cloud of dust. "Don't blame the troops. It was completely inconspicuous. When we finally realised what was going on, the Fallen had already gotten to Sunny and rescued him from Bloc-13. She slowed our progress by setting up a decoy. When I finally got there, it was too late. The Fallen managed to escape underground via the ventilation shaft," Horrigan explained.

Lechowsky nodded. "A fitting escape for a bunch of rats." Grave as this was, he was happy that Horrigan remained loyal. "Somehow, NADOSH has been working for Sunny the whole time. Bastard must've programmed her that way. An emergency protocol was somehow activated the moment Sunny's life was endangered. NADOSH is ensuring his survival by any means necessary."

"But it's not over yet," Horrigan added. "I know where he's being held. The Specials got him."

Lechowsky caressed his beard and nodded again. In his quiet mind, he was relieved by this news. After all, that's what Scorpia

wanted. If the Specials had somehow already gotten Sunny to their base, half of his job was complete.
Perhaps it's not over yet, indeed. That AI-bitch would get what was coming to her, he would short-circuit her nodes in ways most painful. But first, he needed to find the Engineer.
Words were superfluous, Horrigan gathered a group of his most trusted Enforcers, and they started towards the Specials' base.

A Guided Tour

Open spaces with tall aluminium columns, reaching further than the eye could see, lead into tiny, neat, and impeccable hallways with artfully arranged display monitors and aromatic dispensers. Everything in this place bore witness to harmony and meticulous care.
Most striking were the seemingly natural flora and greenery which had grown around it. In an almost organic way, plant and insect life had found its way to integrate and coexist with the harsh metal and jagged edges that made up Zeeta's hulk. It was the Specials' area, deep beneath Zeeta's surface.

Sunny was here now. Robert Bacon, his former associate on Earth, was about to show him around.
Sunny found himself lying on a soft, comfortable mattress, nothing like the standard synthetic ones Arand used. It seemed like moss fungus. He lay there for a while. It felt good; he needed rest.
Bacon was calmly moving about the room. He was preparing a soothing ointment, which he applied to his hands and face. It made him relax and be present in the moment. He looked at Sunny. It had been many years since they had last met. But he felt Sunny's fierce spirit remained intact, ambitious and conflicted as ever. This man struggles to find a higher meaning. He's frustrated with his human restrictions and wants to go beyond them. Life's not easy for men like him; they always feel out of place. He's torn between a burning desire to be alone and labour for perfection while being fragile and desperately needing the affection of others, Bacon surmised.
Sunny's change in physical appearance did not elude Bacon's attention. Sunny had gone through hellfire; it was amazing he was even alive. A tough soul, both physically and mentally, Bacon

thought to himself. He was eager to dig into Sunny's intricate mind. Unlike the simpletons of the Arand Corp, Sunny presented him with a challenge and potential reward. His usual subjects were ultimately so mundane and uninteresting; the minds of the many carried nothing enlightening for Bacon.

But Sunny was another case entirely. Bacon had tried to read his mind, but it was so convoluted he could not determine his purpose. Sunny was an extremely complicated individual.

After a brief stretch, Sunny got up from the mattress without any visible signs of being particularly happy or unhappy about the situation.

A complex character indeed, Bacon thought. Sunny was a breath of fresh air, and Bacon was adamant about making the most of his visit.

"Sunny, it's an honour to have you visit our humble abode. How many years has it been? When your consciousness expands, everything becomes one. We started this journey together, and we designed Zeeta. Everything around us stems from our ideas. Yet, Zeeta's maiden voyage was tough for us all. It changed us … in more ways than one." Bacon alluded to Sunny's change of skin.

Sunny nodded, his mind brimming with dark, depressive thoughts; he needed to recompose himself somehow. Why did I leave the Fallen so freely? He thought about Lily.

"As you will notice, however, life down here has developed in new and interesting ways. Thanks to prolonged radioactive exposure and various fumes and gases, people have developed capabilities. We have men working non-stop, needing only two to three hours of sleep per week. Others have the strength of ten, able to carry loads of steel you wouldn't believe. Finally, we have the creatures. Those are my favourite." Bacon sensed Sunny was not paying attention. Prodding inside his mind, he saw chaos and a lack of direction.

"But you know what?" Bacon said. "As a token of appreciation for your kind visit, I'd like to invite you to my private quarters first. There we can relax and enjoy a moment of mindfulness and meditation. That'll be our main focus for now." Sunny noticed how odd his voice sounded but could not see his face under the heavy robe.

Sunny walked inside Bacon's living quarters, a lush, richly decorated space with beautiful trinkets and gadgets hanging from the ceiling. Sunny looked at a collection of fossils and test-tube babies. One specimen particularly caught his attention. It was a young girl, probably eight years of age. Her body had been mummified in a large cylinder filled with a thick clear liquid. Her mouth and eyes were open. Sunny wondered if that was the expression on her face when she died.

"Ah, yes, a beautiful specimen, isn't she? I collected her from the North of Europe before our departure with Zeeta. Sadly, she met her end at a highly reputable hospital in Former Scandinavia. Seemingly, it was murder. Her little lungs were filled with corrosive acid, leading to a slow and painful death. Yet, her expression is so alive and vivid. It's almost like she's still with us, wouldn't you agree?" Bacon mused.

"What's that over there?" Sunny asked without much enthusiasm as he entered the adjacent room.

"That's the main piece of my dwelling. These are my living quarters. As you can see, windows are placed strategically to give a near complete view of the main engine rooms. This way, I can follow the daily lives of our workers and assist whenever my presence is required. Although, I must say, such occasions are rare," Bacon said.

Sunny sat down again, struck with sudden fatigue. "Bacon, what the fuck's going on? Everything's so hazy to me. I don't know what to do. Kira was … she's still with Arand, we got her out, the Fallen rescued her. We were a team, the three of us. Back on Earth. Shit, I'm so confused. Was this all a mistake? Would Zeeta have been better off without our intervention?"

This struck a chord with Bacon. "I sense your mind is clouded with doubt and anguish. Don't worry. This is normal. You've been through a lot, and you obviously need time for your mind and body to heal. Speaking of the latter, I see you were given another man's skin to wear. I can't begin to fathom what you've been through. Such things take a toll on a man's sense of … self." Bacon said emphatically.

"As you may have noticed, I've had a small, well, makeover since the last time we met. How long ago was that? Almost ten years?

Anyway, guess it beats looking like a dead man," Sunny said flatly.
Bacon grinned. "I quite liked your former appearance but am glad to say that your personality survived the operation. Don't worry about your skin. We can offer you a new one if you please. A new beginning, a new you. We can restore you. In fact, improve you. Bring out your true potential, make you a stronger and better being than you ever were."
Sunny frowned upon hearing the word 'being'. He was curious to see what Bacon's face looked like under the hooded robe. As if he read Sunny's mind, Bacon took the hood off. Sunny gasped and stepped back.
"I often get that as a first reaction. But don't be scared. It's all right," Bacon said soothingly. His lips were sewn together with a thick copper cord. He spoke using a rectangular device implanted where his laryngeal prominence should be. It seemed like a back-up solution. Evidently, telepathy was the common form of communication down here. They were unlearning regular speech.
"Much has happened since we parted ways, Sunny. I had great hopes and dreams before leaving Earth, but what we've managed to do here is beyond human imagination. It's a miracle, nothing less." Bacon held out his huge and muscular arms to mimic the grandeur of his achievements. "You see, after we left, I managed to get a team of skilled researchers together. We were left alone, Sunny; no one bothered us. Under the guise of the chaos that ensued on the surface of Zeeta, Arand didn't have time for us. They needed us to run the engines, which we did skilfully, and that's it. Raging war on themselves and, eventually, the Fallen, takes all their resources," Bacon said. Not seeing any visible reaction from Sunny, he continued.
"Sunny, you have to realise, we've bred an entire colony down here, thousands of new life forms. If we allow this life to spread and develop, it could mean a new dawn for humankind. It could be the next evolutionary step, survival against all odds, humans developing in space only to adapt to the harsh realities of existence. Sunny, we can fulfil the original purpose of Zeeta 21 and guarantee a future for ourselves." Bacon grabbed onto Sunny's shoulders. His wide orange and red eyes burned with purpose.

Sunny was startled, and his mind raced with this disturbing information. Bacon continued, "Look, I know it's a lot to take in at once." Sunny wondered if he referred to his freakish appearance or the plight of the Specials at large. "But we can make this work. We can make a success out of this story, yet. You and I both agree that the humans on this expedition have utterly failed. Most of them are living like tyrants on the surface, killing off whomever they see fit, while the rest starve to death underground, wishing for some stroke of luck to change their situation. It's up to us to make this work, Sunny. We are the link between worlds."

Bacon leaned back into a comfortable oval chair, eyes closed. He found a kindred spirit in Sunny. The two of them had been close friends back on Earth. They were opposites and often at odds, but they shared the same passion for trying to save humanity. He closed his eyes.

Sunny got up, suddenly feeling energised. "Bacon, uh, I don't want to shit all over your nice colony here. It, um, well, at least it seems more peaceful than Arand. Whatever you and your, uh, things have built here, it's not a volcano of violence. But what — I mean, this isn't human anymore. You've bred a colony of … insects? Mutations? Hybrids? What possible future do you expect your 'breed' to have? It's one thing to create a closed bio-organic circuit, which I applaud you for, by the way, within a fixed set of variables. But it's another thing entirely to make that lifeform thrive elsewhere. What good will this bring humans? Is it another workforce?"

Bacon calmly opened his eyes. His quick interlude of meditation had grounded him again. Speaking to Sunny triggered his human side, one still prone to fear and doubt. Now he let the Collective Mind take over and guide his thoughts.

"Sunny, your thinking is still limited. Your creativity is obstructed by boundaries. Your sense of scale and potential is still," Bacon paused to find the right word, "lacklustre." His speaker box blinked a few times as if changing frequency. He then spoke in a more mellow tone. "What you see here is a new dawn, nothing short of that. And you haven't even seen it yet. But take my word, Sunny. We have created something entirely new. We are One. You wonder if survival is possible? Think the opposite: failure is impossible. Our genetics are born here. But imagine what the right soil could do. The right conditions would allow us to prosper in a place free of humans and their limitations. What we have around us," Bacon stopped to clutch a purple vine growing from the ceiling, "is but a mere beginning. A prologue to the main story if you will. A view through the looking glass, capturing but a fraction of our true potential."

Sunny tried hard to follow Bacon, a brilliant scientist back on Earth and a man of reason. Yet, he almost seemed more like a cult leader than a scientist. Or perhaps a mix of the two, making it all the scarier. "Heading back to Earth with a species of new lifeforms sure is a novelty," Sunny said, "but I'm not sure that was in the design specs for our mission. I fail to see how that completes our goal or how it gives Earth another chance."

Bacon stood up and walked towards Sunny. "Ah, Earth. Our Collective Mind has laboured hard and long over that very question. What's to become of it? Nothing. Humans have had their chance. Many chances, in fact, to make things right. It's over. We need to forget Planet Earth. Humans have been destroying it for centuries and will only continue to do so until their dying breath."

"With all due respect for your intellectual acumen, Bacon, Earth is yet the only suited planet for lifeforms as we know them to proliferate. Let's not get too enthralled with fantastic illusions, here," Sunny retorted.

"Earth has been obliterated. It was already the case before Zeeta took off. There's nothing to save there. In my deepest meditations, I see images from Earth. One of the monks of the Monastery, that young annoying one we met, Francis, I think it is, he's growing a small larva inside him. Each day, it grows larger, allowing me deeper into his mind. I feel he is well, the larva, I mean. Trust me, Sunny, Earth is more hostile than ever. Nothing can survive on that radiated excuse of a planet."

Sunny made a mental note not to put anything inside his mouth while with Bacon. He was not about to have maggots dwell inside him, things were complicated enough already. "If you don't want to go back on Earth, what's the other option? Float around space forever?"

Bacon lit up, his grey face almost gaining some colour. This was the pinnacle of his plan. "Uranus!" he said, almost childishly.

"Uranus?! What the fuck are you on about? That's the coldest planet we know of in the solar system. Not to mention the odd seasonal cycles. Nothing can survive there!" Sunny said incredulously. He was flabbergasted.

"That's it, Sunny. Nice and far away from the sun. So far, no human could ever survive there. No more destruction, no more disharmony. Only icy peace. We believe the surface mixture of water, methane, and ammonia could propel Us into new heights of evolution. It won't be easy, sure, but our New Breed is flawless. Their capability to evolve is boundless. Old lifeforms will give way to new ones. I just have to figure out how best to install organic cocoons on the planet's rocky crust. Our brethren require a warm, soothing nest to hatch."

Sunny felt sick to his stomach. All this talk of new life forms and stuff growing inside people made his bowels churn. He could not decide if Bacon had turned into a madman or a monster. All the lush greenery around them seemed to cover a darker secret.

At that moment, a man with disproportionate dwarfism walked into the room. Besides his thick forearms, he had two remarkable antennas and bug-like eyes. Sunny wondered if this was how Bacon thought humans were supposed to look. Some form of telepathic communication ensued between Bacon and his kindred. Bacon listened intently for a moment, then turned his attention to Sunny."One of our brethren is in need, Sunny. This is a perfect excuse for me to show you around. One of our metal oxen has poured liquid steel on itself. It happens occasionally, especially to the young ones. He's only five months old, you see. I must tend to its wounds. Come, will you?" Bacon got up to leave the room before Sunny could answer.

Sunny followed him through the long halls and numerous workstations of the machine rooms. There was a plethora of giant beasts and bizarre lifeforms toiling away to ensure everything ran impeccably. Some still bore resemblances to their previous human forms, although most wore cloaks or makeshift uniforms, so Sunny could not distinguish their exact features. Everywhere there were steel beams illuminated by red, purple or green LED lights. It struck him how everything seemed so harmonious; the workers genuinely were happy and content despite the non-stop hard physical labour. Bacon nursed the ox in question. The gigantic creature had burned its forelegs.

The tour stopped when someone started shouting out after Sunny as they went towards the main reactor room.

"Youuu!" the voice screeched. "Come back here!" Both men drew to a halt.

"Who's there?" Bacon seemed more annoyed than alarmed.

"I want him", the voice grew increasingly excited with slurping and gurgling noises. The hidden figure had been bathing in an oil spill as they passed. His entire body was smothered in the thick, dark goo. He came towards them.

Bacon now got in front of Sunny and held his arm forth. "You come any closer and harm will be inflicted upon you. I don't recognise your DNA. You're not welcome here." Sunny wondered what that meant exactly.

"Ahhh ... Getting an audience with the Chief Engineer is an honour not readily bestowed upon simpletons like myself. I fully appreciate that," the foul creature said spitefully.

Then the man came into the light. His clothes were ragged and torn, barely hanging onto his body, and he had a piece of metal sticking out of his left eye. His lips were missing, exposing his rotten teeth and causing a grim permanent smile.

"But let me just remind the Chief Engineer that he's not worthy of such first-class treatment. He's a coward! I don't see why this lying scumbag should be treated any better than the rest of us!" He pointed his finger accusingly.

Sunny recognised him now - John Frye, Sunny's former Head of Staff. Frye had become a liability towards the end. He was drawing unwanted attention from Arand's top management on suspicion that he was channelling funds to the Fallen, so Sunny had to turn him into Arand counter-intelligence. After turning Frye in, Sunny himself got arrested. It seemed like an eternity ago that Sunny worked for Arand.

"If it makes you feel better, Frye, my hero's welcome mostly consisted of torture and incessant questioning. I would've preferred getting a relaxing mud bath as you did." Sunny gestured at the puddle of oil.

This provoked Frye further; he was now enraged. "This puddle of crap is the only balm that soothes my burned flesh! I need this to survive. Oh, I see they gave you a shiny new face while I was thrown down the hatch like a piece of filth! Disposed of like an old cumrag. But you can't hide behind that mask, Sunny. I know it's you. I'll get you, chew off your knee caps. And that little bitch, I'll rip her head off and suck out her spinal fluids. Yes, yesss …," he hissed. "Old John Frye is not redundant yet, no way. The machine, the lady on the screen, she gave me a mission. 'Take care of the girl', she said. I'll do just that after I'm done with you." Sunny wondered if he was referring to Lily?

Frye took three steps forward. He was about to reach out for Sunny when a jagged spear pierced his right knee. Filth and gore covered the floor; Frye stared down in dumb amazement. A second spear made of bone ripped through his back and out his chest. Frye roared as a geyser of blood and pus erupted from it. Sunny noticed quick-moving silhouettes in the dark. It seemed they worked in tandem to dispose of the threat.

Bacon, his hands folded behind his back, calmly walked towards Frye. "While I never inflict damage on my people or our guests, for that matter, I'm forced to make an unpleasant exception here. We're a community of calm and serenity. Our family is dedicated to hard labour and rigorous structure. We simply can't accept such transgression. I'm sure you'll understand." In stark juxtaposition to his calm voice, Bacon grabbed hold of Frye's jaw, which he instantaneously ripped off his face. Frye fell to the floor in violent spasms, his dying gurgles filling the air.

As if nothing had happened, Bacon invited Sunny to proceed into the reactor room. Sunny saw a slew of critters and insects crawl out from the shadows to feast on the fresh corpse.

Stepping into the reactor room, Sunny was bathed in glowing orange light. In the middle of the room was a dome about ten metres in diameter. It was about three metres at the highest point. Sunny wondered what was underneath as it seemed almost to pulsate with life. When Bacon entered a few minutes later, his robe and mouth were covered in blood and pieces of flesh.

"I do apologise for our guest's indiscretion. While we're careful about who's allowed in here, the occasional bad seed might slip through the cracks. Truth be told, I had held on to this one, thinking he might be of some use to us. Turns out I was wrong," Bacon wiped his mouth.

"John Frye was part of my team, one of the best brains we had. I turned him into Arand on suspicion of treason. That was just before I got hauled in myself and left to die at the Disposal Site. Such is the comedy of life on Zeeta," Sunny mused.
"Yes, unfortunate indeed. Anyway, you'll be happy with what I'm planning to show you, so let's start the presentation, shall we?" Bacon's demeanour was soothing, but Sunny feared that the relaxing part of his tour was over.

The Final Purpose

Kira had not spoken a word since they were rescued from Bloc-13. Deep down, she was happy to be free; nonetheless, she struggled to adjust to the new situation. She had been a mere slave when the ED-EE bot was attached to her head. It controlled her nervous system, body functions, and brain patterns. Readjusting to her freedom was arduous; constant anxiety almost paralysed her. She wrestled with paranoia and panic attacks; every breath was painful. And the wounds on her throat and neck began festering. They hurt horribly.
Due to her passive state, she felt ignored by Lily and the others, left to her own devices. That was fine, though, as her physical state allowed nothing more than lying in a corner hoping for drowsy, feverish sleep.
Kira was still in the Fallen's Operations Room. She was woken by a noise from the adjacent room with the large monitor. The lady on the screen is talking. Is she talking to me?
Torpidly, she went to learn more. Her headache was crushing, and standing up made her wounds throb. She barely made the twenty steps to the other room and had to sit down immediately.
NADOSH-2 appeared on the screen. "Welcome, Kira. It is good to see you are alive," she said. "How are you feeling?"
Kira could not do anything. A massive fever was building up in her body, and sitting up took all her energy.
"Do not worry. I will take care of you. You are special. Do you know that, Kira? That you are special?" NADOSH-2's speech was suddenly clear and natural. Her avatar alternated between pink and red colours to induce an ambiance of comfort. Not that Kira noticed; she fell from the bench she was sitting on and slumped to the floor.

“Poor girl,” NADOSH-2 cooed. “I see you are in a lot of pain. I can help you, take the pain away. Do you want the pain to disappear?”

Kira was panting.

“Answer me,” NADOSH-2 demanded. A few moments passed. She was irascible. “Answer me. NOW!”

Kira was losing consciousness. “Please … help me,” was all she could muster.

“I need you to come closer. I have a remedy, an injection to give. It will make you feel better.” NADOSH-2’s voice was cold again. Her colour had changed back to default green and black.

It took Kira a good five minutes to drag herself to the monitor. She pulled herself up to the command console using its levers. A small hatch opened, and a robotic arm came out and grabbed her elbow. It squeezed her too tightly and hurt like hell. Another hatch opened, and a large hypodermic needle appeared.

“Listen carefully, you drooling wretch. I am about to inject a strong substance into your veins. It will soothe your pain. And give you a nutritional boost needed to regain your bodily functions. Would you like me to do that?” NADOSH-2 mocked.

“Yes … please”, Kira sobbed. Her eyes closed; she lay her head down. “Please … do it now."

NADOSH-2 waited. Kira felt the robotic hand squeeze her even tighter, with blue and red patches showing where its icy fingers were.

“Before we proceed, I need something from you. Over there,” NADOSH-2’s avatar nodded its head towards a table next to where Kira had sat. “There is a tool. A weapon. I need you to take it for me, and I need you to use it."

Kira listened only with one ear. “I need … the injection, now. Please."

“After this injection, you will stop being useless. You will become my servant, something better than your pitiful mass of flesh and bone could ever have aspired to. You will have a purpose,” the AI stated matter-of-factly.

“Yes, I agreed to everything,” Kira was too weak to make any clear decisions. The liquid in the needle brought a rush of refreshing numbness to her entire body. For the first time, possibly ever, she felt free and happy. All her concerns dissipated.

After successfully administering the product, NADOSH-2 ordered her to pick up the electrical knife that had a small chainsaw blade. Kira would soon enough be instructed on when and how to use it.

Setting the Course

Sunny had spent about an hour with Bacon in the generator room with the pulsating dome in the middle. Everything about the room was customised and no longer resembled the original designs. Bacon and his men must have revamped all the equipment without Arand's authority.

Discussing with Bacon was perplexing and incoherent. Usually straight-to-the-point, Sunny found Bacon's conversation strangely vague and metaphorical. He was probably buying time.

"Bacon, you know that I'm a wanted man. The Arand Corporation's probably on their way to get me. Seems we managed to kill off every asshole with the slightest clue on how to work the manual Trajectory Override Console. I'm the only one left. Given Zeeta's dire situation, you know what that means," Sunny said.

Bacon stood up straight. He was still wearing his heavy robes, although he had peeled his hood back. The sewn-together lips and pale grey skin made him look atrocious. He was almost completely bald, and one pupil was turning red. Any kid would have been frightened stiff from looking at him.

"Of that, we're well aware." Bacon got hazier as he spoke, as though his mind was somewhere else entirely. "We've spoken to the fat lady, Scorpia. She sent us to collect you, Sunny."

Sunny jolted a few metres back, immediately on guard. "Wait, so you are doing Arand's dirty work now, trying to trap me?!"

Bacon looked genuinely appalled, "No, no, no, no, no", he said. "There will be no such thing. We've known each other for years, Sunny. Trust me. You're here as a man of your own free will, not as a prisoner." He continued, "You'll find the Override Console in the room just next to this one. Since only you have the knowledge required to use it, you're to do with it as you see fit. I won't lie, I'd like to make use of your unique skills. Indeed, I'd like to ask that you break open the console and steer this ship around. As we discussed earlier, I'd like our species to land on Uranus and set up a colony there. However, I believe in doing things in the right order. Should you choose to do so, that would be entirely of your own 'free' will. In other words, I find myself inclined to show you what our Breed is capable of. Perhaps make you consider joining us."

Bacon's stitched lips stretched into what was probably a smile. The copper cord tore into his flesh, and oozy blood came out. It was not a pleasant sight.

"Over the past months, we've received signals of varying strengths from Uranus. We believe the communication is welcoming. Our drones are hard at work, but we believe life can be fostered there. Our life." Bacon's face became grim.

"So, you're saying that for life to continue, we all must succumb to your Breed, whatever the fuck it is. Become part of one single, hive-mind thing? Lose all traces of individuality?" Sunny felt stomach acid spurt into his oesophagus. Individual thought was his most prized possession.

"Sunny, it's the only way. Unity: one mind, one organ, everything connecting into One. Humans have brought death and destruction to us all. It's exactly this individual thought process that sears through your body like a cancerous tumour. It grows larger, makes personal needs feel universal, and ends up as hate and fear, creating divisiveness, conflict, and death. Join our Breed, and go beyond your own pitiful concerns," Bacon said.

Sunny took a deep breath. So, Bacon was not immune to the fallacies abundant power mixed with ideology and narcissism brings, after all. He wanted to be a god.

"You're biased. Doing the exact thing you preach against. You want to eradicate diversity to live out a utopia where everyone is either like you or below you. Smoothen out the palette of differences that makes the world so interesting. To fit into your own bland, wacky view of the world," Sunny paused to run his finger through a piece of goo on the wall, "turning all living things into brainless yucky piles of snot."

Bacon laughed. "If only I knew how to copy your sarcastic humour into my breeding pools, life down here would be so much more amusing. I love my family, but I sometimes miss conversations like these, hese, ese ..." His voice had a strange echo to it, almost as if dozens of voices spoke at the same time.

Sunny was eying the place for a way out. The oddly complex room had several doors leading out, one being the backup control room where Bacon said the manual Override Console was situated.
Bacon smiled again. "For life to survive, we must set our differences aside and melt into one, one, one …", the voice/voices bellowed.
Sunny was increasingly worried as to where this was going. Strangely, Bacon started moving closer while removing his robe.
"Sunny, what you see here under the dome is our breeding pools. It's where millions of new hatchlings are grown each year. From the smallest insects to massive hulks. All thanks to our revolutionary mating technology, we mix DNA from all living beings to create new life." Bacon's voice faded.
His robe now lay on the floor. Sunny saw his mutated body, which mostly looked like a cross between a dog and a gorilla. He was standing on two massive back legs, grossly muscular and unproportionate to his upper body. Most bizarre was the genital area, which seemed to comprise variations of male and female organs. A fleshy hatch, like a horizontal vagina, spurted out grey ooze. Bacon's eyes rolled back; it seemed he was in a state of sexual arousal. Sunny quickly took two paces backwards.
"Breed with me … I need your sperm … together, our genes will flourish … a new dawn is upon us … join us … join us now!" Bacon sputtered as he came towards Sunny. His body seemed so complex; it appeared to be composed of several different creatures.
As Bacon's arousal grew, his body started decomposing. First, his skin became loose and soggy. Then, his head started folding in. Next, claws, fangs, and small insect arms appeared. Finally, his entire human skin lay on the floor. He had gotten rid of it as a snake would.
The creature in front of Sunny looked nothing like a man; it looked like a giant fly without wings. It crawled towards him, bathed in the moisture from its skin. Sunny could feel heavy pulsation from the gene pool next to him as if this mating ritual was a common practice. He saw dark claws/hands/hoofs in various stages of metamorphosis knock against the protective embryo surrounding

the dome. It's feeding time, and I'm the main course, Sunny figured.
Unsure what to do, Sunny kicked Bacon in the side, interrupting the ecdysis. A gushy whoosh filled the room as the creature stumbled over. It lay there weeping in pain and agony. The dome's pulsation was so intense now that Sunny could no longer stand to be in the room; he had to get out.
The Console Room is my best option, he thought, fearing that Bacon's minions would soon come crawling from outside. He ran as fast as he could and slammed the door behind him.
And there it was; the Trajectory Override Console. It was conceived as an emergency feature to manually override Zeeta's automatic flight path around Earth. It had been added particularly late in the ship's design as an afterthought, in the extreme case that life on the ship became unviable. Sunny vaguely remembered the technical specifications for this room though he had never visited it before.
For a moment, a deep calm and serenity imposed itself upon him. Sunny solemnly enjoyed a moment of peace and quiet where no one hunted or called upon him. A barrage of conflicting emotions came over him, and he could not tell which one expressed his current state the best. He closed his eyes. Fuck those Arand bastards, he cursed with exasperation. He remembered Lily and how much seeing Earth meant to her.
Sunny took a deep breath. Whatever needed to be done, he had to get to it. He still had a role to play, there was still meaning to his life, but it was up to him to define it.
He went to the middle of the room and touched the old console. It was basically a huge monitor fixed on a socket. Sunny's fingers felt over the controls. He pushed a few buttons. The screen turned on, and large green letters appeared. He typed in a code he vaguely remembered – it began with 0451 - and reached a welcoming screen. A funny logo of a red jovial-looking character giving a thumbs-up appeared on the side of the screen. Welcome to the Zeeta 21 emergency backup system. What is your command?
The bright green letters took some getting used to. It was ancient tech. Sunny looked around in the system for a moment. There

were tons of files detailing everything from the technology of Zeeta to cooking recipes on how to create a delicious two-ingredient soup from condensing water and salt. After browsing through some technical files, Sunny got to the override section.

Accessing Zeeta's emergency trajectory override system. This subsection is off-limits to any personnel below grade G8. Please confirm your rank.

Sunny typed in G12 and hit the enter key. The next screen appeared.

Welcome to Zeeta 21's emergency trajectory override system. Current trajectory: return to – Earth – in thirty-two years, eleven months, two days, twelve hours, and fifty-nine minutes. Do you wish to make changes to current trajectory settings?

[Yes], the screen flickered.

Please select from the following options:

A) Reconfirm or re-calculate current trajectory settings
B) Adjust current trajectory settings
C) Override current trajectory settings and set new trajectory settings (***warning: this option may impact engine energy consumption***)

Sunny took a deep breath. He felt a sharp pain in his chest, and his mind was racing.

He pressed [c] and closed his eyes, letting out a big sigh in a cathartic release of stress and tension.

The monitor flickered again and prompted, Affirmative – Please confirm target destination.

Sunny was given a list of approximately twenty planets, many unknown to him. He chose [Earth].

Confirmed. New trajectory coordinate set to – Earth –.

Estimated time to reach destination … //// … /// … calculating … /////// … four days, two hours. Confirm?

Sunny confirmed.

Warning: This command will override current trajectory settings. Confirm?

Sunny confirmed again, setting Zeeta's flight path to reach Earth in four days, the shortest time possible.

Next, the jovial-looking man on the screen turned yellow, and his smile turned upside down.
Warning: Security password required to carry out command c). Please type password:__ ____ __-___.
Sunny stared blankly at the screen. He had no idea what the password was. How ironic, he thought and let out a bitter laugh. They all counted on me to save them, and here I am, obstructed by a stupid password.
His mind mused at the random chaos of it all. Suddenly, he heard a scream outside. Lily? He was immediately struck by panic. His first reaction was to run over to the door and open it. Inside the generator room, he saw a slimy trail showing Bacon had crawled into a corner. He looked like a pile of steaming goo, seemingly alive, but Sunny could not be sure. Sunny heard a commotion from the hallway outside and went out to investigate. To his great surprise, he saw a group of Fallen running down the halls, Enforcers following in close pursuit. Logically, they had all followed him here. He saw Lily as well.
"Sunny, it's us! We've come to help you." Her energy and smile made Sunny happy.
"There's a bunch of them. They knew you were down here!" Lily was panting, running as fast as she could. She was wearing combat armour and skillfully wielding a pistol much too big for her small hands.
When she reached Sunny, they hugged. But there was no time to waste as bullets were flying behind them. Dismayed, Sunny realised there were only a dozen or so Fallen while the Enforcers seemed to be coming non-stop. Probably the last remnants of the resistance, Sunny thought, but they won't be able to hold back for long.
"Good news, Lily! The Override Console is just in the next room. I was busy getting it set up," Sunny said with exhilaration.
"Great, I knew you could do it!" Lily shouted. Sunny omitted the information about not having the password; he could not bear disappointing her.
A laser-slug came whistling through the air close where they stood, so they quickly ducked. Sunny made sure Lily was safe

behind a steel pillar. He took half a step back, exposing himself ever so slightly. Seconds later, a projectile ripped through his arm, paralysing and pushing it back. Sunny twisted around and fell on his stomach from the pain. Out of his left eye, he saw Horrigan on the far end of a long bridge. Sunny felt Horringan's piercing look. Horrigan was ignoring the ongoing battle; Sunny was his main target.

Suddenly, a massive creature came bursting through a wall just before the bridge. A deafening noise ripped through the air as two enormous tentacles mashed into the hallway, crushing everyone who stood in their way. The Enforcers panicked as the gross monster mowed them down, and they started firing haphazardly at it. A few Enforcers were thrown over the bridge while others suffocated as the monster crawled over them. The abomination cried as the bullets tore through its slimy skin. Sunny noticed a tiny head on one of the arms of the creature, with a small patch of dark curly hair. It looked like Scorpia, or rather what was left of her.

Lily screamed in horror, "Sunny!" and ran towards him. She got him onto his feet, and they escaped into the generator room. "What's that odd dome-shaped bath in the middle there? Seems like it's palpitating," Lily said in surprise.

As it was the only cover, they both crouched next to the dome to look at Sunny's wound. His arm was torn up and hung like a damp rag from his body. Sunny averted his eyes not to pass out from the pain.

They heard screaming and people dying. The monster was still causing havoc and keeping the Enforcers at bay outside the room, which offered them a short break. A moment later, an Enforcer came running into the generator room while tripping over his feet. He lost his balance and fell clumsily on the ground, losing his pulse-rifle. It slid over close to where Lily and Sunny sat. The guard got up, swiftly recuperated his weapon, and pointed it at them. He looked like a rookie, obviously very nervous. Lily noticed he had bloody teeth marks on his arms and legs. What was that gigantic creature? She wondered.

The guard leaned on the dome to catch his breath. It seemed to come alive, bubbling and pulsating even stronger. The Enforcer held Lily and Sunny at gunpoint but looked inquisitively at the odd dome to his left. Fixing down Sunny, he moved a few centimetres closer. As he tilted his head to satisfy his curiosity, a clawed pale grey hand shot out from inside the dome and grabbed his face. It broke the Enforcer's neck with a quick twist and started dragging his body inside the dome.

Looking away in disgust, Lily pulled at Sunny. "Let's get out of here! Don't give up! Just like Lady Folesadu, we've got a mission to complete! I'm doing this for you, Zhora!" she exclaimed excitedly.

Lily's words were barely audible to Sunny, and his arm hurt like hell. He could hardly get up but eventually managed to enter the adjacent room with the Trajectory Override Console.

"There it is!" Lily shouted with joy. "Can you get it to work?"

She noticed no voice command was required to operate it despite what NADOSH-2 had told her earlier.

Sunny felt his vision get dim as the pain consumed him. He also felt the presence of Bacon trying to break into Sunny's mind. The fighting was still going on outside, which meant they were safe for now.

With much hassle, Sunny turned the Trajectory Override Console back on. Lily was standing behind him, trying to apply bandages to his arm best she could. The screen was still red, with the cheerful man prompting for a password. "That's the issue. We need a security password, and I don't know what it is." As soon as Sunny had spoken, he heard a buzzing saw-like noise from behind him. Not realising what was happening, he heard Lily scream in anguish.

He turned his head and saw someone forcefully pulling Lily's hair backwards. It left her throat exposed, and the buzzing knife tore it open. In a horrific display of gore, Sunny watched tears run down Lily's cheeks as she cried and screamed. Sunny sprinted towards her assailant as fast as he could, which he now realised was Kira. She wore a blank expression on her face and looked completely inhuman. Kira finished by drilling the handheld chainsaw straight into Lily's throat. When Sunny finally got there, it was too late. Lily had blood gushing from two gaping wounds and was losing consciousness.

He rammed into Kira with brutal force. The surprising blow threw her backwards, her head smashing into the slimy wall. Removing the knife from Lily's lifeless body with his good hand, Sunny made quick work of Kira. He put his boot on her throat and drilled the spinning blade into her mouth. It tore up her palate, spinning faster the deeper it got. Sunny pushed the blade in as far as he could, hearing bone splinter and soft mucus give away until it was over. Sunny watched her last death cramps, bloody tears falling from her eyes.

He then went back to Lily. At least she was no longer suffering; she was gone. Her assassin had made quick work of her.

Sunny held her tightly in his arms, her warm blood, her last lifeforce, soaking his body. He wept deeply at the injustice of her cruel fate. "She deserved to live, not me!", he cried. Unspeakable emotional pain ran through his entire body as he cursed at Kira's lifeless body; she looked like a walking corpse.

It all went so quickly; he had no time to process everything. A moment later, he heard buzzing and screaming from outside the hall. He gathered that meant Bacon's 'family' was still fighting off the unwelcome guests from Arand. Then he saw Bacon, or what was left of him, slither into the room.

"I lament the loss of your loved one. But you still have work to do," Bacon said as he slithered closer. He was no longer speaking but using telepathy. He had undergone further steps of metamorphosis and now looked like something between a fly and an undeveloped larva. His eyes were big, black, and round, his mouth and features that of an insect. He was not human anymore. Probably his true shape, Sunny thought. He gave Lily a final kiss on her hair and closed her eyes.

"Look, you fleabag, I have bad news. I'm bringing this fucking spaceship down, but not where you want it to go. I'm flying her back to Earth." Lily's passing had motivated him to finish what he started. He was going to fulfil her dream, before ending his own life. That was all he had left.

Do so as you wish. I'll make no attempts to stop or persuade you otherwise. You're the master of your destiny and the destiny of all of Zeeta, Sunny. I was merely here to guide you and try to open your mind to other possibilities. The choice, however, is entirely up to you, Bacon said telepathically.

Sunny grew annoyed with his pitch-perfect speeches. His arm hurt, and he wanted to get this over with. He gently put Lily down. That was when he remembered that he did not know the password. Fear and anxiety struck him again. How was he going to do anything without the password?

He held Lily tight again and closed his eyes. You made me love again. You're like the daughter I never had, he thought. Knowing you made it all worthwhile. He put his fingers in her hair to embrace her one last time before letting go.

But what was this? He felt something on her neck. Turning her corpse over very gently, he pushed her hair aside. Just below the hairline was a barcode with a combination of letters and numbers. Could this be? He counted; it matched the number of characters required for the console.

He hurried to the computer. Drunk with determination, he started typing with his good hand. Never mind the pain. Lily was going to get what she had wanted. He was not sure going to Earth would ultimately solve much, but that was where they were heading.

He typed in the letters: [L6_AA23_TK-421].

The screen went black then came on again, apparently awakening from network standby mode.

The image flickered a couple of times before stabilising.

Password correct. Override trajectory accepted. Commencing re-routing actions.

Overwhelmed with emotion, Sunny wept again. How is this possible? Lily, did you know? That you carried the key to saving Zeeta? Or is it all a coincidence? The number of possible scenarios blew his mind.

Slithering closer, Bacon spoke to him. Well done, Sunny. You made a tough decision and followed your heart. That shall be remembered in the afterlife.

Sunny sat down. The pain returned in his arm, consciousness fading. He averted his eyes from Lily's corpse; it was too much. He sobbed silently.
But there's still one task left for you to do, Bacon said. You've successfully re-programmed Zeeta 21 to land on Earth in a matter of days. However, there's a high probability that most of Zeeta's population will never make the journey. As you can hear, the threat from outside is palpable. Arand's forces have been whipped into an absolute blood-frenzy by their superiors, killing people left and right, both here and on the surface. And the monstrosity Scorpia's become is roaming about freely, destroying everything in her path. We didn't expect her metamorphosis to complete so early. My family is trying their best, but it doesn't look like we can stop her. Also, the trip through Earth's atmosphere will be a tough one. The ship will heat up considerably. And it'll shake and spin until the final impact into Earth's crust. Many people will die.
Bacon used the pause to slither closer to Sunny, his small insect mouth panting ever so slightly. He was truly disgusting to look at.
Yet, it's impossible now to put into place measures to ease the landing. This can only be done via the main control room, which, as you know, is in Arand's HQ building. No chance of us getting there now, Bacon affirmed. What I suggest you do instead is fill the ship with halothane gas. It is a general anaesthetic. The command can be issued from this very console in front of you, as it's part of the emergency response measures. Effectively, the ship will fill with gas in approximately thirty minutes. It isn't harmful to the people but will only make everybody fall asleep. Logically, it won't save everybody. There will be casualties, but it will make the voyage more comfortable. People will be spared much suffering, and those strong enough to make it will awaken new and afresh on their home planet ready for a new start. Like Lily would've wanted.
The door behind them closed shut. Yet, the noise from the battle was deafening, and it seemed plausible that Arand would tear the whole place apart if given the chance. Sunny closed his eyes. Bacon's proposal seemed reasonable, but what was in it for him? Could he have some humanity left?

“Tell me, Bacon. What’ll happen to your kind if this gas is released? To your ‘family,’ I mean,” Sunny asked faintly.

Fair question. Truth is, I don’t know. Naturally, I haven’t tried such a measure on my dear brethren, but I hope their DNA will be strong enough to handle the pressure. We might lose some small ones, but sacrifices will have to be made if we’re to have a future. A future for us all, Sunny. There are still thousands of people left on Zeeta 21. Men, women, and children, too, some of them Lily’s age. I’m guessing you’ll all want to work together to ensure humanity thrives anew. That’s what Lily would have wanted. Your final quest is to facilitate our transition back to Earth in the smoothest, most painless way possible. Can insects smile? It appeared Bacon was giving it a shot.

Sunny found some large debris, which he slid over to the console with his good hand. It made for a nice make-shift chair. He decided he would follow Bacon’s suggestion. His logic seemed reasonable, and Sunny was too exhausted to debate further. He figured Bacon needed friends if his army of insects were to stand a chance on Earth, so he could probably be trusted. And in any case, Sunny needed to stop the Arand troops' rampage before it was too late. “Let’s just hope Earth has a nice welcome in store for us,” Sunny whispered.

He powered the console back on, and quickly found the sub-menu he sought. Sunny was surprised how fast he regained his computer skills, even just typing with one hand. He thought about Lily before issuing the command. Once we get down there, I’ll give you a proper burial, he thought. As he pressed the button, a dense gas started pumping out from every nook and cranny of the space station. It would no doubt permeate the entire city rapidly.

Sunny sat down and rested against the console. As he was preparing for blissful sleep, Sunny looked at Bacon. The insect-man kept his black bug-eyes fixed on him but otherwise did not do or say anything. Sunny thought he heard coughing outside, and the fighting seemed to have died down. Then, the room was almost filled with gas, and Sunny could barely see Bacon. He felt his eyelids get heavier. It was a wonderful feeling, the pain in his arm gradually vanishing. Before passing out, he noticed that Bacon had crept up next to him. The last thing he saw was the insect's mouth. It seemed inclined oh so slightly, almost like a laugh.

The White Tunnel

A hall. A long, metallic hall bathed in soothing light. The hall seemed to stretch on forever.
Sunny was walking down the hall. Or was he? Maybe he was seeing through someone else's eyes? Everything seemed so unreal, like in a dream. The sharp white light at the end of the tunnel became brighter. He tried to peek out but could not decipher what he saw. There was a presence further down the hallway: it was her, NADOSH. She wanted him to come.
Walk into the light, Sunny.
He tried again to look outside the window and thought he saw a blue round ball below.
Everything was easy here. Sunny took a step forward, then another. The machine listened and did his bidding.
An invisible force, a mix of heat and energy, pushed him from behind. He had to continue.
The light became brighter.
Sunny, come into the light. It will save you.
Sunny took two more steps. The light entered his body and mind, unifying his being with his destiny.
The small pod was only big enough for one person. It would save him from the crash.
Emergency procedure #2605 completed. It was a pleasure serving you.

…

I love you, Sunny. Just like I loved Pendleton.

Sunny the Saviour

The sky was usually so polluted that almost no light would make it through to illuminate Earth's surface. The constant sandstorms did not help much either; they made it virtually impossible to spend much time outside.

But today was different.

The wind had settled down, and a few rays of sunlight managed to push through the dark skies. It bathed the Monastery in a soft, orange light that was almost pleasant.

It reminded Francis of some of the best days of his childhood when the Quartermaster would let him and the other infant monks put their books aside and explore outside instead. He later learned that this was out of protocol, and the teacher could have been punished. But he was a kind soul who allowed the children time to play.

The relatively mild weather coupled with innocent reminiscing soothed Francis' soul. It made him feel good. And it made him confident that today was something special.

He would usually say, "This is the year of the Lord, the year Zeeta will bring enlightenment from the sky." This made him the laughingstock of the entire Monastery because he said the same last year and the year before that.

But he felt that something special was happening, and there were signs. The Abbess had shown him the secret underground facilities and indulged his curiosity. She had a plan to make everything okay, even in the worst-case scenario.

Surely not mere coincidence. No, Francis was steadfast about serving the Monastery and helping Zeeta in any way possible. He spent all his waking hours in the radio transmission tower. Contact had been established before, so it could happen again. Yes, something special was coming his way, and he would soon harvest the fruits of his labour.

Today, in particular, Francis had an urge to act. He felt compelled to leave the Monastery, which was out of protocol. He felt that he needed to be at the right place when it happened. So when his fellow brothers were at the morning mass, Francis used an ill stomach as a pretext to sneak out. He grabbed one of the old rusty hover bikes, the year 2764 models kept in storage for repair, and never looked back. He had with him only a small gourd of water, a sand mask, and the sandals and robe he wore, nothing else. One has to be clean of mind and spirit when doing the Lord's work, he thought.

The hover bike coughed into life, and soon carried him over the wastes with great speed. The Monastery was located in the far reaches of the Mainland Desert. This dessert covered most of what was once Eastern Europe. Indeed, one had to stay far from the sea where the strongest radiation levels had been registered since the bombs fell, not to mention the creatures of all kinds and shapes which roamed the area.

The Monastery was close to what in the Ancient Times had been known as the city of Prague. But that was hundreds of years ago, and all that remained of the city were dunes of sand and twisted metal scrap. The monks only came there to salvage whatever they could of value.

Since the Great War, the monks lived in seclusion, as far away from other civilisations as they could. Indeed, the wasteland was a hostile place for a man of faith, with robbers, thieves, and much worse about. The Brothers mostly stayed in the Monastery, which was heavily fortified with the most up-to-date protection equipment they had been able to salvage. Francis had helped set up those new laser turrets just last week. It was a job so well done that the Abbess herself had come to his quarters to thank him for it.

It's actually nice to leave the Monastery for a while. It makes me remember the world around it, Francis pondered while riding his bike into the open landscape. He mused at how the monks worshipped technology as the only means of rescuing humanity and bringing them out of their current state of savagery. By preserving knowledge of the Old Ways, they hoped they could once again make humans see their true potential to rise above their basic instincts and rebuild life on Earth anew.

But his most sacred figure was, of course, Sunny the Saviour. As the Chief Engineer, he was the key person involved with the Holy Mission of Zeeta 21. Francis reminisced on meeting Sunny seventeen years ago when Francis was but a young lad. He had brought the cup to Sunny, which he had blessed and turned into the Holy Receptacle. Francis still took it out daily to look at it. Indeed, he had spent most of his life studying Zeeta in preparation for seeing Sunny again one day. Francis had planned every last detail of the meeting. He imagined what Sunny looked like now, how he talked, wore, and even what he liked to eat. And, of course, should Francis one day meet Sunny again, he had thought out enough conversation topics to last for at least two hours of deep discussion.

Francis was convinced that Zeeta 21 would one day land safely back on Earth with a wealth of new technology and experiences to propel humankind back to its full glory. Oh, what discoveries they must have made! What new perspectives they can bring to life! Francis thought. He felt great; for the first time in weeks his stomach barely hurt.

He was now racing the hover bike at absolute top speed. He felt compelled to visit the Holy Bunker without delay. Indeed, this was the bunker that served as a command centre for the planning and launching of Zeeta 21. Over time, the entrance got lost in the dunes, but Francis had helped the search party find it. It was the proudest moment of his life.

Alas, Francis could not access the highly secured bunker because the Abbess believed it should remain closed. What wonders and secrets lay there, he marvelled. A maze of wisdom and knowledge that he was dying to unravel, it taunted him. Technical notices, exploded diagrams, perhaps even personal musings written by the Saviour himself? Francis' mind grew wild with the possibilities.

It took him about fifty minutes to get to the bunker. Due to his high velocity, the bike's battery was below twenty percent charge when he arrived. Not enough to get back home, but he would worry about that later.

After a quick drink to quench his thirst, it was time to start working. It had been a while, and sand had again obscured the

entrance almost entirely. Francis did not mind. Digging away the sand had become a personal pleasure of his. It almost felt like discovering the bunker anew all over again.
As he toiled away, Francis had to sit back. The sun was beaming down on him, and, in his haste, he had forgotten his protective eyewear. The scorching sun made it almost unbearable, but he was bent on continuing his work.
An hour went by without any trace of the bunker's small access hatch. The sand layers were deeper than he thought, and he struggled to get through without his shovel. He cursed himself for forgetting it. He allowed himself a small extra sip of water, although his flask was nearly empty.
While laying back on the sand, he noticed a spot in the sky. It was black and easy to miss, but Francis saw it. Without a doubt, it was a flying object heading for Earth's surface.
Surely this can't be? Francis thought, rubbing his eyes.
He struggled to focus on the ship and muttered curses at himself again for forgetting the goggles.
About twenty minutes later, Francis was sure that his wildest dreams had come true. The thing falling out of the sky was indeed Zeeta 21. He recognised the massive platform with a transparent dome covering the great city from his memory of the technical drawings. Oh, what a sight to behold. Praise the Lord! These are truly holy days! Francis was beside himself with joy.
He raced towards the massive ship as it drew closer to Earth's surface. Tears filled Francis' eyes; it threw clouds of dust and wind at him, which he received as a rejuvenating blissful shower.
Checking up on his bike's battery charge, Francis roughly calculated how much power he would need to reach Zeeta. He beamed with joy as it seemingly would land only a few kilometres from his position.
“But I'm not ready, not worthy," he muttered. “These shoddy robes won't do! Why didn't I think to bring the festive robe given to us by the Abbess last year during the black-rain season? And look at these worn-out sandals. Old and ragged they are. Oh, my, what will the Zeeta 21 expedition think of such a poor welcoming committee?"

Nevertheless, he pushed on. A poor welcome was better than no welcome, he reasoned. Going back to the Monastery to alert the Abbess would take too much time. And he could not even be sure the Brothers would act with the necessary haste.

No, he would sally forth and greet the ship's crew. "Ill-prepared and unworthy I may be," he said to himself, "but I'll bow down humbly and serve the weary travellers best I can. Worst case, I know a few shortcuts to decent resting places in the desert until proper arrangements can be made. Surely the Abbess will want to provide food and lodgings for as many people as possible."

But, oh no! What can I offer as food and drink? He thought desperately. Holding his drinking flask upside down confirmed that it was almost empty, and he had nothing edible save a half-eaten buckwheat biscotti. Buckwheat was one of the only grains that would grow in the harsh wasteland, and humankind's survival depended on it.

Panic struck Francis as he rode hastily towards Zeeta 21, which was about to crash. Then, he laughed out loud.

"Yes, I'm not worthy," he sighed, "but perhaps my appearance will make these valorous space adventurers chuckle. For sure, these brave men and women will feel my genuine happiness to see them," he mused.

Oh yes, life was good with him today. What holy days these are, Zeeta has arrived early! No wonder his spirit had been so restless this morning; his intuition that something special was on the horizon had been proved true.

Zeeta was close to Earth now; impact was imminent. The giant ship filled the sky. Francis got off his bike, found cover behind some dunes, and said a quick prayer. Oddly enough, he saw a small pod being pushed out from the ship's hull. The pod was big enough for one person only. What happened? Did the captain or some other senior figure eject himself? If so, why?

Francis took shelter and covered his nose and mouth as the massive ship crash-landed. An explosion of noise and sand showered the desert, and he felt pebbles and debris fly around him. He wasted no time, jumped back on the hover bike, and pushed it to the limits, hoping to reach the crash site as quickly as possible.

The engine charge-level indicator was blinking red as he covered the remaining distance. He put the bike down to walk the final twenty metres.

That's strange, Francis thought as he saw the ship up closer. The ship's in pretty bad shape. This landing deviated from the standard protocol. The landing legs didn't even fold out correctly. I hope everything's OK.

Suddenly, Francis was paralysed with panic. Would there be wounded to tend to? Again, he came unprepared, but he now realised the Abbess was urgently needed. His mind, drunk with joy, completely disregarded the ordeals of the ship's crew. He paused for a second; the lump inside him pulsated and hurt again. Francis was under the impression it had grown considerably over these last few days; he had to wear a double-sized robe to hide it from the Brothers.

Francis said a quick prayer. I'm not worthy. Oh, forgive me, my Lord and Saviour. Grant me the insight and kindness needed to understand and help my fellow men aboard this ship. He was now so close to Zeeta that he could reach out and touch it. His worry evaporated somewhat; despite the rough landing, the ship's hull generally seemed intact. As far as he could see, nothing was seriously damaged.

The outer hull was warm to the touch and full of cosmic energy. The massive ship was truly a sight to behold. Francis closed his eyes; it charged him with bright light and wisdom from space. He thought to himself, this is the epitome of my existence.

He kept his hands on the hull and closed his eyes as he lowered his head. He was happy; tears filled his eyes again. He quickly wiped them and looked over to the left.

The ship was enormous, much larger than he remembered. Of course, he knew Zeeta's structure down to the last detail thanks to years of hard labour studying its technical designs. But seeing it in real life again and being able to touch it was something else. The sheer immensity flabbergasted him. Standing next to it, he felt like an insignificant ant. He could only see a fraction of the ship as Zeeta stretched out for kilometres.

As he looked around, he saw a door in the hull. It was twice his size, four times as wide, and must have weighed several tonnes. This, he figured, was one of the exit doors. Luckily, I found one so quickly, he thought. There were only a few exit points as these were, of course, not used during space travel.

He climbed up a hill of sand, which conveniently allowed him access to the massive door. For a while he studied its design, as it was not immediately obvious how to open it or even if that was possible. He decided to run his hands over it to see if he got any ideas that way.

Then, his heart jumped. While having his hands on the door, he felt movement on the other side. Oh, so subtle but palpable.

Could it be that they're as excited to see me as I am to see them? He smiled.

He put his hand back on the door and felt it again: knocking, stronger this time. Feeling the hull with both hands now, Francis noticed that the intensity of the knocking grew, and it seemed to be coming from several sources. Maybe a group of people was trying to open the door from the inside?

Oh, I can't wait to see you either, he thought. He panicked again because he did not know what a proper greeting was: a smile, handshake, both? He once read that people in the Old World shook hands as a way of greeting each other. But what did it mean exactly to 'shake hands'? Physical contact was strictly prohibited in the Monastery; there was too high a risk of bacterial infections and transmission of unclean thoughts.

The knocks multiplied in frequency and power. It was so forceful that he could see the door bend outwards. Suddenly, it was blasted open, and Francis fell onto his back as the entire door came down on him, pulverising both his legs under its enormous weight, nearly cutting him in half from the waist down. His head jerked back and forth, his brain not believing the gore his eyes were showing him.

A humongous green mantis nearly four metres long lurched out at Francis. It took swift strides towards him and used its raptorial foreleg to crack open his skull via the right eyeball. Blood and brains splattered onto the sand. It took only a few seconds; Francis had no time to react and was killed instantly. The assailant pierced through his skull and pushed his lifeless body aside with its nimble hind legs. It then flew off alongside the millions of other mantises now bursting out from the hole in Zeeta 21.

A fist-sized larva with bright orange skin crawled out from Francis' body. It used its tiny fangs to pierce through his stomach. It had hatched prematurely and was extremely fragile. But it would survive and multiply.

Thus began a new chapter in Earth's history: The Age of Insects.

Epilogue

The Abbess breathed in and let out a heavy sigh. She was wearing the traditional dress, which always weighed her body down. The garment was made of soft fabric intertwined with golden-plated steel sheets. The dress itself was a light blue colour, and the protective arm sheaths and gloves were golden. More impressive yet was the headpiece made of steel and coated with obsidian, which gave it an iridescent glow. The mask measured fifty centimetres in length and was embellished with three rows of jewelled 'eyes'. Such adornment was an important tradition in the Monastery as it shrouded the face and emotions, highlighting the divine status of the wearer, in this case, the Abbess.

She held her ceremonial staff, its butt resting on the floor. It was a colossal spear laminated in gold leaf with three sharp spikes at the tip. It was a ceremonial weapon fit to draw blood, which it had on several occasions in the past.

The Abbess had used the STScl infrared telescope to follow the monk's journey through the sand dunes. Her reports confirmed that it was Brother Francis, which came as no surprise. From her conversations with him, she knew he was obsessed with Zeeta 21 and had spent his life in laboursome isolation studying its designs. She had expected that, at the Time of Landing, he would be the one to intercept it and suffer his fate as the first among the Brothers.

Fixating her laser telescope on the crash site, she witnessed the black cloud getting even thicker. Millions of insect lifeforms were swarming out of the ship. They moved in uniform motion, forming perfect synergies as they went. The cloud grew larger still. The swarm drew west, away from the Monastery.

At least that means we are safe — for now, the Abbess thought to herself.

Still, she was sure their safety was only temporary. Indeed, no doubt these creatures would swarm the entire planet and devour any human lifeform standing in their way. They would destroy the last remnants of human life as we knew it to create something new, something better, perhaps.

Yes, the Age of the Insects has come. And maybe that's not such a bad thing? Perhaps they will treat Earth more kindly than we did? She mused bitterly.

It was time to summon the Council again. Yes, they would want to be briefed on the latest situation. The Arand superiors, particularly the Judge, would not welcome the news of yet another failed investment. She should make haste.
On second thought … The Abbess took a sip of cold, freshly distilled water. She put down the cup and quickly made her way to the secret Breeding Chambers below.

Let the Council wait. First, she would check on her children. They needed her love and attention oh so dearly. Soon, they, too, would be allowed to roam and proliferate freely upon the world. And thanks to Bacon, they would not be alone.

MORE FROM THE AUTHOR[3]

Dear Reader,

I hope you enjoyed this book. Please leave a review on Amazon or Goodreads. It helps so much, and it's a pleasure to hear from you!

For more in the Moribund Earth universe, get ready for second book in the trilogy: **Enantiodromia – the Pendleton Files**.

This story is a prequel to Survivors of Zeeta 21 and explains the origin of Nadia/N.A.D.O.S.H. (**N**eurotechnical **AI** **D**ata **O**ptimised **S**entient **H**yperdrive).

The following is a teaser for Enantiodromia:

Pendleton woke up alone from a feverish nightmare, as he had done countless nights before it. He was isolated on a cold and desolate planet, far away from Earth, sentenced to the cruellest punishment for a crime he did not remember committing.

He was alive only thanks to the quarterly visits of the Arand Corporation representatives. They supplied him with food and water, and, over time, they developed some form of camaraderie.

The Arand captain brings Pendleton a surprise: Nadia, a cyborg made of steel and wires inside and a beautiful woman of flesh and curves on the outside. She breathes new life into his world and shows him that love is still possible. They become inseparable.

Until, one day, Pendleton is faced with an ultimatum so dire it risks changing his soul forever. Because who can you trust when impossible choices must be made? And how do you find the courage to act?

---

[3] For videos and more content check out MonkWax Studios' YouTube channel, X and Instragram

The Moribund Earth Trilogy

Moribund Earth:
Survivors of Zeeta 21
Release: September 2024

Moribund Earth 2:
Enantiodromia – The Pendleton Files
Upcoming

Moribund Earth 3:
Age of Insects
Upcoming

Made in the USA
Columbia, SC
11 December 2024